Cloaked in shadows: A Jake Riley adventure

Dedication

This book is dedicated to the unsung heroes, the silent guardians, the men and women who operate in the shadows, their sacrifices unseen, their victories uncelebrated. To those who dedicate their lives to the defense of freedom and justice, often at great personal cost, this story is a small tribute to your courage, resilience, and unwavering commitment. Their existence is a testament to human grit and dedication, a reality far more complex and compelling than the fictionalized worlds we craft.

It's dedicated to the countless individuals who choose a path less traveled, one that demands immense self-discipline, unwavering focus, and a capacity for moral ambiguity that many of us cannot comprehend. The path of espionage is a precarious balancing act between the darkness and the light. Those who walk this path do not seek glory; they seek results. They operate in a world of moral grayness, where choices have profound and lasting consequences. They often face impossible dilemmas where compromise is not an option, and the very act of choosing is an act of sacrifice.

This dedication is also for those whose lives have been touched by the clandestine world, those who have lost loved ones or lived with the knowledge that those close to them operate in the silent chambers of intelligence operations. The families who wait, the spouses who worry, the children who grow up with an incomplete understanding of their parents' lives. This is a story of the burden of secrecy, and the weight of a life lived in the shadows, the invisible scars and indelible marks on the minds and hearts of those whose dedication is their silent vow. The silent strength and unseen support of these individuals is the bedrock upon which the clandestine world is built.

It's for the countless hours spent in training, honing skills, both physical and mental, until the body is exhausted and the mind is tested to its absolute limits. It's for the missed birthdays, the forgotten anniversaries, the sacrifices of personal relationships to keep the mission paramount, and the burden of carrying secrets that can never be shared. It's for those who choose service above self, and duty above personal desires. It is for them, in their entirety, that this book is dedicated. This narrative is but a small attempt to capture the essence of their remarkable lives, their unwavering dedication, and the incredible sacrifices they make for a world they strive to protect.

The End of an Era

The crack echoed in the stillness, a sound that shattered more than just a bone. It ripped through the carefully constructed reality Jake Riley had built around himself, a reality woven from years of sweat, dedication, and the unwavering pursuit of a baseball dream. The sun beat down on the perfectly manicured infield of the small-town ballpark, a stark contrast to the icy chill that suddenly gripped Jake's heart. He lay there, the familiar sting of pain replaced by a sickening emptiness, the silence broken only by his ragged breaths. This wasn't just a pulled muscle; this was the end. The definitive, brutal end.

His career, his identity, his whole life, seemed to crumble around him in that instant. The roar of the crowd, the thrill of the game, the unwavering support of his family and friends – all faded into a distant echo, replaced by a deafening silence. The bright, hopeful future he'd envisioned, one filled with the crack of the bat, the cheers of the fans, and the triumphant feeling of victory, was gone, stolen by a single, unlucky play. The perfectly manicured field, once a symbol of his aspirations, now felt like a cruel mockery, a monument to his shattered dreams.

He had poured his entire being into baseball, sacrificing everything for this one goal. He'd spent countless hours honing his skills, pushing his body to its limits, enduring the relentless pressure of competition. Every scar, every ache, every triumph – they were all testament to his dedication, each a thread woven into the tapestry of his identity. And now, the whole tapestry was unraveling, thread by thread, leaving him feeling naked, exposed, and utterly lost.

The small town of Oak Grove, nestled in the heart of the countryside, had always been his sanctuary. A place of familiar faces, friendly smiles, and unwavering support. It was here, surrounded by his close-knit community, that he had grown up, nurtured his talent, and forged lifelong bonds. But now, the familiar comfort felt stifling, the friendly faces seemed to carry a weight of unspoken pity, a silent acknowledgement of his failure. The bonds that had once been so strong now felt like fragile threads, easily broken by the harsh reality of his situation. The close-knit community that had once celebrated his triumphs now seemed to be observing his fall from grace with a mixture of sympathy and awkward distance.

Even his relationship with his father, a man of few words but unwavering support, felt strained. The unspoken words hung heavy in the air, a silent acknowledgment of a shared disappointment, a dream that had died along with Jake's career. His father, a former minor league player himself, understood the profound loss more than anyone. The shared language of baseball, once a bond of connection, now stood as a stark reminder of what was lost. Their conversations, once vibrant with baseball talk and shared memories, now consisted mainly of quiet silences and awkward attempts at consolation. The shared dream, once a powerful force uniting them, had vanished, leaving a void that felt impossible to fill.

His mother, ever the pillar of strength, tried her best to offer comfort and support, but even her unwavering optimism couldn't penetrate the deep-seated despair that consumed him. Her attempts at cheerfulness felt forced, the lightness in her voice a thin veil over the worry that shadowed her eyes. Her unwavering love and concern were a constant, a comforting presence in his life, but even her love couldn't erase the crushing weight of his failure. He found himself withdrawing, retreating into a shell of silence, unable to bear the burden of her concern. The warmth of her love, once a source of comfort, now felt like a heavy blanket, suffocating him under the weight of his unspoken grief.

His friends, his fellow baseball players, offered their sympathy, but their words felt hollow, unable to bridge the chasm that separated him from his former life. They attempted to include him in their routines, but he found himself increasingly isolated, a silent observer of a world he no longer fully belonged to. The camaraderie he once cherished, the shared jokes and inside language, now felt distant and unfamiliar. The easy laughter and shared experiences, which had defined their friendship, now felt like memories from another life, a life that no longer existed. He felt like a ghost, haunting the edges of their world, a constant reminder of their own mortality and the fleeting nature of dreams.

The sun began to set, casting long shadows across the field. The vibrant green of the grass was muted, replaced by the deepening hues of twilight. The beautiful sunset, a spectacle normally capable of evoking awe and wonder, only served to emphasize the darkness that had settled in Jake's soul. The vibrant colors of the sunset seemed to mock his own monochrome existence, a stark reminder of the life he had lost. The shadows that had started to lengthen over the field seemed to creep into his soul, mirroring the emptiness he felt within. It was in this moment of profound loss and despair that the unexpected offer would come, a lifeline thrown into the depths of his despair, an offer that would irrevocably change the trajectory of his life, pulling him into a world far removed from the familiar green of the baseball field. A world of shadows, intrigue, and hidden dangers. A world where his past would become a distant memory, and his future, a terrifying and thrilling unknown. The quiet, sun-drenched baseball field, the scene of his final game, would soon become a distant memory, a stark contrast to the dark and mysterious world that awaited him.

A Chance Encounter

The bar's stale air hung heavy with the scent of stale beer and desperation. Oak Grove's "The Rusty Mug" wasn't known for its ambiance; it was a place where dreams went to die, slowly drowning in lukewarm beer and regret. Ironically, it was here, amidst the wreckage of other people's aspirations, that Jake found himself nursing a whiskey, its burn doing little to soothe the icy ache in his soul. He was a ghost, a shadow of his former self, adrift in a sea of disappointment.

He hadn't touched a bat since the injury. The thought of the diamond, once a sanctuary, now evoked a bitter taste of failure. The silence in his life was deafening, broken only by the occasional clinking of glasses and the muted conversations of the patrons. He'd come here seeking oblivion, hoping the alcohol would numb the sharp edges of his despair, but the whiskey only amplified the silence, the hollowness within.

A cough, dry and raspy, broke through his reverie. He looked up, his eyes scanning the dimly lit room. A man sat at the bar a few stools down, his face obscured by shadows. He was tall, his frame suggesting a strength that went beyond mere physique. There was something about his posture, a certain stillness, that hinted at a life lived on the edge, a life steeped in secrets and shadows. The man's eyes, however, were unmistakable. They held a keen intelligence, a sharp awareness that seemed to pierce through the haze of the bar, directly into Jake's soul.

He didn't approach; he simply held Jake's gaze, an unspoken communication passing between them. The silence stretched, thick and uncomfortable, before the man finally spoke, his voice a low rumble, barely audible above the low hum of conversation. "Riley, isn't it?"

Jake nodded, surprised by the directness of the question, the familiarity with his name in this place, a place he frequented for anonymity. He wasn't a public figure, not anymore. The man's knowledge of his name added another layer to the already strange encounter.

The man took a slow sip from his drink, a dark liquid that glinted in the low light. "Impressive career, short as it was," he murmured, his words laced with a hint of something that could have been either admiration or pity. "Exceptional talent, wasted."

Jake felt a prickle of unease. This wasn't just a random comment; this was an assessment, a calculated observation. The man clearly knew more than he was letting on. "I don't know what you mean," Jake replied, his voice guarded.

The man chuckled, a low, throaty sound that sent a shiver down Jake's spine. "Let's just say I have access to information most people don't. And I'm interested in your particular skill set." He leaned forward, his voice dropping to a conspiratorial whisper. "There are… other fields… where your talents might be better utilized. Fields where failure isn't an option."

Jake's intuition screamed danger. This wasn't a chance encounter; it was a carefully orchestrated meeting. The man's words, though cryptic, hinted at something far removed from the mundane reality of Oak Grove. A world of shadows, a clandestine world he couldn't even begin to comprehend.

"What kind of fields?" Jake asked, his voice betraying a tremor of apprehension. His curiosity, however, warred with his caution. The allure of a new challenge, a chance to prove himself again, fought with the fear of the unknown.

The man smiled, a fleeting, almost imperceptible movement of his lips. "Let's just say it's not baseball," he replied, his eyes glinting with an unsettling intensity. "It's… more demanding. More… dangerous." He paused, letting the weight of his words hang in the air. "And the rewards… far greater."

He slid a small, unmarked card across the bar towards Jake. The card was plain, devoid of any logo or identifying mark. A single phone number was printed on it, etched with an almost invisible precision.

"Call this number," the man said, his gaze unwavering. "If you're interested… in a second chance." He finished his drink, the ice clinking softly against the glass, and then he was gone, melting back into the shadowy corners of the bar as effortlessly as he had appeared.

Jake stared at the card, the number seeming to pulsate in the dim light. The man's words echoed in his mind: "Fields where failure isn't an option." The weight of that statement settled upon him, a heavy burden. The allure of escaping the crushing weight of his failure was strong, but the uncertainty, the inherent danger, was equally daunting. His life had already been shattered once; was he willing to risk everything again, to throw himself into a world of unknown dangers, a world where failure meant far more than a lost game?

The whiskey suddenly tasted bitter, the burn no longer a comforting sensation, but a harsh reminder of the choices he faced. He ran a hand through his hair, his thoughts a chaotic jumble. The silence of the bar felt oppressive, the usual comforting anonymity now feeling claustrophobic. The weight of his decision hung heavy in the air, thick and suffocating, a stark contrast to the light, breezy days on the baseball field. He was facing a crossroads, a pivotal moment that would determine the future, a future he could only begin to imagine. The offer was a dangerous gamble, a high-stakes bet on an unknown future. But it was an offer, a chance to rewrite his narrative, to escape the shadow of his past and forge a new identity in a world far removed from the familiar comfort of Oak Grove.

Days blurred into a haze of introspection. The card remained clutched tightly in his hand, its smooth surface worn from countless nervous strokes of his thumb. The phone number seemed to taunt him, a constant reminder of the choice he needed to make. Sleep offered little respite, his dreams filled with shadowy figures and dangerous pursuits. He replayed the encounter in his mind, dissecting the man's words, searching for hidden meanings, trying to determine the true nature of the offer. Was it a genuine opportunity, a chance at redemption, or a dangerous trap, a path to a darker destiny? The uncertainty was excruciating. He sought refuge in the familiar routines of his days, but even the most mundane tasks felt imbued with a sense of impending doom. His memories of the baseball field, once his sanctuary, felt distant and unreal, replaced by visions of covert operations and clandestine meetings.

His relationship with his parents grew more strained, the silence between them now carrying the weight of his unspoken anxieties. He couldn't explain what he was dealing with, couldn't articulate the conflicting emotions that tore at him. The thought of entrusting them with this secret, of potentially putting them in danger, filled him with a sense of overwhelming guilt and responsibility. Their love and support were a constant anchor in his life, but he felt a growing distance, a widening chasm between his present and his past. The comfort he sought in their presence felt like a betrayal, a weight that added to the crushing burden of his decision.

He revisited the Rusty Mug, hoping to catch a glimpse of the mysterious man again, hoping for further clarification, for some sign of what this opportunity truly entailed. But the bar remained the same; dimly lit, filled with the aroma of despair, and populated by the usual cast of characters lost in their own personal struggles. The only evidence of the previous night's encounter was the worn card in his pocket, a constant reminder of the precipice he stood upon. The silence of the bar was no longer a comforting anonymity, but a stark representation of his own internal conflict, a testament to his isolation in the face of such a momentous choice.

The phone remained untouched, the decision hanging over him like a guillotine. He spent hours debating the implications of this offer, weighing the potential benefits against the daunting risks. Was he brave enough to venture into this world of shadows, to confront the unknown? Could he handle the pressure, the responsibility, the moral ambiguities that undoubtedly lay ahead? The answer wasn't clear, but the weight of the decision, of his inaction, was becoming increasingly unbearable. The ticking clock of his life seemed to have accelerated, each passing moment bringing him closer to a decision that would forever shape his destiny. The sun began to set, casting long shadows that mirrored the darkness that had settled within him. The decision, like the sunset itself, appeared both beautiful and terrifying, a culmination of everything that had come before and the anticipation of everything to come.

Finally, after days of agonizing indecision, Jake reached for the phone. His hand trembled as he dialed the number, the simple act feeling momentous, a step into the unknown. His breath hitched in his throat as the phone rang, each ring echoing in the silence of his apartment, a counterpoint to the turmoil within him. The decision had been made, the die cast. The future, whatever it held, awaited. The darkness was beckoning, and Jake Riley, the failed baseball player, was about to step into it. The call answered with a single word, a whisper so low that he nearly missed it. "Agent." The game had changed. And the stakes had just been raised.

The First Invitation

The voice on the other end of the line was devoid of any inflection, a smooth, neutral tone that offered no hint of personality. "Agent," it repeated, the single word hanging in the air like a cryptic promise. A brief pause, then, "We've been expecting your call, Riley."

A shiver ran down Jake's spine. The formality, the controlled precision of the voice, solidified the reality of his situation. This wasn't some drunken prank; this was real. He was stepping into a world far removed from the familiar comforts of his former life.

The instructions were simple: meet at a designated location, a seemingly innocuous address tucked away in a quiet corner of the city. He was given specific directions, a route meticulously planned to avoid surveillance, a testament to the agency's operational precision. The meeting was shrouded in secrecy, a clandestine rendezvous in a city teeming with millions. The feeling of being watched, the ever-present sense of observation, intensified his anxiety.

The location turned out to be the back entrance of what appeared to be a nondescript office building. There was nothing outwardly remarkable about it – no flashy signage, no overt signs of security. Yet, as Jake approached, he felt an almost palpable sense of unease. The air crackled with an unseen energy, a subtle hum of clandestine activity.

He was buzzed in through a heavily reinforced door, the mechanism silent and efficient, a stark contrast to the flimsy lock of his own apartment. The inside was a stark contrast to the dull exterior. Instead of a cramped office, he was greeted by a pristine, high-tech elevator that silently ascended to a higher level.

The elevator opened onto a spacious, well-lit lobby, more akin to a modern art gallery than a government facility. Sleek lines, minimalist décor, and expansive windows offered panoramic views of the city skyline, a breathtaking vista that belied the covert nature of the building. The silence was remarkable, broken only by the gentle hum of the climate control system.

A woman stood waiting, her appearance strikingly at odds with the austere surroundings. She was impeccably dressed in a tailored pantsuit, her short, dark hair styled with precision. Her eyes, however, held a sharpness that hinted at a steely resolve. She offered a curt nod, not a smile or any unnecessary pleasantries. Her name, she introduced herself as Agent Mallory, and her demeanor conveyed professionalism, efficiency, and a complete absence of warmth.

"Mr. Riley," she said, her voice devoid of emotion. "Please follow me."

She led him down a long corridor, the walls adorned with abstract art, the contrast once again striking. The air felt cool, almost sterile, the silence amplifying the quiet rhythm of their footsteps. He passed numerous unmarked doors, each radiating an aura of mystery and secrecy.

They arrived at a large, imposing door, and Agent Mallory scanned her retina against a sophisticated security system. The door hissed open, revealing a spacious room, a stark contrast to the minimalist corridors. This room was a combination of high-tech and old-school elegance; mahogany desks stood alongside cutting-edge computers, antique maps and globes shared space with state-of-the-art monitoring equipment.

At the far end of the room sat a man, his face obscured by shadows, his back to the door. He was tall and broad-shouldered, his posture radiating an authority that commanded attention. He turned, revealing a sharp, angular face, his eyes piercing and intense.

"Riley," he said, his voice deep and resonant. "Welcome."

He introduced himself as Director Hayes, the head of the agency. He was the embodiment of quiet authority, his presence filling the room. There was no small talk, no pleasantries; it was all business.

Director Hayes outlined the nature of the agency and its clandestine activities. The details were vague, shrouded in secrecy and guarded language. He spoke of covert operations, high-stakes missions, and a world of shadows where deception and subterfuge were paramount. He spoke of protecting national security, combating threats beyond the grasp of conventional intelligence, a world of existential danger where mistakes were not an option.

Jake listened, his mind reeling, struggling to process the sheer scale and scope of the information. The magnitude of it was overwhelming, a stark contrast to the mundane reality of his former life. This wasn't some Hollywood fantasy; this was real, with life-or-death consequences.

Director Hayes spoke of his skills, of the unique combination of athletic ability and mental acuity. He emphasized the rigorous training regimen that awaited him, a program designed to push him to his physical and mental limits. He spoke of the sacrifices he would have to make, the loss of his previous life, the constant threat of exposure and danger.

The risks were immense, the potential for failure catastrophic. Yet, the allure of this new path, the chance to use his abilities for something greater than himself, was equally compelling. The challenge was exhilarating, the stakes impossibly high.

Director Hayes didn't offer empty promises. He painted a stark picture of reality – the potential for serious injury, imprisonment, or death. He made it clear that this wasn't a game, but a life-or-death struggle against powerful adversaries.

He offered a stark choice. Jake could walk away, return to his former life, and accept the defeat of his baseball career. Or, he could embrace the challenge, immerse himself in a world of shadows, and face the unimaginable risks. The choice, he made it clear, was entirely Jake's.

The weight of the decision pressed down on Jake, the enormity of the choice overwhelming. The luxurious surroundings, the high-tech equipment, the air of sophisticated power, felt alien yet strangely compelling. His past life, the disappointment, the crushing weight of failure, seemed distant, a fading memory. This was a new beginning, a new life, full of danger and uncertainty, but also full of potential.

The silence in the room was heavy, pregnant with the unspoken implications of his choice. The city lights flickered outside the window, reflecting the turmoil raging within him. The offer was a gamble, a high-stakes bet on an uncertain future. But it was a chance, a second chance, to redefine himself, to rewrite his narrative. The weight of his former life, the bitterness of his failure, was a heavy burden to bear, a weight he longed to shed. The allure of this new path, this new identity, was irresistible. He knew, with a certainty that surprised even himself, what his answer would be.

He looked at Director Hayes, his eyes unwavering, his gaze reflecting a resolve he hadn't felt in years. "I'm in," he said, his voice firm and resolute. The game had changed, and Jake Riley was ready to play.

Weighing the Options

The silence in the room hung heavy, a palpable weight pressing down on Jake. Director Hayes's words echoed in his mind – the risks, the sacrifices, the potential for irreversible consequences. Outside, the city throbbed with life, a stark contrast to the sterile calm of the agency's headquarters. He looked out at the glittering cityscape, a million lives unfolding below, each with its own story, its own struggles, its own triumphs. And here he was, on the precipice of a new life, one that promised adventure, danger, and a complete erasure of his former self.

His reflection stared back at him from the polished surface of the mahogany desk. He saw the familiar lines etched around his eyes, the evidence of years spent under the relentless sun on the baseball diamond. The lean, athletic physique, honed by years of rigorous training, now seemed incongruous with the elegant surroundings. He was a man out of place, a fish out of water, yet somehow, strangely, at home.

The life he knew was a ghost, a fading memory. The roar of the crowd, the crack of the bat, the camaraderie of the dugout – all of it felt like a dream, distant and unreal. His abrupt departure from baseball had left a void, a gaping hole in his existence. The disappointment, the bitterness, the crushing weight of failure, had almost consumed him. He had wandered aimlessly, adrift in a sea of uncertainty, searching for something, anything, to fill the emptiness. And now, this.

This was a chance, a second chance, to rewrite his narrative. To shed the weight of his past, to redefine himself, to escape the crushing burden of expectation and disappointment. But at what cost? The price of admission was high, impossibly high. He would be leaving behind everything he knew, everything he loved, to step into a world of shadows, a world of deception and danger.

He closed his eyes, picturing his family. His parents, their faces etched with worry and disappointment, their hopes dashed by his unexpected and unceremonious exit from the baseball world. He saw his younger sister, her bright eyes full of admiration, her life still unfolding before her. The thought of leaving them, of abandoning them to a life without his presence, brought a sharp pang of guilt. He had always been the protector, the provider, the strong one. And now, he was leaving them vulnerable, alone.

He thought of the life he was leaving behind. The quiet apartment, the familiar routine, the simplicity of a life unburdened by secrets and lies. The ordinary comforts, the small pleasures, the mundane rhythms of daily existence – he would be trading them all for a life of constant vigilance, constant risk, constant uncertainty. Was it worth it? Was the potential reward worth the unimaginable sacrifice?

His thoughts swirled, a chaotic maelstrom of emotions. Fear mingled with exhilaration, guilt warred with ambition, and longing for the past wrestled with the allure of an unknown future. He was torn between two worlds, two lives, two identities. One, the familiar comfort of a life that was slipping away; the other, a tantalizing unknown, a world of shadows, adventure, and untold danger.

The allure of the challenge was undeniable. The opportunity to use his skills for something greater than himself, to make a real difference in the world, was a siren's call. He had always possessed a strong sense of justice, a deep-seated desire to fight for what was right. And now, he had been given a chance to do just that, to become a force for good in a world shrouded in darkness.

But the weight of responsibility was immense. The lives of others would depend on his actions, his decisions. One wrong move could have devastating consequences, not just for him, but for countless others. The gravity of the situation settled upon him, a crushing weight that threatened to suffocate him.

He reopened his eyes, the city lights blurring through his unshed tears. The decision felt like a physical burden, an immense weight pressing down on his chest. He had spent his life pushing himself to the limit, striving for excellence on the baseball field. But this was different. This was a battle not for a championship title, but for survival itself.

He imagined the rigors of the training program, the grueling physical and mental challenges, the constant pressure, the relentless pursuit of perfection. He pictured the missions, the covert operations, the potential for betrayal, the ever-present threat of exposure. The thought of failure was a chilling prospect, the consequences unthinkable.

Yet, even amidst the turmoil of his conflicting emotions, a sense of purpose began to emerge. A feeling of clarity, of resolve, started to take hold. He was a fighter. He had faced adversity before, overcome obstacles, pushed beyond his limits. This, he realized, was just another challenge, another test of his resilience.

The weight of his past failures began to lighten, replaced by a sense of anticipation, a thrill of excitement. The chance to reinvent himself, to escape the confines of his previous life, was too compelling to resist. He looked at Director Hayes, his eyes fixed, his gaze reflecting a quiet confidence.

He wasn't just accepting an offer; he was embracing a destiny, a calling. He was stepping into a new role, a new identity, one that demanded courage, resilience, and unwavering dedication. He was ready to embrace the darkness, to face the unknown, to fight for something greater than himself. He knew, with an unshakeable certainty, that this was his path. This was his fight.

He inhaled deeply, steeling himself, preparing to embark on this perilous journey. He would face the challenges, overcome the obstacles, and emerge stronger, wiser, and ready to confront whatever lay ahead. He would become something more than just a baseball player; he would become a warrior, a protector, a shadow in the night.

His answer was already decided long ago before he even entered that room. A quiet whisper inside him, a long-dormant ember, had ignited a fire in his soul. It was a fire fueled by the ashes of his past, by the relentless desire to prove himself, to find a purpose that transcended the limitations of his former life. The weight of the decision did not bring him down; instead, it ignited the fighter within him, and with that decision, he began to climb the mountain before him, step by steady step. He would forge his new identity in the crucible of fire and risk, and emerge stronger on the other side. The game had changed, and he was ready. He was in.

Acceptance and the Unknown

The weight of the decision settled upon him, a physical pressure in his chest, a tightening in his gut. It wasn't just a job offer; it was a complete upheaval, a seismic shift in the tectonic plates of his life. He pictured his parents' faces, etched with worry and disappointment, the silent question hanging in the air: *What now?* He saw his sister's hopeful gaze, her implicit faith in him, a faith he was about to shatter with this audacious leap into the unknown. The guilt gnawed at him, a persistent ache in his soul. He was abandoning them, trading the familiar comforts of home for a world of shadows, a life lived in the clandestine corners of society.

But the alternative was a slow, agonizing death, a withering away into insignificance. The baseball field, once a source of pride and accomplishment, had become a graveyard of shattered dreams. The roar of the crowd, the crack of the bat, the camaraderie of the dugout – these were memories now, ghosts haunting the emptiness of his present. He'd chased success on the diamond, only to stumble at the finish line, his career cut short, his future uncertain. The crushing weight of failure had nearly crushed him.

This, however, was different. This was a challenge, a fight against a different kind of opponent – a foe far more elusive and dangerous than any pitcher he'd ever faced. This wasn't about strikeouts and home runs; this was about survival, about the very definition of success and failure. This was about forging a new identity, a new life from the ashes of his old one.

The thrill of the unknown coursed through his veins, a potent elixir of adrenaline and anticipation. He felt a surge of exhilaration, a sudden rush of energy that chased away the shadows of doubt. This was an adventure, a chance to test his limits, to push himself beyond the boundaries of his former life. This was a chance to prove to himself – and to the world – that he was capable of far more than he ever thought possible.

He thought back to his training, the grueling hours spent honing his physical and mental skills, the relentless pursuit of perfection, the unwavering dedication to his craft. Those years on the diamond had prepared him for this. The discipline, the focus, the unwavering determination – it was all still there, dormant but ready to be ignited.

He imagined the training he was about to undertake, a brutal regimen designed to push him to the absolute limit of his endurance. He envisioned the covert missions, the dangerous assignments, the constant vigilance, the relentless pressure. The stakes would be impossibly high, the consequences irreversible. But the thought of failure, of faltering, did not deter him. It only fueled his resolve.

He considered the moral ambiguities, the ethical dilemmas that would inevitably arise. He would be operating in a world of shadows, a world where the lines between right and wrong were blurred, where the ends often justified the means. This would test his values, challenge his principles, and push him to make decisions that would haunt him long after the missions were complete. But he was ready to confront those challenges, to grapple with the complexities, to wrestle with his conscience.

He wasn't simply accepting a job; he was accepting a responsibility, a burden, a destiny. He was accepting a transformation, a shedding of his old self, a rebirth into something new, something stronger. This was a chance to make a difference, to contribute to something greater than himself, to fight for something worth fighting for.

The desire for purpose, for meaning, burned within him, a relentless fire that had been smoldering beneath the ashes of his disappointment. He yearned for a challenge, something that would test his limits, push him beyond his comfort zone, and force him to grow. This was it. This was the opportunity he'd been searching for, unconsciously, perhaps, but undeniably, searching for all along.

The room was silent, the only sound the rhythmic ticking of the clock, a relentless measure of time, a reminder of the urgency of his decision. He looked at Director Hayes, his gaze unwavering, his resolve solidified. He saw not just an employer, but a fellow soldier, a comrade in arms.

He cleared his throat, his voice a low rumble that echoed in the cavernous silence. "I accept," he said, the words firm, decisive, leaving no room for doubt. The weight of the decision didn't crush him; it empowered him. He stood, a different man than the one who had sat down just moments before. He was no longer the dejected baseball player, but a rising warrior, ready to embrace the unknown, ready to embrace the shadows, ready to fight for a purpose that extended far beyond himself.

He stepped forward, crossing the threshold, leaving behind the familiar world of baseball, of comfort and routine, of hopes and disappointments. He was stepping into a world of shadows, a world of secrets and lies, a world where the price of admission was high, but the potential rewards were immeasurable. He was stepping into the darkness, ready to face whatever lay ahead, ready to forge his new identity in the crucible of fire and risk. He was in. The game had changed. And he was ready to play.

The door closed behind him, sealing his past away, leaving him standing in a long, dimly lit corridor. The air hummed with a low, almost imperceptible energy, a tangible sense of the unseen forces at work within this clandestine organization. This was his new world, a stark contrast to the open fields and bright sunlight of his previous life. He felt a sudden chill, not from the temperature of the room, but from the stark reality of his decision. There was no turning back now.

He walked down the corridor, each step firm and deliberate. He was no longer just Jake Riley, the former baseball player; he was now something more. He was a ghost, a shadow, a phantom working in the shadows. The process of transformation would begin now. The rigorous training would strip away the old him, leaving only the essence of what he could become. The physical and mental challenges would be immense, the pressure relentless.

He imagined the faces of the instructors, stern and unforgiving, pushing him to the very brink of his physical and mental capacity. He anticipated the challenges of mastering new skills, the hours of relentless practice, the constant pressure to excel. He was preparing himself for a new kind of battle, one that demanded not only physical prowess but mental fortitude, cunning, and deception.

The uncertainty gnawed at him, a persistent doubt lurking in the shadows of his newfound purpose. But the excitement, the thrill of the challenge, overshadowed his fear. This wasn't merely a change of career; it was a transformation of self. This was a chance to escape the constraints of his past, to shed the weight of expectations and disappointments, and to forge a new identity, a new life from the embers of his old one.

He thought of the mission ahead, the dangers, the risks, the potential for failure. He knew that the lives of others would depend on his actions, his decisions. The weight of that responsibility settled upon him, a heavy cloak of obligation. But he wasn't afraid. He was ready. Years of playing under intense pressure had honed his mental resolve.

He focused on his breathing, steadying his nerves, calming the racing of his heart. He was a soldier now, a warrior, trained to handle pressure, trained to make quick decisions under duress, trained to remain calm in the face of overwhelming odds. He was ready to confront the challenges ahead, to overcome obstacles, and to emerge victorious. He would not fail.

He allowed himself a moment of reflection, a brief pause to absorb the gravity of the moment, the profound shift in his life's trajectory. He was leaving behind one world to enter another, a world shrouded in mystery, a world of intrigue and danger, a world that demanded secrecy, deception, and unwavering loyalty. He would step into the darkness, and he would not flinch.

He reached a heavy metal door, marked only with a small, unassuming number. This was it – the beginning of his new life, his new identity, his new purpose. He paused for a moment, gathering his resolve, drawing strength from the decision he had made. He placed his hand on the cold metal of the door and turned the handle. The door creaked open, revealing a long, dimly lit corridor. He stepped inside, closing the door behind him, leaving the old Jake Riley behind, embracing the unknown, ready for whatever lay ahead. The adventure had begun.

Physical Conditioning

The air hung thick with the scent of sweat and exertion. The training facility was a brutalist monument to human endurance, a cavernous space of steel and concrete, devoid of any comfort or decoration. Sunlight never penetrated the thick, reinforced walls; the only illumination came from harsh fluorescent lights that hummed a relentless, oppressive rhythm. This was not a place for the faint of heart; this was a crucible, designed to forge warriors from raw material.

Jake's first encounter with the physical regimen was a shock to the system. He'd been a professional athlete, accustomed to rigorous training, but this was on a different plane of existence. The instructors, hard-faced veterans with eyes that missed nothing, treated him as just another recruit, another body to be broken down and rebuilt in their image. There was no coddling, no special treatment for a former star athlete.

The days began before dawn, with a series of calisthenics designed to push his body to its absolute limits. Hundreds of push-ups, sit-ups, and squats were just the warm-up. Then came the brutal runs, miles and miles of punishing terrain, over hills and across rough, uneven ground, often in the dead of night, under the watchful eyes of his instructors. His muscles screamed in protest, lactic acid building up in his limbs, burning like fire. He pushed through the pain, driven by a stubborn refusal to quit, a determination forged in the fires of his failed baseball career.

The weight training was equally merciless. He'd worked out in state-of-the-art gyms, but this was different. The equipment was older, more basic, but its purpose was the same: to break him down and rebuild him stronger. He lifted weights far exceeding anything he'd ever handled, his muscles straining under the relentless pressure. He pushed himself beyond exhaustion, beyond pain, into a realm where only sheer willpower kept him going.

There were obstacle courses, designed to test his agility, strength, and endurance. He scaled walls, crawled under barbed wire, navigated treacherous terrain, and swung across chasms. His body was battered and bruised, his skin scraped raw, his muscles aching, his lungs burning. He fell, he stumbled, he failed, but each failure was a lesson, a step towards improvement, a step towards becoming something more.

The instructors were relentless. They pushed him past his perceived limits, past the point where he thought he could go no further. They screamed at him, berated him, pushed him to the brink of collapse. But they never gave up on him. They saw something in him, a spark of resilience, a fire that refused to be extinguished. Their cruelty was a kind of perverse affection, a recognition of his potential.

One particularly grueling training exercise involved a series of timed sprints up a steep, rocky incline, with weights strapped to his ankles. The ascent felt impossible; each step was a battle against gravity, against his own failing body. His lungs burned, his legs trembled, his heart hammered in his chest like a trapped bird. He thought he was going to collapse, to succumb to the pain, to the exhaustion. But he didn't. He pushed onward, driven by a primal instinct to survive, to prove himself.

He reached the top, gasping for air, his body drenched in sweat, his muscles screaming in agony. He collapsed onto the ground, exhausted, spent, but triumphant. The instructor, a granite-faced veteran named Sergeant Miller, simply nodded, his expression devoid of any emotion. It was a silent acknowledgment of his perseverance, a tacit approval of his determination.

The training was not just physical; it was mental as well. He was subjected to sleep deprivation, sensory overload, and psychological manipulation. He was interrogated, questioned, challenged, pushed to the limits of his sanity. He learned to control his emotions, to keep his thoughts private, to remain calm and focused under immense pressure.

The solitary confinement was particularly difficult. He was locked in a small, dark cell, deprived of sleep and sensory stimulation. The silence was deafening, the darkness suffocating. He fought against the insidious creep of paranoia, the gnawing sense of isolation. He battled his inner demons, his doubts, his fears. He emerged from the experience stronger, more resilient, more resolute.

The hand-to-hand combat training was brutal. He sparred with seasoned fighters, larger, stronger, more experienced opponents. He was beaten, bruised, bloodied, but he learned. He learned to defend himself, to strike with precision, to anticipate his opponent's moves. He learned to rely on his instincts, to trust his body, to fight with a ferocity that surprised even himself.

The weapons training was equally rigorous. He learned to handle a variety of firearms, explosives, and other weaponry, mastering their use with deadly efficiency. He learned to dismantle and reassemble weapons blindfolded, to shoot accurately under pressure, to handle explosives with precision and care. He became a master of his craft, a deadly weapon in his own right.

The survival training was perhaps the most challenging aspect of his ordeal. He learned to navigate unfamiliar terrain, to find food and water in the wilderness, to build makeshift shelters, to survive in extreme conditions. He learned to rely on his instincts, to trust his judgment, to adapt to changing circumstances. He learned to endure hardship, to overcome adversity, to emerge victorious.

The training was never-ending, relentless, always pushing him to the very edge of his capabilities. But it wasn't just about physical strength and endurance. It was about shaping his mind, molding his character, creating a warrior who could not be broken. It was about forging a new identity, one forged in the fires of adversity, a testament to his relentless will and indomitable spirit. He was being transformed, stripped down to his essence, rebuilt into something stronger, something more capable, something lethal. The crucible had begun its work, and Jake Riley was ready to be reborn. He would emerge from this hell not just a survivor, but a force to be reckoned with. The transformation was complete, or so he thought. The real test lay ahead.

Espionage Tactics

The relentless physical training was only the foundation. The true crucible began with the introduction of espionage tactics. Gone were the grueling runs and weightlifting sessions, replaced by a curriculum designed to turn Jake into a ghost, a shadow moving unseen through the most secure environments. The first lessons focused on surveillance. Jake learned to blend into crowds, to observe without being observed, to become a chameleon, adapting his demeanor and appearance to match his surroundings. He practiced shadowing targets, maintaining a safe distance while remaining visually connected, learning to anticipate their movements, their habits, their routines. This wasn't just about observation; it was about prediction, about anticipating their next move before they even made it. He spent hours studying human behavior, learning to read body language, to decipher micro-expressions, to identify deception. He practiced in bustling city streets, crowded marketplaces, and quiet residential areas, honing his skills until they were second nature.

The instructors introduced him to a variety of surveillance equipment, from sophisticated listening devices to high-powered binoculars and cameras equipped with advanced zoom lenses. He learned how to deploy and conceal these tools, how to use them effectively without leaving a trace. He mastered the art of covert photography, capturing images without attracting attention, learning to use various techniques to enhance and edit his images, obscuring identifying features, and creating false trails. He even learned how to build his own covert listening devices using readily available components, proving his resourcefulness and adaptability. Each successful surveillance operation, each unnoticed observation, was a small victory, a step closer to mastering the art of the invisible.

Infiltration training was equally demanding. Jake learned to forge documents, create believable identities, and manipulate computer systems to gain unauthorized access. He mastered lock-picking, gaining entry to secure locations without leaving a trace. He studied security systems, identifying weaknesses, finding loopholes, understanding the psychology behind security protocols. He practiced breaking into simulated secure facilities, each attempt more complex and challenging than the last. The instructors, ever vigilant, tested his abilities, pushing him to his limits, forcing him to think outside the box, to adapt to unexpected challenges. He learned to navigate complex maze-like corridors, avoiding motion sensors and pressure plates, moving with the grace and precision of a phantom.

The simulated environments were incredibly realistic. One exercise involved infiltrating a high-security government building, navigating intricate corridors, circumventing sophisticated security systems, and accessing a specific file. Another simulated a diplomatic mission, requiring him to blend into a high-society gathering, extract sensitive information, and escape undetected. Each infiltration exercise ended with a debrief, a critical analysis of his performance, identifying areas for improvement, highlighting his strengths and weaknesses. The goal was not just to succeed; it was to perform flawlessly, leaving no trace, no evidence of his presence. He learned to anticipate and counter potential threats, to remain calm under pressure, to think critically and strategically, turning every obstacle into an opportunity.

Hand-to-hand combat training evolved beyond the brutal sparring sessions. He learned advanced grappling techniques, disabling holds, pressure points, and close-quarters combat strategies. He practiced on specialized training dummies, their resilience designed to simulate the force of a human body. The instructors, masters of their craft, patiently guided him, correcting his posture, refining his technique, honing his reflexes. He learned different fighting styles, adapting his approach based on his opponent's size, strength, and skill. He honed his awareness, learning to predict an opponent's moves, reacting instinctively, defending himself effectively, and striking with precision. The focus was not on brute force, but on efficiency, on taking down an opponent quickly and silently, minimizing collateral damage.

Weapons training took on a new level of complexity. Beyond proficiency with firearms, he learned the subtle art of marksmanship, practicing precision shooting from various positions and distances. He mastered advanced weaponry, including silenced pistols, specialized rifles, and explosive devices. He learned how to disarm opponents, to handle explosives safely and effectively, to utilize weapons in close-quarters combat. He practiced in various simulated environments, from urban battlefields to wilderness scenarios, learning to adapt his tactics based on the environment and the mission objectives. He learned to anticipate weapon malfunctions, handling failures with calmness and precision, always maintaining control and situational awareness.

The training extended beyond the physical and technical aspects, delving into the psychology of espionage. Jake underwent extensive deception training, learning to create false narratives, to manipulate individuals, and to project a persona tailored to specific situations. He mastered the art of interrogation, learning both coercive and persuasive techniques, pushing subjects to reveal information without leaving a trace of his methods. He learned to control his emotions, to remain calm and composed under pressure, to think strategically and adapt to unexpected developments. He underwent extensive polygraph testing, learning to control his physiological responses and manipulate the results. The psychological training was designed to shape him, to mold his mind, to make him resilient to pressure, unwavering in his focus, and utterly resistant to manipulation. This was not just about training his body; it was about shaping his very essence, forging a master spy, a formidable instrument of the state.

The final phase of training focused on integration. Jake learned to operate in teams, to coordinate with other operatives, to trust his colleagues implicitly. He participated in simulated missions, replicating real-world scenarios, working with different specialists, adapting his skills to the demands of the task. He learned how to maintain operational security, how to communicate covertly, and how to handle emergencies. He practiced escape and evasion techniques, learning to disappear without a trace, to blend into unfamiliar environments, and to exploit any opportunity to escape. The training was both physically and mentally exhausting, but each challenge was a step closer to his goal, shaping him into the ultimate spy, ready to operate in the shadows, to execute missions with precision and efficiency, always leaving no trace behind. The crucible had finished its work; Jake Riley was forged anew, ready for his first real mission. The world awaited, and he was ready.

Psychological Warfare

The physical and technical training, brutal as it was, proved to be only half the battle. The instructors, figures shrouded in an almost mythical aura of competence and ruthlessness, now turned their attention to Jake's mind, to the very core of his being. This phase, the psychological warfare, was designed not just to test his resilience but to break him down and rebuild him in their image – a weapon of unparalleled precision and unwavering loyalty.

The setting shifted from the sprawling training grounds to a stark, isolated compound, a secluded fortress nestled deep within the wilderness. The atmosphere was different here; the air thick with a palpable sense of tension, a silent pressure that bore down on Jake with an almost physical weight. The instructors, their faces now devoid of the gruff camaraderie of the physical training phase, seemed to radiate an icy calm, their eyes penetrating, unwavering, as if they could see right through him, into the very depths of his soul.

The psychological challenges began subtly, with seemingly innocuous exercises designed to probe Jake's vulnerabilities. He was subjected to sleep deprivation, relentless questioning designed to unravel his carefully constructed defenses, and forced to endure extended periods of sensory deprivation in soundproof chambers, the silence amplified to an unnerving intensity. He found himself battling not just fatigue, but the creeping tendrils of paranoia, the insidious whispers of doubt that gnawed at the edges of his sanity.

One particular exercise involved prolonged interrogation sessions, orchestrated by masters of manipulation. These weren't the straightforward, brute-force methods of interrogation depicted in movies; these were refined, subtle techniques designed to unravel a subject's carefully constructed defenses. They presented conflicting information, sowing seeds of doubt and confusion. They used psychological projection, mirroring Jake's own anxieties and fears back at him, magnifying them until they became overwhelming. They employed subtle forms of gaslighting, twisting his perceptions and making him question his own sanity. The goal wasn't just to extract information, but to break down his resistance, to instill a deep sense of insecurity and vulnerability. Jake found himself questioning his own memories, his own judgment, battling the insidious creep of self-doubt.

Another challenge involved navigating complex social simulations, scenarios designed to test his ability to deceive and manipulate. He was placed in situations requiring him to extract information from individuals who were themselves highly trained in deception. He learned to subtly plant misinformation, to create false narratives that were both convincing and easily verifiable. He had to maintain his composure while being subtly manipulated by skilled actors, whose expertise in reading body language and detecting deception far surpassed anything he had encountered before. Success here demanded not just a mastery of deception, but also the ability to anticipate and counter the tactics of his adversaries. He was taught to create believable false identities, to seamlessly adopt different personas to infiltrate various social circles, moving undetected amongst people who could instantly recognize a fabricated persona.

The pressure scenarios escalated in intensity. Jake found himself in simulated hostage situations, forced to negotiate under extreme duress, making life-or-death decisions with limited information and under immense time pressure. He learned to control his emotions, his heart rate, his breathing, to project an image of calm authority even when his mind was racing, his instincts screaming for action. He was placed in simulated environments mimicking real-world emergencies, requiring quick thinking, strategic decision-making, and the ability to remain calm under pressure, situations where failure had dire consequences. He was challenged with moral dilemmas, forcing him to make choices that tested his ethical boundaries, testing his ability to compartmentalize, to operate within the moral gray areas of the espionage world.

The training also extended into the realm of advanced psychological operations. Jake learned to identify and exploit psychological vulnerabilities in individuals, using his observations of their behavior, their body language, and their micro-expressions to gain an advantage. He studied various psychological manipulation techniques, from subtle forms of influence to overt attempts to control and dominate. He practiced manipulating the emotions of his targets, creating false hopes and anxieties, planting doubts and fears. He learned to use empathy and understanding as tools of manipulation, skillfully exploiting the trust and goodwill of others.

But it wasn't just about manipulating others; it was also about mastering his own mind, his own emotions. He was trained in mindfulness techniques, learning to control his breathing, to focus his attention, to calm his mind under pressure. He underwent extensive cognitive behavioral therapy, learning to identify and challenge his negative thought patterns, to develop greater resilience and adaptability in the face of adversity. He practiced emotional regulation, learning to control his reactions, to manage his stress levels, and to maintain his composure under pressure.

The instructors relentlessly tested his ability to withstand psychological stress, pushing him to the brink of mental exhaustion. They used a variety of methods, from sleep deprivation and sensory overload to social isolation and emotional manipulation. They sought to break him down, to expose his weaknesses, to see if he could withstand the pressures of the job. They wanted to see how he reacted under intense duress, how he adapted to changing circumstances, and how he maintained his focus and his composure in the face of overwhelming adversity.

Throughout the entire process, the instructors offered little in the way of comfort or reassurance. Their methods were brutal, relentless, their goal not to help Jake, but to break him and rebuild him into something more lethal, something more resilient. There were no pats on the back, no words of encouragement; only the cold, hard reality of the mission ahead. The instructors remained stoic and unyielding, their faces impassive masks revealing nothing of their thoughts or intentions, leaving Jake to grapple alone with the relentless psychological assaults. The lack of human connection, the isolation, served as another form of psychological warfare, adding another layer to the already intense mental and emotional challenge.

The psychological training concluded with a series of complex, multifaceted simulations, each designed to test his skills under pressure. He was placed in a series of ever-escalating scenarios, each designed to push his skills, his resilience, his resolve to the absolute limit. Each simulation required him to use everything he had learned – physical prowess, technical skills, and his newly honed psychological resilience. These simulations were not just tests of his ability; they were a crucible, refining him, forging him into a weapon of unprecedented effectiveness. The intensity of these scenarios was designed to mimic the chaos, the uncertainty, and the intense pressures of real-world espionage operations. The simulations ended only when the instructors were convinced that he had the mental strength, the adaptability, and the resilience to succeed in the clandestine world he was now entering.

The final test was a grueling, multi-day simulation involving a complex infiltration operation, a mock assassination attempt, and a high-stakes negotiation, all conducted under intense psychological duress. It was a final, ultimate test of his ability to maintain composure, strategic thinking, and operate effectively under extreme pressure. This was a grueling, all-encompassing ordeal, pushing Jake to his absolute limits, physically, mentally, and emotionally. The constant pressure, the relentless mental assault, and the ever-present threat of failure combined to make this the most challenging experience of his life. Only when he successfully navigated this ultimate test did the instructors deem him ready for his first real mission. Jake Riley, the former baseball player, had finally been transformed. He had become something more; something far more dangerous. He was ready to enter the shadows.

Adapting to the Shadows

The shedding of Jake Riley, the baseball player, wasn't a singular event, but a slow, agonizing process of erosion and reconstruction. It began subtly, with the confiscation of his personal belongings – the worn-out baseball glove, the faded photographs of family and friends, the letters from his college sweetheart. Each item, a tangible piece of his past, was meticulously cataloged, then locked away, becoming symbolic sacrifices on the altar of his new life. The instructors didn't offer explanations; their silence was a chilling testament to the finality of his transformation.

The replacement wasn't a simple matter of adopting a new name and a fabricated backstory. It was a deep dive into the creation of a new identity, a new persona meticulously crafted from scratch. He spent weeks immersed in the study of different personalities, analyzing mannerisms, speech patterns, and behavioral quirks. He learned to mimic accents, to subtly alter his posture and gait, to feign emotions he didn't feel. He practiced adopting different personas, seamlessly shifting between them as if changing clothes. He wasn't just learning to play a role; he was learning to *be* the role, to inhabit it completely, to make it an extension of himself.

This involved not only the external facade but also the internal landscape of his mind. He underwent intense sessions of cognitive restructuring, learning to suppress his natural inclinations and adopt the behaviors of his new identity. This was a painful process; a constant battle against his innate personality, a forced suppression of his own thoughts and feelings. He was taught to control his reactions, to mask his emotions, to remain impassive in the face of adversity. The line between Jake Riley and his new persona became increasingly blurred, creating a sense of internal dissonance that added another layer to the mental and emotional toll.

The psychological exercises escalated in intensity. He was subjected to prolonged periods of solitary confinement, where the silence became a suffocating presence, amplifying his doubts and fears. He participated in elaborate role-playing scenarios designed to push him to his psychological limits. He was forced to interact with skilled actors who played the roles of his targets, interrogators, and potential allies, each scenario testing his ability to deceive, manipulate, and remain calm under pressure. The simulations were often emotionally draining, forcing him to confront his vulnerabilities and to grapple with the moral ambiguities inherent in his new profession.

One particularly harrowing exercise involved a simulated interrogation under duress. Bound to a chair, subjected to sleep deprivation and psychological manipulation, he had to maintain his composure while resisting the relentless attempts to extract information from him. He was confronted with seemingly irrefutable evidence, planted to create doubt and confusion. His interrogators used a combination of intimidation, subtle flattery, and psychological projection, mirroring his own fears and insecurities back at him in an attempt to break his resolve. He found himself battling not just the external pressures but the internal whispers of doubt, the insidious creep of paranoia that threatened to undermine his carefully constructed facade. The experience was brutal, pushing him to the brink of mental exhaustion, but he emerged with a hardened resilience, a renewed sense of his capacity to withstand immense pressure.

The training also focused on the art of deception, going beyond simple lies to encompass a deep understanding of human psychology. He learned to read body language, to interpret micro-expressions, to identify subtle cues that betrayed a person's true thoughts and emotions. He practiced creating believable cover stories, developing intricate backstories for his new persona, ensuring that his fabricated history was consistent and airtight. He studied various forms of deception, from subtle misdirection to outright fabrication, learning to manipulate others without raising suspicion.

He wasn't just learning how to deceive; he was learning how to anticipate and counter deception. He was trained in identifying and exploiting vulnerabilities in others, learning to use their own biases and preconceptions against them. This involved intensive studies of human behavior, including personality types, psychological profiles, and the various methods of influencing and manipulating people. He learned to recognize deceptive techniques, to detect subtle lies and inconsistencies, and to maintain his composure while being subtly manipulated by others. He was forced to navigate complex social interactions, where his every word and action was scrutinized, where a single misstep could expose his true identity.

The transformation wasn't simply about adopting a new persona; it was about burying the old one deep within. He was taught to suppress his past, to sever ties with his former life, to erase any trace of his previous identity. This involved not only physical separation but also emotional detachment. He was encouraged to detach himself from his loved ones, to distance himself from those who knew him before. It was a painful process, a necessary sacrifice on the altar of his new life. He was learning to exist in the shadows, a phantom moving through the world, unnoticed and unremembered.

This emotional detachment wasn't a simple act of will; it was a carefully orchestrated psychological process. His instructors employed various techniques designed to weaken his emotional ties to his past. This included sleep deprivation, sensory overload, and prolonged periods of isolation. The goal wasn't simply to weaken his emotional attachments but to replace them with a unwavering loyalty to his new mission and his new identity. His instructors were ruthless in their pursuit of this goal; they were sculptors shaping him into a weapon, and emotional attachments were considered weaknesses to be eradicated.

As the training progressed, the line between reality and simulation blurred. He found himself questioning his own memories, his own identity. The constant pressure, the relentless psychological manipulation, and the emotional detachment took their toll. He experienced moments of doubt, moments of self-questioning, moments where the weight of his transformation threatened to overwhelm him. But he persevered, driven by a combination of determination, ambition, and the fear of failure.

The final stage of his transformation involved a grueling, week-long simulation designed to test every aspect of his new identity. He was given a complex mission requiring infiltration, deception, and the extraction of sensitive information from highly trained professionals. He had to maintain his cover for an extended period, navigate complex social interactions, and remain calm under intense pressure. He was observed throughout by his instructors, who scrutinized every move, every word, every expression. The pressure was immense, the stakes unbearably high, and the emotional cost immeasurable. He emerged from this final crucible transformed, ready to enter the shadows and play his part in the clandestine world. He was no longer Jake

Riley. He was a ghost, a shadow, a weapon forged in the crucible of deception. He was ready for his first mission.

Forging a New Identity

The steam from the shower clouded the mirror, momentarily obscuring the face staring back at him. It wasn't the face he remembered. Gone was the youthful exuberance of the baseball player, replaced by a sharper, leaner visage, etched with the lines of hardship and discipline. The eyes, once bright with the promise of a carefree life on the diamond, now held a steely glint, a calculated coldness that mirrored the depths of his training. He ran a hand over his jaw, feeling the stubble that had become a permanent fixture, a testament to the relentless schedule that had consumed his life for the past months. This wasn't merely a physical transformation; it was a fundamental reshaping of his very being.

He watched as he meticulously applied the faintest trace of stubble coloring, blending it seamlessly with his skin. It was a detail, almost imperceptible, but crucial in completing his new persona. He studied the face in the mirror—the subtle asymmetry of the jawline, the slight downturn of the left corner of his mouth, the almost imperceptible slant in his eyes. These were the carefully crafted imperfections that made him believable, that rendered him indistinguishable from the persona he now inhabited. The hours spent studying photographs, analyzing mannerisms, and practicing expressions had paid off. The transformation was complete. He was no longer Jake Riley. He was… someone else entirely.

The details were painstakingly etched into his memory. His new name, Alexander Dane, flowed effortlessly from his tongue, a name that felt as natural as his own skin, despite its foreign nature. His backstory, meticulously researched and flawlessly crafted, was a complex tapestry of believable details. He knew the exact location of his fictional childhood home, the names of his non-existent friends, the details of his fabricated educational history and career path, even the nuances of his purported family relationships. He knew where his supposed parents were living now, their jobs, their likes, and dislikes, down to the make and model of their car. The depth of his preparation was terrifying, but this was no longer some academic exercise. This was his life now.

This newfound identity extended beyond the surface. He had learned to speak with the precise cadence, accent, and inflection required for his new persona. His posture, his gait, even the way he held his hands and looked at people were all meticulously curated to match his new role. He could mimic emotions with a chilling accuracy, feigning interest and empathy when the situation demanded it, masking his true feelings with a mastery that came only after countless hours of practice. He had become a master of deception, a chameleon capable of seamlessly blending into any environment.

The training had pushed him beyond his physical and mental limits. The psychological conditioning was the most grueling. The sleep deprivation, the isolation, the relentless simulations, all designed to break him down and rebuild him in the image of his new identity. He recalled the interrogation scenarios, the chilling precision of his instructors, their ability to exploit his deepest vulnerabilities, his most profound insecurities. He had faced the darkest corners of his mind, his own capacity for self-doubt and fear. He had learned to confront these weaknesses and to transform them into strengths. He emerged not just physically changed, but emotionally hardened, resilient, and resolute.

His physical conditioning was equally rigorous. He had undergone an extreme transformation of his body. He was faster, stronger, more agile than he had ever been. His hand-to-hand combat skills were lethal, honed to a razor's edge through countless hours of intense sparring and brutal simulations. He possessed a detailed understanding of weaponry, both conventional and unconventional, and he could disassemble and reassemble a handgun blindfolded. The physical demands were extraordinary, pushing him to his absolute peak performance. He felt the power coursing through his veins, the strength that was both his protection and his weapon.

He spent countless hours practicing surveillance techniques, learning to blend seamlessly into crowds, to observe without being noticed, to extract information without leaving a trace. He mastered the art of covert communication, learning to use encrypted channels and hidden messages to transmit critical information discreetly. He became proficient in various forms of infiltration and exfiltration, mastering techniques for breaching security systems, utilizing advanced technology, and escaping detection. He was a ghost, capable of disappearing and reappearing at will.

He had learned to control every aspect of his physical presentation, even under intense pressure. He knew how to maintain a consistent demeanor, how to manage his body language and micro-expressions to convey the desired impression, regardless of his internal state. He was a master of observation, able to glean information from the slightest of cues, from a fleeting glance or an almost imperceptible shift in posture. He could read people like an open book, understanding their motivations, their weaknesses, their vulnerabilities. He had become a master of manipulation, capable of influencing others subtly and discreetly, achieving his objectives without raising suspicion.

The final test, a week-long, immersive simulation, had been a harrowing crucible. He had been thrust into a complex, ever-shifting scenario that demanded absolute perfection. He had infiltrated a high-security facility, navigated treacherous social interactions, gathered critical intelligence, and exfiltrated successfully without raising suspicion. He had played a role, not merely acted one out. He had become Alexander Dane, and he had excelled. His instructors had watched him relentlessly, scrutinizing his every action, every word, every expression. And he had not faltered.

He looked again at his reflection, a stranger staring back. The eyes reflected not fear or uncertainty, but a quiet, steely confidence, a sense of purpose. This man, Alexander Dane, was a culmination of years of dedication, of brutal training, and of complete self-transformation. He was a weapon crafted in the fires of necessity, honed to a lethal edge. He was ready for the shadows. He was ready for his first mission. He was ready for the war that awaited him. The war he wasn't even certain he understood.

The cold certainty that settled within him wasn't just a reflection of his training, but a realization of the profound shift in his own identity. The man staring back at him from the mirror was a ghost of his former self. The baseball player was gone. The naive, optimistic Jake Riley was a distant memory. In his place was a finely tuned instrument of espionage, a blank slate, a phantom in the world, free from all the bonds and burdens of his past.

The freedom, however, felt oddly cold. It wasn't the liberating sense of escape he had once envisioned. It was a chilling realization of just how much he had lost. The price of his transformation had been steep. He had forfeited everything to become this new man, this phantom, this ghost. He had sacrificed his friends, his family, his dreams.

In the quiet stillness of the bathroom, he felt a profound isolation, a stark loneliness that cut through him like a knife. The emptiness was tangible, a silent witness to the sacrifices that had been made. It was the chilling price of his new life.

This new identity was a carefully constructed facade, a performance he was expected to maintain at all times. Any slip, any lapse in his fabricated persona, could have devastating consequences. He lived with this constant awareness. Every conversation, every interaction, was fraught with the potential for exposure. His life was a tightrope walk above an abyss of risk and uncertainty. The weight of this constant vigilance was immense. It was a heavy cloak he wore, never to be removed.

He knew the risk he faced if his identity was ever compromised. The potential for retribution was chilling, and the thought of his old life being discovered sent a cold shiver down his spine. He had been trained to anticipate and mitigate threats, but the reality was that failure was not an option.

There was a certain satisfaction, though, in this perfect control. The precision of his actions, the precision of his disguise, the flawless execution of his deceptive strategies. This was a skill he had mastered, and the ability to pull off a flawlessly crafted deception was intoxicating. It was the thrill of being the master of his own destiny, the puppeteer pulling the strings.

He knew there would be moments of doubt, of self-questioning, of the insidious creep of self-doubt. This was inevitable, given the profound psychological transformation he had undergone. But he had been trained to deal with this; to confront these vulnerabilities, to master his own psyche.

He was a warrior, hardened and resolute, prepared for whatever lay ahead. He was ready to face the shadows.

The Briefing

The heavy oak door hissed open, revealing a dimly lit room. The air was thick with the scent of old paper and stale coffee, a familiar aroma that spoke of countless clandestine operations and whispered secrets. Jake, or rather, Alexander Dane, stepped inside, his footsteps echoing faintly on the polished concrete floor. The room was spartan, almost monastic in its simplicity, yet the air crackled with a palpable tension. Maps, sprawling and detailed, covered much of the walls, their intricate lines tracing the contours of a foreign land – a labyrinthine city nestled amidst a chaotic landscape. Stacks of intelligence files, bound in thick, unmarked folders, were piled high on a steel table, their weight hinting at the gravity of the information contained within.

A single figure sat behind the table, silhouetted against the faint glow of a computer screen. He rose as Jake entered, revealing a tall, gaunt man with eyes that seemed to pierce through the carefully constructed façade of his new identity. This was Mr. Hayes, his handler, the enigmatic figure who had overseen his transformation. Hayes didn't offer a greeting, his silence as imposing as any verbal command. He gestured to a chair, and Jake sat, the cold metal biting into his thighs.

"The target is known only as 'The Serpent,'" Hayes began, his voice low and measured, each word carrying the weight of a thousand unspoken dangers. "He operates within the city of Al-Zahra, a city renowned for its labyrinthine alleyways, its dense population, and its impenetrable security."

Hayes tapped a finger on a large map of Al-Zahra. The city, a tapestry of twisting streets and crowded souks, was a visual representation of chaos. The map itself was a testament to the meticulous intelligence gathering that had been undertaken. "The Serpent" was a shadowy figure, a ghost within the city's shadows, his identity shrouded in mystery, his operations a tangle of veiled transactions and clandestine meetings. His true purpose remained elusive, though intelligence suggested links to a network involved in the illicit trafficking of weapons technology.

"Your mission," Hayes continued, his gaze unwavering, "is to infiltrate his inner circle, to ascertain his identity, his operations, and his ultimate goals."

The task was daunting. Al-Zahra was a city of secrets, a place where whispers carried more weight than shouts, where loyalty and betrayal danced in a deadly waltz. Infiltrating a city was challenging enough, but to burrow into the heart of the Serpent's operation would be a test of courage and intellect, a trial that pushed the boundaries of human endurance.

"We know very little about the Serpent's organization," Hayes said. "What we do know is that they operate from within the heart of the old city. The souks are a maze of narrow passageways and hidden courtyards, making surveillance difficult, if not impossible. You will need to rely on your wits, your instincts, and your training."

Jake nodded, his outward composure masking the churning storm of uncertainty that roiled within him. He was prepared for challenges, he had undergone training that stretched the limits of human endurance. But this, this felt different. It was an undertaking so complex and treacherous that the mere contemplation of it caused a cold sweat to break out on his skin.

Hayes continued, outlining the operational details. Jake would be working alone, a lone wolf in a den of vipers. He would be supplied with minimal resources, a testament to the clandestine nature of the operation. A small team of specialists were operating on the periphery, providing remote surveillance and logistical support, but his every move, every decision, would rest squarely on his own shoulders. He would be operating beyond the reach of conventional extraction methods; he would be entirely self-sufficient.

"You will be working under deep cover," Hayes stressed. "Your cover identity has already been established. You are Hassan Al-Rashid, a merchant dealing in rare antiques." He handed Jake a thick folder containing a wealth of carefully crafted biographical information. The dossier was astonishingly detailed; family history, business associates, and even financial records, meticulously fabricated to create a believable façade.

"Be aware that your cover is extremely fragile," Hayes cautioned. "Any deviation from the established persona could result in catastrophic failure, and failure in this mission is not an option."

The stakes were impossibly high. The success of the mission depended entirely on his ability to blend into this alien environment, to master deception, and to outwit those who were masters of deception themselves. He was stepping into a world of shadows and moral ambiguities, and the risks were not limited to his own safety and security. There were political implications that extended far beyond the scope of this mission.

"The intelligence we have gathered suggests that 'The Serpent' is not merely involved in weapons trafficking," Hayes revealed, leaning forward. "There are indications that he is involved in activities that have the potential to destabilize the entire region. This is a high-stakes operation, Alexander. The consequences of failure are far-reaching."

Jake felt a cold shiver run down his spine. The weight of responsibility settled heavily upon his shoulders. He had been trained to deal with pressure, but the scale of this mission, the sheer magnitude of its implications, felt different. It was no longer a game; this was a high-stakes gamble with potentially devastating consequences.

The briefing concluded with a detailed explanation of the communication protocols, the emergency extraction procedures, and the contingency plans. Hayes detailed the use of encrypted communication channels, the activation procedures for emergency support, and the means of relaying gathered intelligence. Every aspect of the mission, every contingency, had been meticulously planned, but even with the best preparation, nothing could fully prepare him for the inherent uncertainties and risks.

"You leave in 24 hours," Hayes stated flatly. He handed Jake a small, sealed envelope. "This contains your travel documents, along with your initial funds. Remember, Alexander, your actions will determine not only your fate, but the fate of many others."

Jake took the envelope, his fingers tracing the crisp edges of the paper. The weight of the mission settled upon him, a crushing burden that made his chest heavy. He stood, the silence broken only by the faint hum of the computer and the rhythmic ticking of a clock on the wall. The room felt suddenly cold, the air thick with the chilling certainty of his approaching departure. He had trained for this; he had sacrificed everything for this. He was ready. Or at least, he had to be. He turned and walked towards the door, the echoes of Hayes' final words ringing in his ears. He stepped out into the night, a ghost walking into the shadows, a phantom heading into the labyrinth of Al-Zahra, where his true test would begin. The Serpent awaited.

Infiltration and Surveillance

The Al-Zahra airport swarmed with a chaotic energy, a vibrant tapestry of faces, languages, and smells assaulting his senses. Jake, or rather Hassan Al-Rashid, moved through the throng with practiced ease, his newly acquired persona settling comfortably upon him. He was a merchant, yes, but a merchant with a keen eye for detail, a man who observed and absorbed everything around him. His carefully crafted backstory played out in his mind, a well-rehearsed script ready to be delivered at a moment's notice.

His initial objective was simple: establish a foothold. He checked into a modest hotel near the old city, a labyrinthine warren of narrow streets and bustling souks. The hotel, a relic of a bygone era, was more a collection of crumbling rooms than a functional establishment. It was perfect. Its disrepair offered a cloak of anonymity, allowing him to blend seamlessly into the background.

The next few days were a blur of calculated movements and meticulous observation. He spent his days wandering through the labyrinthine streets, visiting the bustling souks, his eyes scanning for anything out of the ordinary. He learned the rhythms of the city, the subtle shifts in the crowd, the unspoken cues that revealed the underlying power dynamics. He mingled with the locals, adopting their mannerisms, their speech patterns, the way they conducted business, all adding layers to his disguise.

His cover identity as Hassan Al-Rashid, a merchant specializing in rare antiques, provided him with a degree of legitimacy. He frequented the antique shops, engaging in conversations with the merchants, learning their trade secrets, gleaning information about the city's underbelly. He was building a network, a web of connections that would eventually lead him to the Serpent. He used his training – the subtle art of extracting information, the ability to read body language, the mastery of deception – to weave himself into the fabric of Al-Zahra's social structure.

Each contact, each transaction, was meticulously planned, each interaction designed to yield a piece of the puzzle. He learned about the city's power brokers, its hidden networks, its unspoken rules of engagement. He even managed to subtly insert himself into a high-stakes poker game held within a dimly lit backroom of a bustling tea house, a hidden gathering place for Al-Zahra's elite.

The poker game proved invaluable. He observed the interactions between the players, overhearing snippets of conversations that hinted at the Serpent's activities. He noted the subtle gestures, the veiled allusions, the coded language that whispered of secret deals and clandestine meetings. He even managed to win a significant sum of money, establishing a level of trust and respect among the players, gaining access to their inner circles.

Through careful observation, he noticed a pattern, a recurring motif that linked several of the individuals he'd encountered. The symbol of a coiled serpent, subtly embroidered on clothing, etched onto a ring, or even a marking on a rare book. It was a subtle but significant detail – a breadcrumb trail leading directly to the Serpent's organization.

He initiated contact with one of the players, a seemingly innocuous individual who he quickly identified as someone close to the Serpent's inner circle. He started by engaging in casual conversation, skillfully weaving in his knowledge about the intricacies of the antique trade, demonstrating his understanding and expertise of local culture. He presented himself as someone of considerable wealth, discreetly hinting at his connections within the international network of collectors.

The subtle exchange of information became an art form in itself. He discovered that the Serpent's organization was far more complex than he initially anticipated, a network of individuals operating in different sectors – arms dealing, drug trafficking, financial fraud. It was a web of intricate connections that demanded a higher level of understanding and skill to unravel. His skills in code breaking, information gathering and deception became invaluable tools as he navigated these dangerous waters.

His surveillance efforts were never overt. He relied on his keen observational skills, blending in with the crowds, observing from a distance, utilizing the city's natural cover. He employed a variety of methods – inconspicuous observation from rooftops and balconies, subtly recording conversations, and using hidden cameras that sent encrypted images to his remote support team. But technology only took him so far. He needed human intelligence, and that required navigating the treacherous social landscape of Al-Zahra.

His training kicked in. He used his physical prowess, honed during his time in military intelligence, to evade those who attempted to follow him, navigating the city's maze-like streets with the skill of a seasoned professional. He was a phantom in the city's heart, moving with speed and precision, disappearing before he could be detected.

Days turned into weeks. He gradually gained the trust of several individuals connected to the Serpent's organization. He played his role meticulously, carefully calibrating his demeanor to fit each situation. His patience and perseverance paid off, and he gradually began to identify key figures, map their hierarchies, and decipher their methods. He was getting close. The Serpent's web was beginning to unravel.

But as he delved deeper, he realized the true extent of the Serpent's ambitions. The weapons trafficking was just a piece of a larger puzzle. His network seemed intricately linked to political figures, influencing events on a regional scale. The implications were staggering, far beyond the initial scope of his mission. The stakes had escalated dramatically.

He was operating in a gray area, and moral ambiguities started haunting him. He was involved in deception, manipulation, even potential betrayal, but the overall cause, the protection of international security, justified it in his mind. The weight of responsibility pressed upon him, a chilling reminder of the potential consequences of failure.

He knew that soon, he would have to make a decision. Would he follow established protocols and report his findings? Or would he take a more drastic approach, one that was high-risk and outside the confines of his mission's original parameters? The path ahead was fraught with danger, a treacherous tightrope walk between success and catastrophic failure. The labyrinth of Al-Zahra had tested his limits, but the true challenge had only just begun. The Serpent was closer than he had ever anticipated. And the time to strike was drawing near.

Unexpected Allies

The dimly lit backroom of the "Serpent's Kiss" tea house reeked of stale jasmine and desperation. Jake, or rather Hassan, felt the weight of a hundred eyes on him, even though the room was sparsely populated. Across the low table, Omar, the seemingly innocuous poker player, steepled his fingers, his gaze unnervingly intense. Omar had been his contact for weeks, a seemingly insignificant cog in the Serpent's vast machine, yet he held a key.

"You have information, Hassan," Omar stated, his voice a low rumble. He didn't ask; he stated it as a fact, a testament to the intelligence network that had already painted a picture of Jake's clandestine activities.

Jake feigned a casual shrug, letting the tension build. "Information is a valuable commodity, my friend. And valuable commodities command a price."

Omar smiled, a slow, chilling curve of his lips. "We both understand the value of information, Hassan. You know what we seek. The details of the upcoming arms shipment. The rendezvous point, the buyers... the entirety."

Jake leaned forward, his eyes narrowed. He knew the risks of revealing too much too soon. "I have fragments, yes. But to assemble the complete picture... that would require an investment, a significant one."

Omar chuckled, a sound that felt like ice cracking. "You're playing a dangerous game, Hassan. The Serpent doesn't appreciate games. He appreciates results."

Their negotiation was a dance of veiled threats and subtle promises. The air crackled with unspoken power, each word a calculated step in a deadly game of chess. Eventually, after hours of tense maneuvering, a deal was struck, a dangerous alliance forged in the shadows. In exchange for the information Jake possessed, Omar offered him something unexpected: a contact within the Serpent's inner circle—a woman named Layla.

Layla, it turned out, was not who she appeared to be. She was a disillusioned operative, weary of the Serpent's brutality and corruption. She'd been planning her escape for months, and Jake's information, particularly the details of the upcoming arms deal, provided her with the leverage she desperately needed. Layla was a skilled hacker, a digital ghost capable of accessing the Serpent's encrypted communications and financial records. She viewed Jake as a means to her own escape, a way to dismantle the organization from within. Their alliance, however, was built on shifting sands of mutual self-interest, a precarious truce in a war zone.

Their first joint operation was a heart-stopping infiltration of a heavily secured warehouse on the outskirts of Al-Zahra. Layla, using her expertise, remotely disabled the security systems, creating a window of opportunity for Jake. The warehouse was a labyrinth of stacked containers, each potentially concealing deadly cargo. The tension was palpable as Jake navigated the maze, his senses heightened, his every move deliberate and calculated.

He discovered the arms shipment—a cache of sophisticated weaponry far exceeding the initial intelligence reports. The scale of the operation was far greater than he initially suspected, the potential consequences far more devastating. As he was cataloging the weapons, he discovered another unexpected element – a small, unassuming package hidden within one of the crates. It contained a series of coded documents, hinting at a far more sinister plot than simply arms trafficking.

But their operation wasn't without peril. They were discovered. The warehouse alarms blared, sirens wailed in the distance. A firefight erupted, bullets ricocheting off metal containers, sending sparks flying in the dimly lit space. Jake's military training kicked in, his movements fluid and precise as he returned fire. Layla, despite her lack of combat experience, proved surprisingly resourceful, using her technological skills to create diversions and disorient the guards. Their combined expertise allowed them to escape the warehouse, but not without a few close calls.

Their escape was a hair-raising chase through the labyrinthine streets of Al-Zahra, a breathtaking pursuit that pushed their skills to the limit. They weaved through crowded marketplaces, scaled crumbling walls, and used their knowledge of the city's hidden alleys to evade their pursuers. The chase ended abruptly when they found themselves cornered in a dead end, surrounded by heavily armed guards.

Just as it appeared all hope was lost, an unexpected ally emerged: a group of local rebels, members of a clandestine resistance movement actively fighting against the Serpent's influence. They had been watching the chaos unfold, and recognizing the plight of the two individuals battling against a powerful and oppressive force, they chose to intervene, opening fire on the guards, creating a diversion that allowed Jake and Layla to escape.

These rebels, initially unknown to Jake, now represented another unexpected piece in the complex puzzle of Al-Zahra.

Their presence hinted at a broader network of resistance, a hidden army fighting against the Serpent's tyranny. It was a glimmer of hope, a sign that not everyone had succumbed to the Serpent's corrupting influence.

The coded documents found in the warehouse held the key to the Serpent's ultimate plan—a plot to destabilize the entire region by triggering a series of coordinated attacks on key infrastructure. The implications were catastrophic, a scenario that could plunge the region into chaos and war. Jake and Layla realized that their alliance, initially formed out of self-interest, had evolved into something far greater – a shared mission to prevent a global catastrophe.

The discovery of the documents also revealed a crucial piece of information: the location of the Serpent's secret headquarters—a hidden bunker beneath the city, a place of unimaginable secrecy and security. The bunker, it turned out, was heavily fortified, equipped with state-of-the-art surveillance systems, and surrounded by a network of heavily armed guards. It was a fortress, a symbol of the Serpent's absolute power.

The escape from the warehouse had been harrowing, but it had also exposed Jake and Layla to the dangers they faced. They sought refuge with the rebel group, pooling their resources and expertise to plan their next move—an infiltration of the Serpent's headquarters. This time, however, they wouldn't be alone. The rebels, armed with their local knowledge and intimate understanding of the city's underbelly, were invaluable allies. Together, they formed an unlikely coalition, a force bound by a common goal: to expose the Serpent and dismantle his empire. The challenge ahead remained daunting, yet the combined might of unexpected allies might just be the key to their success. The final confrontation with the Serpent was fast approaching, and the fate of the entire region hung precariously in the balance. The labyrinth of Al-Zahra had only revealed a fraction of its secrets; the deepest, darkest layers remained to be uncovered.

Ethical Dilemmas

The adrenaline still thrummed in Jake's veins, a phantom echo of the firefight. He sat with Layla, the flickering candlelight casting long shadows on their faces, in the cramped, earthen-floored room offered by the rebels. The air was thick with the scent of woodsmoke and damp earth, a stark contrast to the sterile, technological environment of the Serpent's warehouse. The coded documents, now carefully deciphered with Layla's help, lay spread between them, a roadmap to a catastrophe in the making.

The information revealed a chillingly intricate plot. The arms shipment wasn't simply a matter of profit; it was a meticulously orchestrated prelude to a series of attacks on key infrastructure—power grids, water treatment plants, communication networks. The Serpent wasn't just a criminal; he was a puppet master, pulling the strings of regional instability for his own nefarious purposes. The potential for mass casualties was staggering, the humanitarian cost immeasurable.

Layla, her face grim, pointed to a specific paragraph. "This… this indicates collaboration with a foreign power. We're not just dealing with a local crime syndicate; we're talking about international espionage, state-sponsored terrorism."

Jake felt a knot tighten in his stomach. The mission had expanded exponentially. What had begun as a simple arms deal investigation had morphed into something far larger, far more dangerous. He had signed up for espionage, but this was… different. This felt morally repugnant. The implications extended far beyond the immediate threat to Al-

Zahra; the entire region, perhaps even the globe, hung precariously in the balance.

He considered the information they possessed. The data pointed to a series of carefully timed detonations, carefully designed to maximize chaos and suffering. Stopping the Serpent meant preventing those detonations, but how? The magnitude of the task felt overwhelming. His training had prepared him for close-quarters combat, infiltration, and data extraction—but not for this. This required a level of strategic thinking, of global awareness, that dwarfed his operational experience.

Layla, sensing his internal struggle, broke the silence. "The rebels are willing to help, but they're low on resources, and their network is limited. We need to get this information to someone… someone with the power to stop this before it happens."

"And who is that?" Jake asked, his voice barely a whisper. The burden of responsibility felt crushing. He'd crossed ethical boundaries before, accepting risks he knew were significant, but this was a different order of magnitude. The potential loss of life, the potential for widespread suffering… it was staggering.

Layla suggested contacting his agency, but the thought chilled Jake to the bone. His initial contact, the seemingly benign Omar, had been a deceptive agent of a vast, dangerous machine. The potential for betrayal by the very agency he worked for was substantial; the idea of exposing this information to his superiors, only to have it either ignored, manipulated, or become another tool of political maneuvering weighed heavily on his mind. The moral ambiguity was suffocating.

The rebels, too, presented their own moral quandary. Their fight was driven by righteous anger and a desire for freedom, but their methods, while effective in their local context, weren't exactly by-the-book. Their willingness to engage in acts that might be considered terrorism by other international actors meant that they were operating outside international legality and could be potentially compromised by the very individuals they opposed. Their loyalty could be purchased or their integrity could be bought or broken.

Jake wrestled with a profound sense of moral exhaustion. Was he merely a pawn in a larger game, a tool used by both sides to achieve their goals? Was his allegiance to his handlers or to the innocent lives at risk? Was there even such a thing as a "good" outcome in this scenario, or was the entire conflict a downward spiral of escalating violence, regardless of his actions?

The days that followed were a blur of frantic activity. Jake and Layla worked tirelessly, coordinating with the rebels, sharing information, and plotting their next move. The rebels provided maps and local intelligence, detailing the Serpent's security network and highlighting potential weaknesses. The task was fraught with risk, each step forward a gamble.

They debated their options. Contacting international organizations was considered, but the time frame was limited and the risk of infiltration and compromising their operation was high. Could they trust anyone outside their immediate circle? Every contact, every alliance, carried the potential for betrayal. Each decision had unforeseen consequences. A small misstep, a single miscalculation, could lead to disaster. The weight of their responsibility was palpable.

The rebels suggested a different approach: disrupting the Serpent's supply lines, crippling his operations before the planned attacks could be launched. This plan, however, meant engaging in actions that walked a fine line between self-defense and direct aggression. It required venturing into territory where the lines between right and wrong were blurred, where the justifications were more shades of grey than clear-cut black and white. Would sacrificing some to save many truly be an ethical choice?

The moral dilemmas piled up. Each choice felt loaded, each step fraught with consequences, both intended and unforeseen. The weight of potentially countless lives rested on their shoulders. Jake, hardened by his military training, felt a profound sense of moral exhaustion. He struggled with the profound ethical choices confronting him, questions that went to the very core of his identity and purpose. The mission had become more than just a job; it was a personal crusade, a relentless fight against a tide of overwhelming evil, a fight he wasn't sure he could win, but one he was determined to undertake regardless of the cost. The line between survival and justice, between duty and morality, was becoming increasingly faint, and Jake had to navigate this treacherous territory, guided by little more than instinct and a flicker of fading hope.

Mission Success or Failure

The warehouse pulsed with a nervous energy, a palpable tension that vibrated in the concrete floor beneath Jake's boots. He'd infiltrated the Serpent's secondary munitions depot, a sprawling complex hidden beneath the guise of a legitimate import-export business. The air hung heavy with the scent of gunpowder and oil, a suffocating aroma that clung to the back of his throat. Layla, her movements fluid and silent as a wraith, was already in position, her sniper rifle trained on the main entrance. The rebels, a ragtag group armed with a mixture of antiquated weaponry and surprisingly modern explosives, were strategically positioned throughout the compound, ready to strike.

The plan was audacious, bordering on suicidal. They aimed to trigger a controlled explosion, destroying a significant portion of the Serpent's arsenal while minimizing civilian casualties. The success of the operation hinged on precision timing and flawless execution; a single mistake could transform the calculated chaos into a catastrophic massacre. Jake's heart hammered against his ribs, a frantic drumbeat against the backdrop of the silent, expectant warehouse.

His mission wasn't merely to destroy the weapons; it was to gather intelligence, to identify the Serpent's collaborators, and to unravel the intricate web of corruption that extended beyond Al-Zahra's borders. The coded documents from the first raid had revealed a chilling truth – the Serpent wasn't a lone wolf; he was a pawn in a larger game, a puppet manipulated by unseen hands pulling strings from faraway capitals. Jake needed to uncover those hands, to expose the puppet master before he could unleash his deadly symphony of chaos upon the world.

The tension ratcheted up as the first rays of dawn painted the sky in hues of orange and grey. He checked his equipment one last time, the familiar weight of his weapons comforting in their lethality. He had no illusions about the risks involved; this was a gamble with the highest stakes imaginable. He could feel Layla's gaze on him, a silent acknowledgment of the precariousness of their situation. Their fate, and the fate of countless others, hung precariously in the balance.

The explosion rocked the warehouse, a deafening roar that ripped through the silence. Jake felt the earth tremble beneath him, a violent tremor that sent shockwaves through his body. The ensuing chaos was a whirlwind of dust, smoke, and fire. The rebels moved with practiced efficiency, their actions a ballet of destruction and controlled mayhem. Jake, utilizing his tactical training, navigated the inferno, neutralizing threats with calculated precision. He moved like a ghost, a phantom gliding through the smoke-filled labyrinth, his every move deliberate, every action honed to deadly perfection.

The fight was brutal, a desperate struggle for survival. The Serpent's men, initially surprised, quickly rallied, their desperate resistance fueled by adrenaline and fear. The warehouse became a battleground, a maelstrom of gunfire and explosions. Jake found himself in a desperate hand-to-hand combat, wrestling with a hulking mercenary, the fight a brutal dance of strength and skill. He utilized his military training, his every move precise, deadly, his experience giving him a slight edge in the chaotic melee. The mercenary, despite his superior size, found himself outmatched by Jake's superior tactics.

As the dust settled, a grim tableau emerged from the wreckage. The warehouse lay in ruins, a testament to the violence that had transpired. The Serpent's arsenal was decimated, a significant blow to his operations. But the victory was bittersweet. Several rebels had been wounded, their sacrifices a heavy price for the tactical success. Layla, despite her sharpshooting skills, had suffered a minor injury, a graze on her arm a stark reminder of the perils of their profession.

Yet, Jake's primary objective remained incomplete. The Serpent had escaped, vanishing into the chaotic aftermath. The intelligence gathering proved more elusive than expected, the intricate network of corruption proving much more complex than initially anticipated. The documents they had managed to secure were partially destroyed, the information fragmented and incomplete.

The following days were a whirlwind of debriefings, analysis, and frantic attempts to piece together the puzzle. The information they had gleaned pointed towards a shadowy organization, far larger and more sophisticated than anything they had initially anticipated. The scale of the conspiracy stretched far beyond Al-Zahra, its tendrils reaching into the highest echelons of power. The moral ambiguity intensified. They had struck a blow against the Serpent, but the larger threat remained, a looming specter that cast a long shadow over their success.

The mission was a success in terms of immediate tactical goals – they had destroyed a significant portion of the Serpent's arsenal and disrupted his operations. However, strategically, the outcome was far less clear. The Serpent himself was still at large, and the shadowy network behind him remained largely untouched. The initial victory felt hollow, tainted by the knowledge of the larger, more insidious threat that lingered. Jake found himself wrestling with a deep sense of unease. Had they merely won a small battle in a larger, more devastating war? The answer remained elusive, a shadow hanging over their hard-won success. The ambiguous victory left a bitter taste in their mouths; a reminder that in the shadowy world of espionage, even a seemingly successful mission could be just one step in a much longer and more treacherous game. The true cost of their success was yet to be fully realized, as the uncertainty of the future loomed large.

The emotional toll of the mission was profound. Jake had witnessed death and destruction on a scale that tested his psychological resilience. The ethical questions, the moral compromises they had made, weighed heavily on his mind. The line between right and wrong blurred, often disappearing entirely. The line between justice and survival became a razor's edge that Jake had to tread, constantly balancing on the knife's thin edge. He had faced life-or-death situations, but the mental and emotional battles proved just as brutal. Sleep offered little respite, haunted by the faces of the fallen and the echoes of gunfire.

The experience transformed him, hardening him while simultaneously shattering his illusions about the nature of good and evil. He had crossed lines he never thought he'd cross, committing actions that challenged his own moral compass. He questioned his allegiance, his purpose, his very identity. He wrestled with existential questions, questioning the nature of his role and the world he had become a part of. The victory was a hollow one, a pyrrhic victory at best. The mission had changed him, irrevocably marking his soul with the indelible scars of war, conflict, and moral ambiguity. The shadows of the labyrinth clung to him, a constant reminder of the darkness he had encountered and the compromises he had made in his pursuit of justice.

PostMission Debriefing

The fluorescent lights hummed, a sterile counterpoint to the chaotic symphony still playing in Jake's head. The room, a stark, minimalist office somewhere deep within the agency's labyrinthine headquarters, felt colder than the Antarctic. He sat across from General Petrov, his superior, a man whose granite features betrayed nothing of his inner thoughts. The air was thick with unspoken questions, the silence more oppressive than any interrogation. A single, half-empty glass of water sat between them, a symbol of the parched landscape of Jake's emotions.

The debriefing wasn't about the tactical successes – the destruction of the Serpent's munitions depot, the disruption of his operations. Those were facts, cold and hard, already documented in countless reports. This was about the unseen battles, the ones fought in the shadows of his own mind. It was about the cost of victory, a price rarely tallied in official assessments.

"Riley," Petrov began, his voice low and measured, the kind of voice that could calm a raging storm or shatter a man's spirit. "The mission report is…comprehensive. The tactical objectives were achieved. However, there are… unquantifiable elements."

Jake remained silent, his gaze fixed on the water glass. The reflection distorted his face, a stranger staring back at him from a world away. He could still smell the acrid scent of gunpowder, the metallic tang of blood, the haunting sweetness of fear. He felt the phantom pains in his muscles, the lingering ache in his ribs, a testament to the brutal hand-to-hand combat. But it wasn't the physical wounds that bothered him.

"The psychological impact…that's what concerns us," Petrov continued, his eyes piercing, as if attempting to see beyond Jake's guarded exterior. "Your performance was exceptional, borderline reckless. The reports indicate a disregard for your own safety, a level of aggression that… exceeded expectations."

"I was trained to be effective, General," Jake replied, his voice low, deliberately neutral. "And I was successful."

"Success is a relative term, Riley. We achieved a tactical victory, yes, but at what cost?" Petrov leaned forward, his gaze intense. "Your actions, while undeniably effective, bordered on insubordination. Your deviation from the planned protocol… explain that."

Jake hesitated, choosing his words carefully. He couldn't simply admit to acting on instinct, on a visceral reaction to the overwhelming chaos. That would reveal a vulnerability that could be exploited. "The situation on the ground…it evolved rapidly. Adaptability was key."

"Adaptability, or recklessness?" Petrov pressed, his tone sharper now. "Your actions endangered not only yourself, but Layla as well."

He thought of Layla, her pale face etched with exhaustion and pain in the aftermath of the explosion, her arm bandaged, her usual sharp wit dulled by the ordeal. Her resilience was astonishing, but even Layla couldn't escape the psychological toll. The image of the fallen rebels, their faces forever frozen in moments of agony, flashed before his eyes. The guilt gnawed at him, a relentless beast feeding on his conscience.

"She's a professional, General," Jake replied, defending Layla, if not himself. "She understood the risks."

"And yet," Petrov said, his voice softening slightly, "the reports indicate she requested a leave of absence following the operation. An unusual request for someone with her experience."

The weight of responsibility pressed down on him, a crushing burden. He hadn't just endangered himself and Layla; he had endangered the entire mission, jeopardizing years of planning and countless resources. The shadows of doubt, initially faint and fleeting, now loomed large, menacing and inescapable. He had faced death countless times in the warehouse, but the true fight began here, in this sterile office, in the battle for his own sanity.

"The Serpent escaped," Petrov stated, breaking the silence. "Your failure to secure him... that's a significant setback."

"He was a ghost, General," Jake explained, the memory of the chaotic aftermath still vivid. "He vanished into the crowd, leaving no trace."

"Yet the intelligence gathered... it's incomplete, fragmented. We have only glimpses into a far larger network, a conspiracy that extends beyond our initial understanding."

The larger network. The puppet master. The unsettling realization that their victory had only scratched the surface of a deep, dangerous conspiracy sent a shiver down his spine. He had faced down heavily armed mercenaries, navigated a burning building, and engaged in brutal hand-to-hand combat. But the psychological battle was far more complex, far more insidious. The war wasn't over; it had just begun, and the true enemy was now an invisible, faceless network of power, manipulation, and deceit.

"We need you to focus, Riley," Petrov said, his voice regaining its measured calm. "This isn't just about the Serpent. This is about something much larger, much more dangerous. Your skills are vital. Your…adaptability…we need you to channel that effectively."

The words hung in the air, a double-edged sword. Petrov was acknowledging his exceptional abilities, but also implicitly recognizing his dangerous recklessness. He needed to control his instincts, to reign in the aggression that had almost cost him everything. But the fight in the warehouse, the adrenaline, the visceral need to survive… it was ingrained in his system now. Could he truly be contained?

The debriefing continued, the questions ranging from tactical assessments to psychological evaluations. He answered with precision, his military training kicking in, but the subtle tremors in his voice betrayed the turmoil within. He spoke about the moral ambiguities, the lines he had crossed, the choices he had made under immense pressure. He described the moral landscape of the conflict, the shades of gray so pervasive they obscured any definitive black and white.

Petrov listened intently, his expression unreadable, the silence punctuating the gravity of their conversation. He was trying to assess not just Jake's physical capabilities, but his psychological resilience, his ability to handle the intense pressure and moral compromises inherent in their world. He would need to prove he could function effectively under pressure, control the aggressive instincts, and yet retain the edge that made him such a valuable asset. The psychological evaluation was as important as, or perhaps even more important than, the tactical analysis of the mission's success. The line between effective operator and unstable liability was razor-thin, a precarious balance he now had to maintain.

As the debriefing concluded, Petrov rose, offering a curt nod. "We will monitor your progress, Riley. Therapy sessions are mandatory. We'll provide you with the best resources available. Your next assignment... it will be… challenging."

Jake remained seated, the weight of the unspoken words pressing down on him. The "challenging" assignment would test not just his physical and tactical abilities, but his resilience in the face of the mental and emotional scars he carried. The war within was just as dangerous as any external threat. He had survived the warehouse, but the true battle for his soul had just begun. The shadows of doubt, once fleeting, were now a constant companion, a chilling reminder of the price of victory in the world of espionage. The mission was over, but the fight had only just begun.

Internal Conflict

The spartan apartment felt colder than usual, the minimalist furnishings amplifying the silence. Jake stared out the window, the city lights blurring into a hazy, indistinct mass. The sterile efficiency of the agency's debriefing room had given way to the raw, unyielding solitude of his own space, a space that mirrored the growing chasm within him. He wasn't just physically exhausted; he was emotionally drained, the weight of his actions pressing down on him like a physical burden.

The mission's success felt hollow. The destruction of the Serpent's depot, the disruption of his operations—these were tactical victories, cold hard facts. But the human cost, the moral compromises, the lines blurred and crossed under the pressure of lethal combat… these were the things that gnawed at him, leaving him hollow and filled with a profound sense of unease. He replayed the events of the warehouse in his mind, each image as sharp and visceral as if he were still there, the scent of gunpowder thick in the air, the sound of gunfire echoing in his ears.

Layla's face swam into focus – her pale face, the exhaustion in her eyes, the way her hand instinctively went to her bandaged arm. He'd endangered her, his reckless abandon putting her life on the line. He justified his actions, initially, with the necessity of the mission, the urgency of the situation. He was trained to be effective, trained to eliminate threats, trained to prioritize the mission above all else. But the cold, hard logic of military training seemed pathetically insufficient in the face of the raw, emotional reality of what he'd done. He'd acted instinctively, driven by adrenaline and the sheer will to survive, yet his actions bordered on insubordination, endangering both himself and Layla.

The escape of the Serpent was another weight on his conscience. The man was a ghost, vanishing into the teeming chaos of the city, leaving behind only fragmented information, a tantalizing glimpse into a larger, far more insidious network. The mission's success, therefore, felt incomplete, a pyrrhic victory at best. He'd taken down one pawn, but the game continued, the true players still hidden in the shadows.

The echoes of Petrov's words reverberated in his mind: "Your performance was exceptional, borderline reckless." The compliment was laced with a sharp undercurrent of warning. His superiors recognized his effectiveness, his raw talent, but they also saw the dangerous unpredictability that threatened to derail the entire operation. The agency needed him, but could they trust him? Could he trust himself?

He thought about the rebel fighters, their bodies strewn across the warehouse floor, their lives extinguished in the crossfire. He had been trained to see them as enemies, as obstacles to be eliminated. But their faces, frozen in moments of agony, haunted his dreams. Their deaths, even though justified within the context of the mission, carried a weight of responsibility that he couldn't easily shake. Was it truly necessary? Had he made the right choices?

The moral ambiguities gnawed at him, the shades of gray swirling into a chaotic vortex. The clear-cut lines of right and wrong, so carefully defined in his military training, had been blurred beyond recognition. He was no longer a simple soldier following orders; he was a clandestine operator, operating in the shadows, making life-or-death decisions with far-reaching consequences. He questioned the ethics of his profession, the sacrifices demanded, and the potential for collateral damage.

He poured himself a drink, the amber liquid doing little to soothe the turmoil within. He wasn't simply questioning his actions; he was questioning himself, his identity, his very purpose. He had been a baseball player, a man of routine, predictability, and teamwork. Now, he was a spy, a lone wolf operating in a world of deception and betrayal, where trust was a rare and precious commodity. The transformation had been brutal, leaving him isolated, alone in the echoing chambers of his own mind.

The mandatory therapy sessions loomed. He'd initially scoffed at the idea, believing himself immune to the psychological pressures of the job. He was a soldier, trained to withstand unimaginable stress and hardship. But the warehouse had shattered that illusion. The psychological wounds were deeper, more insidious, than any physical injury. He was haunted by memories, the faces of the dead, the fear in Layla's eyes, the chilling knowledge that the Serpent remained at large.

He thought back to his baseball career, the camaraderie, the predictable rhythm of practice and games, the simple joy of teamwork. The transition to the clandestine world had been jarring, stripping away the familiar comforts and replacing them with a constant state of alertness, suspicion, and danger. He'd traded the cheers of the crowd for the chilling silence of shadows and deception, the camaraderie of teammates for the isolating solitude of a life lived in the margins.

The apartment, once a haven, now felt like a prison, the walls closing in on him, amplifying his isolation. He picked up a worn baseball glove, its familiar leather texture a poignant reminder of his former life, a life that seemed impossibly distant. The glove was a relic of a simpler time, a time before the shadows of doubt had consumed him. He traced the worn stitches, the leather soft and yielding under his fingertips, yet the comfort it offered was fleeting, unable to reach the core of his torment.

The upcoming assignment, described as "challenging," hung over him like a dark cloud. It wouldn't simply test his physical and tactical skills; it would be a crucible, a trial by fire that would determine if he could handle the pressure, the moral ambiguities, the crushing weight of responsibility. He wasn't just battling enemies in the field; he was battling himself, wrestling with the demons born from the moral compromises he'd already made. He knew that the shadows of doubt, once fleeting and distant, were now deeply ingrained, a constant, chilling reminder of the cost of victory in the world of espionage. The true battle was not over; it was just beginning, fought not on a battlefield, but within the confines of his own troubled mind. He was a soldier, a spy, a man battling not just external enemies, but the internal war that threatened to consume him.

Haunted by the Past

The rhythmic crack of the bat against leather echoed in his mind, a phantom sound from a life that felt both impossibly distant and achingly close. He squeezed his eyes shut, the image of the stadium lights blazing down, the roar of the crowd a deafening wave, flooding back with unexpected force. The smell of freshly cut grass, the feel of the sun on his skin, the camaraderie of the dugout – these sensory details, once commonplace, now felt like fragments of a dream, vivid and unreal. He was Jake Riley, the promising young baseball player, a man defined by his talent, his teamwork, his predictable routine. That man felt like a stranger, a ghost from a past life he could barely remember.

The sterile, minimalist apartment offered no such comforts. It was a stark contrast to the vibrant chaos of the baseball field, a space designed for efficiency and anonymity, not warmth or familiarity. The city outside, a symphony of honking cars and distant sirens, mirrored the relentless, unpredictable nature of his new life. It was a cacophony of sounds that constantly reminded him of the ever-present threat, the constant state of vigilance that had become his second skin.

He traced the worn outline of a faded photograph tucked into the corner of his desk. It was a team photo, a sea of smiling faces frozen in a moment of triumph. He recognized the players' names, each a trigger to a flood of memories. The easy jokes, the shared triumphs and defeats, the unspoken language of the field – these things were once his bedrock, his sense of belonging. Now, they were fragments of a lost world, a world of simplicity and predictability that seemed almost impossibly far away.

The memory of Mark, his closest friend on the team, his former roommate, his confidant, tugged at him. Mark had been his rock, his anchor in the stormy sea of professional sports. They'd spent countless hours talking, strategizing, sharing their hopes and dreams, and their fears. Mark's belief in him, his unwavering support, had propelled Jake forward. He wondered where Mark was now, if he knew what had become of him, if he'd even believe it. The thought brought a pang of guilt, a sharp stab of regret for the silence between them, the unspoken chasm that now separated them.

The silence in the apartment was broken only by the hum of the refrigerator, a sound that somehow amplified the emptiness. He felt a profound sense of isolation, a loneliness that went beyond simple solitude. It was the isolation of deception, the knowledge that he could trust no one completely, not even those he worked alongside. The camaraderie of the baseball field had been genuine, a bond forged in shared struggle and mutual respect. This new world, this world of espionage, was different. Trust was a commodity to be carefully rationed, a luxury he could not afford.

He remembered the rigorous training, the brutal physical conditioning that had pushed him to his limits and beyond. His body ached, a constant reminder of the sacrifices demanded. The psychological conditioning, the manipulation of his emotions, had been even more arduous. He'd been forced to confront his fears, his vulnerabilities, to shed his former identity, layer by layer, until there was little left but the raw, essential him.

This new, hardened self was efficient, deadly, and emotionally detached. This new Jake Riley was a ghost, a shadow flitting through the city's underbelly, executing missions with chilling precision, always one step ahead, always ready for the next confrontation. But the ghost of the old Jake Riley still lurked within, clinging to memories that seemed increasingly out of place.

Layla's face appeared in his memory, her face etched with worry and fear. He saw her again in the warehouse, the adrenaline-fueled chaos of the mission swirling around them. He remembered the way her eyes had flickered to his when the situation had gotten critical, the unspoken understanding that passed between them despite their limited time together. He wondered if she was haunted too, if she wrestled with the same moral ambiguities that consumed him.

The image shifted, morphing into the faces of the enemy combatants, their lives extinguished in the chaos. He'd trained to see them as enemies, targets to be neutralized. But now, their lifeless eyes haunted his waking moments and plagued his dreams. Their faces were not merely statistics, not just collateral damage in a necessary mission. They were individuals, each with a story, a life that had been violently cut short. He could almost hear their silent screams. The weight of their deaths, the knowledge that he was responsible, lay heavy on his conscience.

He poured another drink, the liquor burning a path down his throat, but failing to ignite anything resembling warmth. The cold reality of his actions crashed over him again, the weight of the decisions he had made and the consequences that would echo for years to come. He wondered if he could ever atone for the lives he had taken, if he could ever truly reconcile himself with what he had become. The shadows of doubt, once peripheral, now enveloped him, a suffocating presence that threatened to consume him entirely.

He looked at his hands, noticing the calluses, the slight tremors, the subtle signs of the intense pressure he endured every day. These were the marks of his new life, a life that was as brutal and unforgiving as it was exciting and dangerous. He saw the reflection of his own haunted eyes, the reflection of a man torn between his past and present, caught between the life he had known and the one he now lived.

The upcoming assignment loomed, a stark reminder of the precariousness of his existence. It was a test not just of his physical and tactical prowess, but also of his mental fortitude, his ability to withstand the gnawing uncertainties of his life. He was a soldier, a spy, a man forever marked by the ghosts of his past and the chilling shadows of his present. The battle was within, a fight for his soul, his sanity, his very identity. And the war, he knew, was far from over. The game, far from finished. He was just a player, haunted by the past, and deeply, deeply alone.

Questioning Loyalty

The gnawing unease had begun subtly, a low hum beneath the surface of his meticulously crafted persona. It started with inconsistencies, minor discrepancies in the mission briefings that didn't quite add up. A misplaced detail here, an ambiguous phrase there – things that wouldn't raise an eyebrow in the heat of an operation, but which, in the quiet solitude of his apartment, sparked a nagging sense of unease. He'd dismissed them initially, attributing them to the inherent chaos of the clandestine world, the calculated ambiguities designed to test loyalty and maintain plausible deniability.

But the inconsistencies grew, morphing into something more substantial. He noticed patterns, recurring themes in the missions assigned to him: each one seemingly leading to another, each one unveiling a deeper layer of the organization's clandestine operations. It was as though he was being carefully guided, not towards a specific objective, but towards something much larger, something more sinister.

His handler, a shadowy figure known only as "Director," remained an enigma. Their meetings were always brief, their instructions clipped and precise, devoid of the personal touches that often characterized relationships in his past life. There was a chilling efficiency to Director's communication, a calculated distance that served to underscore the absolute control they wielded. He was given orders, never explanations. He was a tool, not a colleague.

This realization chipped away at his carefully constructed emotional detachment. He'd trained himself to operate in a world of shadows, to compartmentalize, to leave emotion out of the equation. But this was different. This wasn't a matter of eliminating a target, neutralizing a threat. This was a question of loyalty, of questioning the very foundation of the organization he'd pledged his life to serve.

One evening, sifting through the encrypted messages, a particular phrase caught his eye. It was a seemingly innocuous remark, buried amidst a stream of technical jargon. But repeated analysis revealed it was a code, a subtle reference to a seemingly unrelated incident from his past, a detail he'd meticulously buried, long forgotten. This raised a terrifying question: how much did they truly know about him? How much of his past life had been revealed and manipulated against his will?

The realization sent a chill down his spine. He felt like a chess piece, moved across a board by an unseen hand, his every move meticulously orchestrated, his life reduced to a series of carefully calculated gambits. The weight of this revelation was overwhelming. He was no longer simply a spy, but a pawn in a game far larger than himself, a game whose rules were unknown, whose stakes were incomprehensible.

He decided to test the waters. During his next meeting with Director, he subtly shifted the conversation, asking oblique questions, testing for weaknesses in their well-rehearsed facade. He inquired about the history of specific operations, the identities of key personnel, probing for any inconsistencies that might betray the organization's true objectives. Director's answers were flawless, their responses carefully crafted, yet Jake sensed an almost imperceptible tension, a hint of unease beneath the surface. It was a small victory, a sliver of doubt in an otherwise impenetrable wall of secrecy.

His next mission presented another opportunity. It involved infiltrating a seemingly insignificant arms dealer, a seemingly straightforward assignment. But as he delved deeper into the operation, he discovered a discrepancy. The arms dealer, it turned out, was a former associate of his old team, someone he vaguely remembered from his baseball days. This was no coincidence. It was a deliberate placement, a calculated move designed to test his loyalty, to gauge the depth of his commitment to the agency.

This was the crux of the dilemma. Was he willing to betray a friend, someone who had been a part of his past life, a life he still struggled to reconcile with? The weight of the decision pressed down on him, threatening to crush him under its immense pressure. His past life, with its simplicity and predictable routines, felt like a distant memory, a fading dream. Yet, the values forged during those years, the principles of honesty and loyalty that he'd learned on the baseball diamond, still resonated within him.

He spent days agonizing over this ethical labyrinth. He knew that to refuse the mission would arouse suspicion, to betray his new identity. To follow the orders, however, meant betraying the trust of someone who'd once been close to him. The pressure intensified with each passing hour. Sleep became a luxury, a welcome respite from the incessant churning of his mind, a fleeting refuge from the agonizing weight of his decision.

His physical capabilities, once his greatest asset, seemed to fail him. His body, accustomed to the rigors of his training, felt depleted, strained to its breaking point. The relentless pressure of his new life was beginning to take its toll. The muscles were aching; his mind was weary; his spirit, frayed.

The day of the mission arrived, shrouded in a veil of tension and uncertainty. He stood poised on the edge of a precipice, ready to leap into a void filled with uncertainty. He was a spy, operating in the shadows, but he was also a man struggling with his conscience, battling with his own sense of morality. The game, he realised, extended far beyond the mission. It was a test of loyalty, not only to the shadowy organization he served, but to himself and the principles he still clung to.

The decision he made was a silent one, a whisper in the dark, but it would forever alter his path, forever change the course of his life. He played his part, but his eyes were now open. The shadows of doubt were no longer merely peripheral. They were the dominant force, shaping his actions, influencing his decisions. The game was far from over, but he had just entered into a completely new phase—one where the enemy wasn't just out there, but potentially hiding in plain sight, within the very ranks of the organisation he'd sworn to serve. The consequences of this new reality were potentially devastating, but the seeds of rebellion had been sown. The battle for his soul, his identity, and his future had truly begun.

A Path Forward

The biting wind whipped across the desolate coastline, stinging his face, mirroring the turmoil within. He hadn't slept properly in days, the weight of his decision pressing down on him like a physical burden. The rhythmic crash of waves against the jagged rocks was a counterpoint to the frantic rhythm of his thoughts. He stood on a remote cliff overlooking the churning grey sea, the wind a constant, relentless companion in his solitude. This isolated headland, discovered during one of his clandestine missions, had become his sanctuary, a place where he could confront the demons that haunted him without fear of observation.

He'd chosen this location deliberately. The vastness of the ocean, the relentless power of the elements, mirrored the immensity of the choices he faced. The agency, with its shadowy operations and ambiguous loyalties, had become a labyrinth, a maze of deceit where truth and falsehood were inextricably intertwined. He had glimpsed a glimpse of its true nature, its sinister machinations, and the knowledge had shattered the carefully constructed façade of his new life. Yet, something held him back from abandoning it entirely.

The training, the honed skills, the adrenaline rush of the dangerous assignments – these were not merely aspects of his profession; they had become ingrained in his very being. The agency represented a challenge, a test of his resilience and intellect. He had excelled in everything he had set his mind to – baseball, and now, this. To simply walk away felt like surrender, a betrayal of his own capabilities. But the moral compromises, the potential for inflicting harm, weighed heavily on his conscience.

He'd considered confessing everything, spilling the secrets he'd uncovered to a trusted authority, perhaps even to the authorities. But such a revelation would be fraught with dangers. Who could he trust? He was dealing with an organization that operated outside the bounds of conventional law, an entity capable of manipulating governments, erasing identities, and eliminating threats with ruthless efficiency. Such an act would be tantamount to declaring war, and he wasn't sure he possessed the resources or the support to wage it.

Moreover, there was the matter of his past, the life he'd left behind. The baseball life he'd once treasured, felt distant now, almost unreal, like a fading photograph. He had consciously shed that identity, embracing the cloak of anonymity that his new life offered. Yet, the values he'd learned – integrity, loyalty, teamwork - still resonated deep within him. These values clashed sharply with the shadowy world of espionage, and the dissonance created an unbearable tension.

He had learned that the enemy wasn't always the easily identified enemy. The greatest threats could emerge from within, disguised as allies and friends. The arms dealer, his former teammate, had been a pivotal point in this realization. He hadn't betrayed his friend; he had instead used the opportunity to gather more information about the agency's true intentions. But he knew it was just one step.

The next move had to be carefully calculated. He needed a plan, a strategy that would allow him to simultaneously protect his own identity while uncovering the secrets of the organization. He had to find a way to balance his dedication to his new mission with his unwavering adherence to his principles. It was a delicate act, a high-wire walk over an abyss of uncertainty.

As the sun dipped below the horizon, casting long shadows across the desolate landscape, a plan began to take shape in his mind. It was a bold strategy, risky and potentially dangerous, but it was the only path forward that he could see. It involved using his position within the agency to gather information, subtly manipulating events to uncover the hidden truths. He would play their game, but on his own terms.

The key was patience, meticulous observation, and the careful cultivation of trust, a skill he had honed during his baseball days, the ability to read people, to discern their motives, to understand their weaknesses. He would exploit their internal power struggles, their rivalries, and their conflicting ambitions to his advantage. He would become a master manipulator, weaving his way through the maze, gathering intelligence from seemingly insignificant sources, piecing together the puzzle of the organization's true goals.

The agency's methods were sophisticated, their communications encrypted, their operations clandestine. But Jake was a master of deception, and he would use their tools and methods against them. He would infiltrate their secure networks, access classified files, and decipher encrypted messages, piecing together the fragments of information into a coherent narrative, revealing the sinister plot at the heart of the organization.

His transformation into a spy had been a metamorphosis, a shedding of his old identity to embrace a new one. He was no longer the naive athlete. He had undergone rigorous training, he had learned to kill, to lie, to manipulate, to survive. But his ability to adapt, to transform, was a double-edged sword. He could use this adaptability to unravel the agency's secrets, to expose the truth.

He would use his past against the agency, allowing his former self to inform his current actions. His baseball instincts for teamwork, his uncanny ability to read opponents, could now be employed to decipher the hidden dynamics of the organization. He was their tool, yet he would use their own tool against them. He would become a phantom, a shadow moving unseen, a force of disruption within the heart of the agency.

The path ahead was perilous. There would be moments of intense fear, periods of agonizing uncertainty, and potentially life-threatening situations. Yet, a newfound resolve had taken hold, a sense of purpose that went beyond the simple completion of missions. This was no longer about following orders; this was about a battle for truth, a fight for his own integrity. He was no longer a pawn; he was the player.

The setting sun painted the sky in hues of fiery orange and deep violet, a breathtaking spectacle that mirrored the turbulent emotions within him. He turned his back to the sea, the wind still whipping at his coat, and started his descent, a changed man, ready to embark on the most dangerous mission of his life, a mission not against an enemy on the battlefield but against the system itself. He was ready to walk into the shadows once more, but this time, he would be walking in them, in control, ready to expose the truth that hid within their darkness. His journey was far from over. The battle had just begun. The shadows, once sources of fear and doubt, now contained the seeds of his rebellion. He was no longer just a spy; he was a warrior for justice.

The Cost of Secrecy

The hum of the fluorescent lights in the anonymous motel room was a constant, irritating drone, a stark contrast to the silence he craved. He stared at his reflection in the cracked mirror, barely recognizing the gaunt, shadowed face staring back. The carefully cultivated persona he presented to the world – the affable, slightly rumpled businessman – felt like a costume, a mask he wore to conceal the turmoil within. He was a chameleon, adapting to each environment, each role, yet feeling increasingly disconnected from himself. The loneliness was a gnawing emptiness, a constant companion in this clandestine existence.

This wasn't the adrenaline-fueled excitement he had initially anticipated. The missions, though thrilling in their execution, left a residue of unease, a lingering sense of moral ambiguity. He had justified his actions, telling himself that he was working for the greater good, that his contributions were essential in protecting national security. Yet, the faces of those he'd had to manipulate, the lives subtly disrupted, the potential for irreversible harm – these haunted him.

The cramped motel room, a recurring motif in his undercover life, was a stark reminder of his sacrifice. It was a world away from the spacious comfort of his former life, a life of sunshine, cheering crowds, and the camaraderie of his baseball team. He missed the uncomplicated joy of the game, the shared ambition, the genuine connection he had with his teammates. Now, his companions were shadows, their true identities obscured by layers of deception. He was surrounded by people he couldn't trust, people who were just as skilled at deception as he was.

He ran a hand through his tired hair, the weariness etched deep in his features. He longed for the simple act of a friendly conversation, a genuine laugh, a shared meal with people who knew the real him, not the fabricated persona he presented to the world. But such moments were luxuries he couldn't afford. He was a ghost, flitting through the shadows, his existence a constant game of cat and mouse.

One particular assignment, a seemingly mundane meeting in a bustling city cafe, had left an indelible mark on him. He'd been tasked with extracting information from a seemingly harmless, middle-aged woman – a supposed accountant with ties to a sophisticated money laundering operation. He'd played the role of a charming, albeit slightly dishevelled, businessman, engaging her in innocuous conversation. He had extracted the necessary data, his skills honed to perfection, but the woman's quiet dignity, her resigned acceptance of her predicament, stayed with him. It wasn't the thrill of the successful mission that resonated, but the weight of her unspoken story.

The clandestine nature of his work had extended beyond the operational level. Even his most trusted contacts within the agency seemed to operate at arm's length, their communication cryptic, their motives often ambiguous. He learned to read between the lines, interpreting subtle cues, sensing underlying tensions and shifting allegiances. The trust he'd once placed in his superiors was slowly eroding, replaced by a healthy dose of skepticism. He realized they were as much a danger as the enemies he hunted, their own agendas often clouding the bigger picture.

His training had prepared him for physical challenges, but it had failed to equip him for this deep-seated emotional toll. The constant deception, the constant vigilance, the ever-present threat of exposure, were eroding his sense of self.

The line between his professional persona and his true identity blurred. The longer he operated in this shadowy world, the more difficult it was to remember the person he used to be. He longed for the simple, uncomplicated life he once had.

He found solace only in his secluded sanctuary, the windswept cliff overlooking the churning sea. There, surrounded by the raw power of nature, he could confront his demons, his doubts, his regrets. The vastness of the ocean, the relentless crashing of waves, mirrored the immensity of the sacrifice he'd made. It was a sacrifice not only of his former life but of a part of himself, a piece of his soul chipped away with every mission, every lie, every manipulation.

The cost of secrecy was far greater than he'd imagined. It wasn't merely the risk of exposure, or the physical dangers of his clandestine operations. It was the erosion of trust, the loss of genuine connection, the relentless solitude. It was the constant fear of betrayal, not just from external enemies, but also from those within his own organization. It was the emotional burden of carrying secrets that were too heavy to bear alone.

His undercover life involved frequent changes of location – a small apartment in a bustling European city, a rented house in a quiet suburban neighborhood, a luxury hotel in a tropical paradise. Each location, though superficially glamorous, was merely a temporary stage in his ongoing drama. The transient nature of his existence amplified his sense of isolation. He had no roots, no home. He was always looking over his shoulder, never fully able to relax, always anticipating the next threat.

He'd been to places most people only dreamed of – exotic locales that shimmered with an alluring mystery. He'd sampled the finest cuisines, enjoyed luxurious accommodations, and experienced cultures vastly different from his own. Yet, beneath the superficial veneer of adventure, a deep sense of emptiness lingered. These experiences were hollow victories, empty moments of pleasure, tinged with the knowledge that he was living a lie.

His nights were filled with troubled sleep, fragmented dreams haunted by the faces of those he had wronged, those he had deceived. Even in his unconscious moments, the cost of secrecy continued to exact its price. He woke each morning with a heavy heart, the weariness of his secret life weighing down on his shoulders, his soul, his spirit. He knew that to continue down this path would lead to an irreversible shattering of himself. He could only hope he could unravel the agency's secrets before it unravelled him first. He had a plan now, a strategy to expose the agency's inner workings and find his way back to something approaching normalcy, but the road ahead remained fraught with danger. The cost of secrecy was steep, and he was beginning to wonder if it was a price he could truly afford to pay. The weight of the world rested on his shoulders, a burden he was determined to shed, even if it meant walking alone into the darkness, with the weight of the world pressing on him, he pressed on.

Strained Relationships

The phone call came late, the jarring ring slicing through the quiet of the pre-dawn hours. It was his mother. Her voice, usually brimming with a cheerful energy that belied her age, was thin, strained. "Jake," she whispered, her words laced with a tremor he hadn't heard before. "Your father... he's not doing well."

The news hit him like a physical blow. He hadn't spoken to his father in months, the silence a deliberate choice, a necessary precaution to protect them both. His father, a proud, stubborn man, would never understand his life now. He couldn't explain the shadowy world he inhabited, the constant danger, the moral compromises he'd made. Even if he could, the knowledge might break his father's heart.

He made excuses to his handlers, claiming a sudden family emergency. The agency, always pragmatic, simply provided a new identity and a flight. He found himself on a commercial jet, clutching a hastily packed bag, a knot of anxiety tightening in his gut. The luxury of the first-class seat felt utterly inappropriate, a cruel irony in the face of the heartache threatening to overwhelm him.

The hospital smelled of antiseptic and despair. He saw his father, frail and pale, lying in a sterile bed, his chest rising and falling with labored breaths. The man who had taught him to throw a baseball, who had cheered him on from the stands, was reduced to a shadow of his former self. The once-strong hands, calloused from years of manual labor, now lay limp on the crisp white sheets.

His mother rushed to him, her eyes red and swollen. She embraced him tightly, her frail body trembling with a mixture of grief and relief. "Thank God you came," she whispered, her voice choked with emotion.

He spent the next few days by his father's bedside, caught in a whirlwind of conflicting emotions. Guilt gnawed at him, a constant companion, fueled by his prolonged absence, by the lies he had told, by the life he had chosen. He longed to explain, to share the weight he carried, but the words wouldn't come. The chasm between his two lives felt insurmountable, an unbridgeable gap.

His attempts at conversation with his father were strained, awkward. The man looked at him with a mixture of confusion and disappointment. The unspoken questions hung heavy in the air, unanswered accusations that pierced him deeper than any bullet. His father was slipping away, and Jake was powerless to stop it. The weight of his silence felt heavier than any burden he'd ever carried on a mission.

His sister, Sarah, arrived a few days later. The reunion was equally fraught with tension. Sarah, a successful lawyer, always had a pragmatic approach to life. She didn't judge him outright, but the subtle shifts in her demeanor, the slight tightening of her lips, the carefully chosen words, spoke volumes. Her attempts at casual conversation felt forced, each sentence a carefully constructed bridge across a vast and widening chasm.

She had always been his confidante, his rock, the one person who truly understood him. But now, a wall had been erected between them, a barrier constructed from lies and omissions. He could see the hurt in her eyes, the disappointment in her voice, the unspoken questions hanging in the air like a suffocating cloud. He yearned to bridge that gap, to reclaim the bond they had once shared, but he didn't know where to begin. He was a stranger to her, a phantom flitting in and out of her life, his true identity shrouded in secrecy.

The guilt he felt extended beyond his immediate family. His old baseball team – the camaraderie, the shared triumphs and failures, the unwavering support – felt like a distant dream. He'd received a few hesitant calls, awkward attempts at reconnection, but he'd found himself unable to respond. He couldn't explain the truth, couldn't share the details of his new life. The risk of exposure was too great, the potential consequences too devastating.

Even the friends he had maintained contact with before his recruitment into the agency were drifting away. Their conversations grew infrequent, punctuated by long silences and vague explanations. He felt like an outsider, looking in on a life that no longer belonged to him. He was becoming a ghost, a phantom existing on the periphery of their lives. The people he cared about were receding, slipping away like sand through his fingers.

The strain wasn't just emotional; it was physical. The exhaustion he felt wasn't merely the fatigue of long hours and dangerous missions. It was the exhaustion of deception, the toll of keeping a constant vigil, the burden of secrecy weighing heavily on his mind and body. He found himself snapping at his handlers, his patience wearing thin, his temper short. His sleep was restless, plagued by nightmares of betrayal and exposure.

One night, after a particularly grueling mission, he found himself staring out at the city lights from his anonymous hotel room. The city was beautiful, a shimmering tapestry of lights and shadows, but the beauty was hollow, superficial, without the warmth of human connection. He longed for the simple pleasures of a normal life – a genuine conversation, a shared laugh, a moment of unburdened intimacy. These were luxuries he couldn't afford.

The realization hit him with the force of a physical blow. He had sacrificed everything – his career, his relationships, his sense of self – and for what? The work itself was exhilarating, the thrill of the chase a powerful drug, but the cost was exorbitant, a price far greater than he had ever anticipated. The weight of secrecy was crushing him, slowly but surely eroding his sanity, his spirit, his very soul. He needed to find a way out, a path back to the life he'd lost, even if the journey was fraught with peril. The future was uncertain, but one thing was clear: he couldn't continue down this path. The price of secrecy had become too high. He had to find a way to reclaim his life, to rebuild the bridges he had burned, to reconcile the man he was with the man he had become. The journey ahead would be fraught with danger, but he was determined to fight for his life, for his family, and for the chance to finally shed the weight of the world from his shoulders. The fight for his life would be his next mission, even if he had to face it alone.

The Search for Connection

The sterile scent of the hospital still clung to him, a phantom smell that mirrored the phantom existence he'd carved out for himself. He flew back to his anonymous city apartment, the plush comfort of the first-class seat feeling like a cruel mockery of the desolation within him. The apartment itself, a sterile, modern space, felt more like a holding cell than a home. He'd never decorated it, never personalized it, always anticipating the next move, the next relocation, the next fabricated identity. He was a man without a place, adrift in a sea of shadows.

His handlers, ever efficient, offered no solace, no words of comfort. Their concern was operational, not personal. He was a tool, a highly trained asset, and his emotional state was irrelevant to their objectives. Their calls were brief, to the point, scheduling his next assignment, briefing him on the latest intel, never deviating into the realm of human empathy. The emptiness echoed in the silence that followed each call, a void that gnawed at his soul.

He tried to connect, desperately reaching for something, anything, to fill the void. He found himself in dimly lit bars, the stale beer doing little to numb the ache in his chest. He'd try to strike up conversations, casual encounters with strangers, but the words felt hollow, forced, the mask of his carefully constructed persona slipping at the edges. He couldn't relax, couldn't truly be himself, couldn't share the weight of his secrets. The conversations remained superficial, a veneer of normalcy covering the chasm of his isolation.

One night, in a smoky jazz club, he met a woman. She was a writer, her eyes sharp and intelligent, radiating a quiet confidence that drew him in. He found himself drawn to her, captivated by her wit and her easy grace. For a few precious hours, he forgot the weight of his burdens, the constant threat of exposure, the crushing burden of secrecy. He spoke to her about his life, or rather, a version of his life, carefully avoiding any details that could compromise his security. He told her he was a freelance journalist, a writer himself, a man who dealt in secrets and shadows, a description that skirted the truth without quite lying. He watched her carefully, her expression carefully guarded, never giving away what she truly thought.

The evening was intoxicating, a brief respite from the constant vigilance, a glimpse of what life could be like without the shadow of his double life always looming. He felt a flicker of hope, a fragile flame in the darkness. He drove her home, the silence in the car filled with unspoken hopes and fears. He wanted to tell her the truth, to pour out his heart to her, to finally shed the burden he carried. But the risk was too great, the consequences too devastating. He kissed her goodnight, the lingering touch a promise of something more, a longing for a connection that he knew he couldn't have.

The following days were spent in a blur of assignments, briefings, and covert operations. The fleeting connection he had found in the jazz club became a distant memory, a bittersweet reminder of the normalcy he had lost, the life he could never have. His work was relentless, demanding, and his solitude deepened. The physical and mental strain was relentless. His sleep was haunted by fragmented memories, dreams that blurred the lines between his two worlds – the man he once was and the phantom he had become.

He tried other avenues for connection, small, insignificant attempts at bridging the gap he had created. He went to coffee shops, he sat in parks, he tried striking up conversations with strangers, but the barriers remained. He couldn't shake the feeling of being an outsider looking in, a phantom observing a life that had moved on without him. He felt disconnected, alienated from the world, adrift in a sea of loneliness.

He went to museums, hoping to find solace in art, in beauty, but even the masterpieces felt detached, their vibrant colors muted by the grayscale reality of his existence. He would watch families, couples, friends laughing and sharing moments together, and the pangs of isolation grew sharper, more intense. He yearned for simple human connection, for shared moments, for meaningful conversation, but the walls he had built around himself were too high, too strong.

He tried reconnecting with his sister, Sarah, cautiously, tentatively, through a series of carefully worded emails. She responded with a polite coldness, her words distant, formal. The unspoken accusations hung heavy between them, a chasm that seemed to widen with each strained exchange. His attempts at explaining his life, his reasons for his absence, were met with skepticism and a weary resignation. He had betrayed her trust, broken the unspoken bond they shared, and the damage was irreparable.

The realization that his self-imposed isolation was an inescapable consequence of his chosen life struck him with the full force of its implications. He had sought to protect his family by keeping them at arm's length, but the result was an agonizing distance, an unbearable loneliness. He wasn't just a spy; he was a recluse, a ghost, forever detached from the life he once knew.

He tried reaching out to old friends from his baseball days, but their responses were hesitant, cautious. His carefully constructed excuses, carefully veiled hints at his 'travel writing,' were met with polite but distant responses. The truth, he knew, would shatter the fragile vestiges of their friendships. He was a stranger to them, a ghost from their past, and the knowledge was a bitter pill to swallow.

His work continued, unrelenting and demanding. Each mission, each successful operation, felt more hollow, more devoid of meaning. The adrenaline rush, the thrill of the chase, couldn't compensate for the absence of human connection, the void in his heart. The price of secrecy was too high, far exceeding the paltry rewards it offered. The emptiness consumed him.

He realized that the isolation wasn't just a consequence of his job; it was a self-fulfilling prophecy, a consequence of his own choices, his own deliberate retreat from the world. He had become a prisoner of his own making. The weight of secrecy was a physical burden, crushing his spirit, suffocating his soul.

One evening, sitting alone in his apartment, staring out at the city lights, he made a decision. The life he was living, though exciting, was killing him. The isolation, the constant deception, the fear of discovery – it was all too much to bear. He needed to find a way to reconnect with the world, to rebuild the bridges he had burned, even if it meant risking everything. The path ahead was uncertain, fraught with peril, but for the first time in a long time, he felt a spark of hope, a glimmer of light in the surrounding darkness. The weight of secrecy was still immense, but he was finally ready to start fighting to shed it. The fight for connection would be his next, and perhaps, his most dangerous, mission yet.

Finding a New Support System

The decision, once made, felt both liberating and terrifying. The weight of secrecy, previously a crushing burden, now felt slightly lighter, replaced by a nervous anticipation. He needed a support system, a lifeline in the treacherous waters he navigated. But where could he find it? His past life was gone, the people he knew either too far removed or too deeply implicated in his current reality. He couldn't risk exposing them, not after all he'd been through.

His next mission took him to a bustling metropolis in Southeast Asia, a city teeming with life, a stark contrast to the sterile anonymity of his apartment. He was embedded, observing a high-level arms deal, his every move calculated, every breath measured. The tension was palpable, the air thick with secrets and deceit. He was a shadow, observing, analyzing, waiting for the opportune moment to strike.

During a lull in the operation, a chance encounter changed everything. He found himself in a small, dimly lit tea house, the scent of jasmine and spices filling the air. He'd sought refuge from the relentless heat and the oppressive humidity, hoping for a moment of quiet contemplation. He ordered a jasmine tea, its delicate aroma momentarily soothing his frayed nerves.

A woman sat at the table next to his, engrossed in a worn leather-bound book. She was older than he'd initially estimated, her face etched with lines that spoke of wisdom and resilience. Her eyes, however, held a spark of mischief, a glint that caught him off guard. She was dressed simply, a flowing silk dress in muted tones, but her elegance was undeniable. He couldn't place her; she didn't fit the profile of anyone he'd encountered in his line of work.

He found himself watching her, captivated by her air of quiet confidence. She looked up, catching his gaze, and offered a small, knowing smile. There was something about her that felt familiar, a sense of shared understanding that transcended the casual observation. It wasn't a flirtatious look; it was something deeper, a recognition of shared experiences in a world of shadows.

Hesitantly, he offered a polite nod, a hesitant greeting. She responded in kind, her voice soft but firm, carrying a hint of a foreign accent he couldn't quite place. She spoke in perfect English, yet a subtle melodic undertone hinted at a rich and varied background.

"Beautiful day, isn't it?" she remarked, her gaze lingering on the bustling street outside.

He chuckled softly, "Beautiful in its own way. Chaotic, but beautiful."

She laughed, a low, melodious sound. "Indeed. Chaos and beauty often go hand in hand, don't you think?"

Their conversation flowed effortlessly, an unexpected oasis in the desert of his solitary existence. He found himself revealing more than he intended, sharing anecdotes about his "travel writing," carefully sidestepping any details that could compromise his identity. She listened intently, her expression unwavering, her responses insightful and engaging.

He learned her name was Anya Petrova. She claimed to be a translator, working on various projects around the globe, a profession that offered her a similar level of travel and anonymity. He sensed a certain ambiguity about her words, a carefully crafted narrative that mirrored his own. There was a shared understanding, an unspoken acknowledgment of the clandestine nature of their lives.

They met again the following day, and the next, their conversations becoming deeper, more intimate. He began to relax, to shed the layers of deception he'd built up over the years. With Anya, he found he could be himself, or at least, a more authentic version of himself. She didn't pry, didn't push, but she offered unwavering support and understanding.

She spoke of her own experiences, hinting at a past filled with its own share of danger and secrecy. She didn't offer details, but the implication was clear – they were kindred spirits, navigating a similar landscape of shadows and deceit. Her strength, her resilience, her quiet confidence, were inspiring. He found himself relying on her, not just for conversation, but for a sense of shared understanding, a sense of belonging he hadn't felt in years.

Anya wasn't just a chance encounter; she was a lifeline. She wasn't part of his agency, wasn't involved in his operations, and yet, she offered a different kind of support, a much-needed counterpoint to the cold efficiency of his handlers. She offered friendship, companionship, and a sense of normalcy in a world that had become increasingly surreal.

Their bond deepened, not into romantic entanglement, but a powerful, mutually supportive friendship. They shared meals, explored the city, and spoke late into the night, their conversations spanning everything from literature and art to the complexities of the human condition. He shared his struggles with isolation, the weight of secrecy, the constant fear of exposure, and she listened, offering quiet understanding and unwavering support.

Her perspective, her experience, offered a fresh perspective on his life. She wasn't judgmental, nor did she offer simplistic solutions. Instead, she provided a safe space, a place where he could be vulnerable, a place where he could be himself without the constant fear of judgment or betrayal.

He began to see the possibility of a different future, a future where he wasn't defined solely by his work, a future where he could have meaningful connections, genuine relationships. Anya wasn't a replacement for the life he'd lost, but she was a beacon of hope, a testament to the possibility of human connection in even the darkest of circumstances.

He continued his missions, but with a renewed sense of purpose. His work was still challenging, still dangerous, but the weight of secrecy felt less overwhelming. He had found an anchor, a connection that helped him navigate the treacherous waters of his double life.

Their friendship was a testament to the resilience of the human spirit, a beacon of hope in a world shrouded in shadows. It was an unexpected gift, a lifeline in a world of deceit and danger. The possibility of future relationships, whether romantic or platonic, hinted at a brighter future, a future where the weight of secrecy might eventually be lifted. For now, though, the support and understanding of Anya Petrova was enough. It was a starting point, a foundation upon which he could build a new, more fulfilling life, a life where the darkness wouldn't completely swallow him whole. The road ahead was still uncertain, still fraught with peril, but with Anya by his side, he felt a renewed sense of hope, a renewed belief in the power of human connection, a belief that even in the shadows, there could be light. And that light, he realized, was worth fighting for.

Acceptance of the Life

The Himalayan foothills offered a stark contrast to the urban jungles he'd grown accustomed to. The air, crisp and clean, carried the scent of pine and damp earth, a world away from the smog-choked cities and clandestine meeting places that had become his reality. He stood on a precipice, gazing at the sprawling panorama below, a vast tapestry of emerald green valleys and snow-capped peaks piercing the azure sky. It was a breathtaking vista, a scene of unparalleled beauty, and yet, it was the quiet solitude, the sense of removal from the world of shadows he inhabited, that resonated most deeply within him.

This remote monastery, nestled high in the mountains, was his chosen sanctuary, a temporary retreat from the relentless demands of his life. He had earned this respite, this period of quiet reflection. His transformation was complete. The rigorous training, the brutal missions, the constant vigilance – it had all forged him into something new, something… different. He was no longer just Jake Riley, the promising baseball player whose career had been cut short. He was something else entirely, a ghost, a shadow, a phantom operating in a realm beyond the comprehension of ordinary life.

The acceptance didn't come easily. There were nights when the memories of his former life would flood back, the echoes of laughter and camaraderie, the roar of the crowd, the crack of the bat. He'd wake up in a cold sweat, the phantom pain of a past injury reminding him of the life he'd left behind. But those nights were becoming less frequent, the sharp edges of grief slowly smoothing into a dull ache, a manageable sorrow.

He'd learned to compartmentalize, to separate the two halves of his existence. The Jake Riley he'd once been remained a cherished memory, a ghost that haunted the quiet corners of his mind, but he no longer allowed it to consume him. His new life, though fraught with danger and moral ambiguities, was his reality, and he'd learned to embrace it, to find a strange sort of peace within its chaos.

The monastery, with its ancient stones and the rhythmic chanting of the monks, offered a paradoxical sense of grounding. It was a place of stillness, a stark contrast to the relentless activity and perpetual tension of his missions. Here, surrounded by the silent majesty of the mountains, he could finally breathe, could finally allow himself to feel the weight of his experiences without being overwhelmed by them.

He spent his days meditating, his mind gradually quieting, the ceaseless stream of thoughts and anxieties slowing to a gentle trickle. He found solace in the simplicity of the monastic life, the repetitive rituals, the quiet contemplation. The physical exertion of his training had prepared him well for the rigors of the mountainous terrain. He hiked through the forests, climbed the slopes, his body responding instinctively to the demands of the landscape, mirroring the physical and mental discipline he'd honed over the years. He found a rhythm in his days, a sense of purpose in his solitude.

His handlers had sanctioned this leave. They understood the necessity of rest, of allowing their operatives a chance to reset, to recharge their batteries before returning to the shadows. They knew that a burned-out agent was a liability, a broken tool. This wasn't a vacation, but a strategic retreat, a necessary step in maintaining operational effectiveness.

Yet, even in this solitude, the weight of secrecy never fully lifted. It was an intrinsic part of his being now, a second skin that he could never shed completely. The constant awareness of his double life, the need to maintain a facade of normalcy, the perpetual tension of hidden knowledge – these were the hallmarks of his new identity. But the acceptance was growing, blossoming like a tenacious wildflower clinging to the rocky mountainside.

He spent hours reading, poring over ancient texts, philosophical treatises, works of fiction that offered different perspectives, different realities. He sought out stories of resilience, of survival, of redemption, searching for parallels to his own experiences. He found comfort in the written word, a reflection of his own internal struggles and a glimpse into the shared human experience. He realized that he was not alone, that even in the darkness, there was light, a flicker of hope, a belief in the possibility of a brighter future.

He began to journal, to write down his thoughts, his feelings, his memories, a cathartic process that allowed him to externalize his experiences, to confront his demons without succumbing to them. The act of writing brought a sense of order to the chaos within, a semblance of control in a world often beyond his grasp. The journal became a confidante, a silent witness to his transformation, a record of his journey from the shadows into the tentative light.

One evening, as the sun dipped below the horizon, painting the sky in hues of orange, purple, and gold, he sat by the monastery's ancient prayer wheels, the gentle turning a soothing counterpoint to the turmoil within. He felt a profound sense of peace, a quiet acceptance of his life, his identity, his destiny. The weight of secrecy remained, but it no longer felt like a crushing burden. It was a part of him now, an integral aspect of his being, but it no longer defined him. He was more than just a spy; he was a man who had survived, who had adapted, who had found a measure of peace in the midst of chaos.

He understood that his life would always be lived in the shadows, that the constant vigilance, the inherent risks, were unavoidable facets of his existence. But he also understood that he wasn't alone. He had Anya, a beacon of light in the darkness, a symbol of human connection in a world that often felt devoid of empathy. And he had this newfound sense of self, a resilient core that had been forged in the crucible of his experiences. He had learned to embrace the weight of his secrecy, not as a curse, but as a defining characteristic, a testament to his resilience and his capacity for survival. He had accepted his life, not with resignation, but with a quiet, determined acceptance.

His mission had changed. It was no longer solely about fulfilling the agency's objectives, but about preserving his own humanity, about maintaining the fragile balance between the life he led and the life he longed for. He carried the weight of secrecy, but he carried it with a newfound grace, a quiet strength that allowed him to move forward, to navigate the treacherous currents of his double life, and to find a measure of peace in the heart of the storm. The Himalayan peaks served as a silent witness to his transformation, a backdrop to his quiet triumph over adversity, a symbol of his enduring spirit. He was ready to return, ready to face whatever challenges lay ahead, knowing that even in the darkest of shadows, he could find his way towards the light. His acceptance wasn't a passive surrender; it was a powerful affirmation of his strength, his resilience, and his indomitable spirit. He was ready. He was whole. He was at peace.

Seeds of Discontent

The crisp mountain air, once a balm to his soul, now felt thin and strained, a reflection of the growing unease that had settled over him like a shroud. His leave was over. The return to Langley felt less like a homecoming and more like a descent back into the suffocating pressure cooker of his double life. The serene monastery, with its quiet rituals and breathtaking views, was a distant memory, replaced by the sterile, echoing corridors of the agency. The familiar scent of coffee and stale air hung heavy, a constant reminder of the intense, clandestine world he inhabited.

The change was palpable. A subtle shift in the atmosphere, a tension that vibrated in the hushed conversations and hurried footsteps. It wasn't just the usual clandestine atmosphere; this felt different, charged with a palpable sense of unease. Whispers followed him like shadows, the unspoken anxieties circulating like a toxic gas, poisoning the air. He saw it in the furtive glances exchanged between colleagues, in the clipped, terse exchanges that replaced the usual camaraderie. Even Anya, his usually unflappable contact, seemed burdened with a silent worry.

His first meeting with his handler, Marcus Thorne, was short and businesslike, devoid of the usual easy banter. Thorne, a man whose expression rarely betrayed emotion, seemed strained, the lines around his eyes deeper than usual. The briefing, concerning a routine asset extraction in Prague, felt rushed, almost perfunctory, as though he was holding back information. The usual meticulous detail was absent; the mission parameters were vague, the contingency plans hastily sketched. It was a departure from their usual thoroughness, a sign that something was amiss.

Later, during a seemingly innocuous meeting in the agency cafeteria, he overheard a hushed conversation between two analysts. They spoke in code, their words carefully chosen, but Jake, honed by years of training, picked up on the undercurrent of anxiety. They spoke of a "leak," a "mole," and a "compromised operation." The casual reference to a catastrophic failure sent a shiver down his spine. His sharp ears caught the names whispered—names he recognized, names of people he trusted, names he'd shared missions with. The seeds of doubt were sown, the whispers transforming into a cacophony of suspicion.

The following days were filled with a sense of mounting dread. He noticed subtle shifts in the patterns of his colleagues' behavior, the unusual absences, the late-night work sessions, the hurried, clandestine meetings in dimly lit corners. The casual camaraderie, once a defining feature of their shared environment, had vanished, replaced by an atmosphere of intense suspicion and distrust. The agency, usually a well-oiled machine operating with precision and efficiency, seemed to be falling apart at the seams.

One evening, while reviewing his files, he stumbled upon a discrepancy. A minor detail, almost insignificant, yet it raised a red flag. A document had been altered, a date changed, a name substituted. The alteration was subtle, easily overlooked, but his trained eye caught it immediately. It was a subtle manipulation, designed to mislead, a sign of something far more sinister.

He confided in Anya, his instincts telling him that something was deeply wrong. Anya, usually his unwavering confidante, seemed hesitant, her usual openness replaced by a guarded silence. She confirmed his suspicions, albeit indirectly, her words carefully chosen, hinting at a deeper level of conspiracy than he could have imagined. She spoke of infighting, of power struggles, of a dangerous game being played at the highest levels of the agency.

The information she revealed was both shocking and terrifying. There was a mole within the agency, someone high up, feeding crucial information to an unknown enemy. The leak wasn't just compromising operations; it was risking the lives of agents in the field, jeopardizing years of meticulous work, and threatening the very existence of the agency itself. The betrayal ran deep, the tentacles of deception spreading through the organization like a malignant tumor.

Anya described the deep-seated rivalry between two factions within the agency: The traditionalists, clinging to older methods and distrustful of new technology, and the progressives, eager to embrace new technologies and strategies. This internal conflict had festered for years, but now, it had erupted into a full-blown war, with each faction desperately trying to gain control.

The mole, she explained, was likely someone from either faction, a person close enough to sensitive information to cause maximum damage. Anya hinted at a possible connection to an ongoing operation, a complex mission that involved multiple assets and several foreign governments. The failure of this operation could trigger a chain reaction of events with devastating consequences.

Jake felt a cold knot of fear tighten in his stomach. The seemingly routine assignment to Prague now took on a new and sinister meaning. He realized that he was a pawn in a much larger game, caught in the crossfire of a deadly internal conflict. The betrayal was not just a violation of trust; it was a calculated act of war.

The next few days became a blur of clandestine meetings, covert surveillance, and frantic efforts to uncover the identity of the mole. The atmosphere at the agency was poisonous, the air thick with suspicion and paranoia. Everyone was a suspect, every conversation a potential trap.

Jake's investigation led him down a rabbit hole of deceit and intrigue, uncovering a network of hidden alliances and secret agendas. The lines between friend and foe had become blurred, trust had eroded, and the future of the agency, and possibly the world, hung precariously in the balance. The seeds of discontent had grown into a poisonous vine, choking the life out of the organization he had sworn to serve. He knew then that his new mission, more critical than any he'd faced before, was not just to protect national security but to survive the treachery within. He had to expose the mole, before it was too late. His life, and the lives of countless others, depended on it. The game had changed, and Jake knew he was playing for keeps. The calm acceptance he found in the Himalayas was a distant, almost forgotten dream. Now, only the fight remained.

Shifting Loyalties

The Prague extraction, initially presented as routine, now felt like a carefully laid trap. The vague briefing, the rushed preparations – it all pointed towards a deliberate obfuscation, a calculated attempt to mislead. The more Jake dug, the more unsettling the inconsistencies became. He revisited his training records, poring over the details of his mission profile, seeking any clues that might illuminate the shadowy machinations at play. He found nothing explicit, only a creeping sense of unease, a nagging feeling that something was fundamentally wrong.

His investigation led him to a shadowy figure known only as "The Serpent," a legendary operative whose existence was barely whispered within the agency's hallowed halls. The Serpent was a ghost, a phantom whose actions echoed through the corridors of power, leaving behind a trail of chaos and uncertainty. Rumors suggested he was a master manipulator, a puppet master pulling strings from the shadows, orchestrating events to his own advantage. Some whispered that he was a double agent, others that he was a rogue operator acting independently. His true identity and motivations remained shrouded in mystery, a riddle that seemed impossible to solve.

Jake's search for answers took him to unexpected places. He infiltrated a clandestine meeting held in a dimly lit bar in Georgetown, a gathering place for disgruntled agents and disillusioned insiders. The atmosphere was thick with resentment, a toxic cocktail of betrayal and suspicion. He listened to hushed conversations, overheard snippets of coded messages, and gleaned valuable information from the disgruntled whispers. He learned of a secret faction within the agency, a cabal of agents who had grown disillusioned with the organization's direction, its increasingly aggressive tactics, and its willingness to compromise its moral principles.

This faction, known only as "The Shadow Syndicate," was led by a charismatic but ruthless operative named Viktor. Viktor was a former KGB agent who had defected to the West years earlier, bringing with him a wealth of experience and a deep-seated distrust of authority. He had cultivated a network of loyalists within the agency, agents who shared his discontent and his ambition for power. The Shadow Syndicate was operating in the shadows, subtly manipulating events, undermining the agency from within.

Jake's presence at the Georgetown meeting was discovered. A tense standoff ensued, a deadly game of cat and mouse in a dimly lit back room. He managed to escape, but not without leaving a trail of unanswered questions and deepening his suspicion that the mole was closer than he'd initially thought.

Anya, his usual reliable source of information, became increasingly elusive. Their communication became cryptic, her responses laced with hints of fear and a growing sense of desperation. She warned him to be cautious, to trust no one, and to tread carefully. Her messages were brief, coded, and delivered through a series of seemingly innocuous encounters, adding a layer of complexity to his already precarious situation.

The tension within the agency escalated. The air grew thick with suspicion, as colleagues eyed each other with distrust, every conversation carefully measured, every move scrutinized. The camaraderie that had once been a defining characteristic of their shared profession had evaporated, replaced by a suffocating atmosphere of paranoia.

Jake's investigation led him to a series of encrypted messages, hidden within seemingly innocuous documents. These messages revealed a complex conspiracy involving a high-ranking official within the agency, a man named General Petrov, who had secretly been collaborating with a foreign power. Petrov, a staunch traditionalist, resented the agency's embrace of new technologies and its growing dependence on advanced surveillance methods. He had been feeding sensitive information to a rival nation, compromising ongoing operations and endangering the lives of countless agents.

The revelation of Petrov's betrayal sent shockwaves through the agency. The discovery of the mole at such a high level confirmed Jake's worst fears. It was a betrayal of the highest order, a profound violation of trust. It revealed a rot that had festered for years, a cancer that had metastasized throughout the agency's core. The consequences were catastrophic.

The ensuing power struggle between the traditionalists and the progressives intensified, threatening to tear the agency apart. Jake found himself caught in the crossfire, his loyalties tested, his judgment clouded. He had to navigate the treacherous currents of intrigue and deceit, while simultaneously uncovering the truth and exposing the mole.

Anya's final communication was a desperate plea, revealing a rendezvous point for a clandestine meeting. The message was fraught with danger, a thinly veiled warning that she was in grave danger. Jake raced against time, trying to locate Anya before it was too late. The agency was a labyrinth of deceit, a maze of secret corridors and hidden rooms. Each step he took was fraught with peril, every encounter a potential trap.

He arrived at the rendezvous point, a deserted warehouse on the outskirts of Washington, only to discover a brutal ambush. A fierce firefight ensued, a deadly ballet of bullets and shadows. He fought his way through a barrage of gunfire, dodging bullets with the agility honed from years of training. The attackers were highly skilled, ruthless mercenaries who showed no mercy.

He eventually overcame the ambush, but Anya was nowhere to be found. He found a cryptic message, a single playing card – the Queen of Spades – tucked into a concealed compartment. It was a clear signal, a message with a hidden meaning. He knew then that the game had just begun, and the stakes were higher than ever before. He had to decode the message, and quickly. Anya's life and potentially the future of the agency depended on it. The Queen of Spades was only the first piece in a much larger puzzle, a complex and deadly game with far-reaching consequences. The fight for survival had become a desperate race against time, and Jake Riley was determined to win. The betrayal ran deeper than he had ever imagined, and the road ahead would be long and perilous. His journey, filled with moral ambiguities and life-or-death choices, was far from over.

Exposure of a Mole

The Queen of Spades. The image burned itself onto Jake's mind, a chilling symbol of the escalating danger. Anya's fate hung precariously in the balance, a victim of the insidious betrayal that had poisoned the agency from within. The ambush had been brutal, a calculated attempt to eliminate both Anya and him. He'd survived, but the near-death experience only intensified his resolve. He had to find Anya, expose the mole, and unravel the conspiracy before it was too late.

His first move was to revisit the encrypted messages he'd discovered earlier. He spent hours hunched over his laptop, the glow illuminating his determined face, his fingers flying across the keyboard. He utilized every decryption tool at his disposal, sifting through layers of code, deciphering complex algorithms, searching for any clue that might lead him to Anya or provide insight into the identity of the mole. The pressure was immense, the stakes impossibly high. Each failed attempt chipped away at his confidence, yet he persisted, driven by a fierce determination to uncover the truth.

Finally, a breakthrough. A seemingly innocuous sequence of numbers, embedded within a seemingly routine financial report, revealed a hidden pattern. Using a newly discovered algorithm – a piece of software he'd stumbled upon during a clandestine data-mining operation – he decrypted the code. The message was short, chillingly direct: "They know. Meet at the old clock tower. Midnight." The message was unsigned, but the context was clear. "They" referred to the mole, and the rendezvous was undoubtedly a trap.

The old clock tower. It was a forgotten relic, a dilapidated structure on the outskirts of the city, a place shrouded in shadows and steeped in a history of forgotten secrets. Jake knew he was walking into a lion's den, but he had no choice. Anya's life depended on it.

He arrived at the clock tower just before midnight. The air was cold, heavy with the scent of rain and decay. The moon cast long, eerie shadows, enhancing the desolate ambiance. He moved cautiously, his senses heightened, his instincts screaming at him to be wary. Every rustle of leaves, every creak of the aging structure sent shivers down his spine. He checked his weapons, his heart pounding in his chest. He was alone, vulnerable, and completely exposed.

He found Anya waiting for him, but not as he had hoped. She was bruised, her clothes torn, her face pale, her eyes filled with a haunting mixture of fear and resignation. She spoke in hushed whispers, revealing a chilling tale of torture and betrayal. She'd been captured, interrogated, and forced to reveal information she couldn't have known without access to highly classified intelligence. The information was a complex series of coordinates and dates, the coordinates of a clandestine meeting between high-ranking officials, and the dates of planned covert operations. This was no ordinary mole; this was a catastrophic breach of national security.

The mole wasn't just leaking information; they were manipulating events, orchestrating chaos, and potentially setting up an elaborate double-cross. The implications were terrifying. The very foundation of the agency was crumbling under the weight of this massive betrayal.

Anya's capture had been a calculated move, a calculated risk by the mole to lure Jake into a trap. The ambush at the warehouse had been a feint, a distraction to keep him occupied while they extracted information from Anya. It was a masterful display of deception, a demonstration of the mole's cunning and ruthlessness.

Anya's capture, however, inadvertently provided Jake with a crucial clue – a tiny, almost imperceptible scratch on her arm. It was a symbol, a coded message etched into her skin. He recognized it – a stylized representation of the Ouroboros, an ancient symbol of cyclical renewal and infinity. It was the same symbol he'd seen in a coded message from Viktor, the leader of the Shadow Syndicate.

The pieces of the puzzle were finally falling into place. Viktor was the mole, his infiltration of the agency a meticulously planned operation that had spanned years. He had been playing both sides, manipulating events to his own advantage, sowing seeds of discord, and undermining the agency's authority. He was the puppet master, pulling strings from the shadows, orchestrating chaos to achieve his own ultimate goal – seizing control of the agency and establishing his own power base.

The confrontation was inevitable. Jake, armed with this new knowledge, pursued Viktor, a relentless hunter tracking his prey. The chase led him through the agency's labyrinthine corridors, a deadly game of cat and mouse played in the shadows, a battle of wits and will. The confrontation took place in the agency's secure server room, a sanctuary of secrets and technology, the heart of their communications network.

The final showdown was brutal. Viktor, a skilled operative, fought with the ruthless efficiency of a seasoned assassin. He used the technology around him – the monitoring systems, the surveillance cameras, even the computer systems themselves – as weapons. But Jake, using his tactical skills and knowledge of the facility's layout, countered every move. The server room became a battleground, the air thick with tension, the sounds of shattering glass and metal echoing through the corridors.

After a protracted struggle, Jake subdued Viktor. The victory was hard-won, but he knew this was only the beginning. The exposure of Viktor was a significant blow to the conspiracy, but there were likely others involved – a network of accomplices who had aided and abetted Viktor in his treachery.

The aftermath was a period of intense scrutiny, soul-searching, and rebuilding. The agency was deeply wounded, shaken to its core. Trust had been shattered, alliances broken, and loyalties tested. The exposure of Viktor, however, paved the way for systemic reforms, increased security protocols, and a renewed focus on trust and accountability.

Anya, though traumatized, recovered. She became an invaluable asset in the investigation, providing crucial insights and assisting in the dismantling of the remaining elements of the Shadow Syndicate. The case of the mole became a watershed moment in the agency's history, a stark reminder of the dangers of unchecked ambition, the fragility of trust, and the ever-present threat of betrayal.

Jake, having faced the ultimate test of loyalty and survival, continued his career within the agency, but with a newfound awareness of the ethical complexities and moral ambiguities of his profession. The scars of his experiences were deeply etched into his soul, a constant reminder of the high stakes and the constant vigilance required in the world of espionage. He had become a seasoned operative, stronger, wiser, and more determined than ever before. The battle was won, but the war was far from over. The shadows always lurked, and the hunt for those who sought to undermine the fabric of national security would continue. Jake Riley would be at the forefront, the guardian of secrets, the silent protector, ever vigilant, ever ready to fight for what he believed in. The Queen of Spades, a symbol of betrayal and danger, would forever serve as a reminder of the price of victory.

Trust and Treachery

The Ouroboros. The symbol, etched so subtly onto Anya's arm, pulsed in Jake's memory, a venomous serpent consuming its own tail, a perfect representation of the cyclical nature of betrayal within the agency. Viktor, the seemingly incorruptible leader of the Shadow Syndicate, was the mole. But he couldn't have acted alone. A vast network of deceit, carefully woven over years, had to be unraveling, threatening to bring the entire agency crashing down.

His immediate priority was to inform his superiors. He knew the ramifications of revealing Viktor's treachery would be seismic. The agency, already reeling from the recent attacks, would be thrown into absolute chaos. He found his superior, Director Thorne, in his dimly lit office, the faint glow of the computer screen illuminating his weary face. Thorne listened, his expression shifting from skepticism to grim acceptance as Jake laid bare the evidence – the decrypted messages, Anya's testimony, the Ouroboros symbol. The weight of the situation was palpable, the air thick with unspoken fears.

"This is… catastrophic, Riley," Thorne finally uttered, his voice barely a whisper. "This goes beyond a simple leak; this is a systematic dismantling of our operations."

The following days were a whirlwind of activity. Jake, now thrust into the forefront of the investigation, worked tirelessly alongside Anya and a select team of trusted operatives. They meticulously pieced together Viktor's web of deceit, tracing his movements, analyzing his communications, and identifying his collaborators. Each new discovery only deepened the chasm of betrayal. The list of compromised agents grew longer with each passing hour, and the lines between friend and foe became increasingly blurred.

Their investigation led them to a series of safe houses scattered across the city, each meticulously hidden, each a testament to Viktor's meticulous planning. The safe houses weren't just storage locations for stolen data; they were operational hubs, nodes in a vast network of clandestine activities. In one safe house, tucked away in a seemingly innocuous warehouse district, they uncovered a hidden laboratory, where advanced weaponry was being developed and tested—weapons far more sophisticated than anything in the agency's arsenal. This was no mere intelligence leak; it was an act of industrial espionage on a grand scale.

Another safe house, a secluded villa overlooking the ocean, held the key to Viktor's ultimate goal. Inside, amidst carefully organized files and encrypted hard drives, they found the blueprint of a clandestine operation codenamed "Project Nightingale." The project involved the infiltration of a rival nation's most secure defense systems and the theft of highly sensitive information, the kind that could trigger a global crisis. The magnitude of Viktor's treachery was staggering. He wasn't simply seeking power within the agency; he was aiming for global dominance.

The investigation also brought Jake face-to-face with the devastating human cost of Viktor's treachery. They found evidence of blackmail, coercion, and even murder. Agents, once considered loyal and trustworthy, had been manipulated and exploited by Viktor, their lives irrevocably damaged. Jake found himself grappling with the moral ambiguities of his profession. He had to make difficult decisions, separating the wheat from the chaff, deciding who to trust and who to arrest.

One particularly harrowing encounter involved a former colleague, Agent Sarah Walker. Sarah, a woman Jake had considered a close friend, was implicated in Viktor's network. The evidence was overwhelming: coded messages, financial transactions, and witness testimony. Confronted with the evidence, Sarah confessed, her eyes filled with remorse and despair. She had been blackmailed, her family threatened, her loyalty bought. Jake felt the sting of betrayal deeply; a friend, a comrade, had been compromised. He understood the power of manipulation, the insidious nature of treachery.

The investigation extended beyond the agency's walls. They discovered that Viktor had cultivated connections with foreign governments and criminal organizations, building a vast network of support and influence. These connections reached into the highest echelons of power, demonstrating the reach and depth of Viktor's conspiracy. Their pursuit took them through dimly lit back alleys, clandestine meetings in dimly lit bars, and covert operations in foreign countries.

The final confrontation with Viktor's remaining operatives took place in a desolate, abandoned factory on the outskirts of the city. The ensuing firefight was intense, a brutal ballet of gunfire and hand-to-hand combat, testing Jake's skills and resolve to their limits. He fought alongside Anya and a small team of loyal operatives, their combined skills and tactical prowess enabling them to overcome Viktor's remaining forces.

The culmination of the investigation and the dismantling of Viktor's network was a long and arduous process. The agency underwent a complete overhaul, its structure reorganized, its protocols strengthened, its culture reexamined. The trust that had been shattered had to be painstakingly rebuilt. The betrayal exposed by Viktor's actions served as a harsh, but necessary, lesson. The agency emerged from the ashes, stronger, more resilient, and more vigilant than before.

Jake, though physically and emotionally scarred, had become a cornerstone of the newly reformed agency. His experience had hardened him, sharpened his instincts, and deepened his understanding of the human cost of espionage. He had witnessed firsthand the fragility of trust and the insidious nature of treachery, and those lessons would forever shape his approach to his profession. He knew the shadows would always lurk, and the hunt for those who sought to undermine the agency would continue. But he was ready. The Queen of Spades had dealt a devastating blow, but Jake Riley had survived, and he would continue to guard the secrets, the silent protector, ever vigilant.

Choosing Sides

The biting November wind whipped around Jake, stinging his cheeks as he stood in the cavernous emptiness of the abandoned warehouse. The air hung thick with the scent of dust and decay, a stark contrast to the sterile, technologically advanced environment he was used to. This was Viktor's final play, a desperate gamble, and Jake was right in the middle of it. He wasn't here to arrest Viktor; that ship had sailed. Viktor was gone, a ghost in the machine, his network fractured but not destroyed. The fight now was for the remnants, for the loyalists still clinging to his corrupted ideology, for the future of the agency itself.

Anya stood beside him, her usually vibrant eyes shadowed with concern. "They're here," she whispered, her voice barely audible above the wind whistling through the broken windows. "Three operatives. All heavily armed. They're waiting for the transfer."

The transfer. The final piece of Viktor's insidious puzzle. A cache of highly classified data, enough to cripple several allied nations, was scheduled to be moved from this dilapidated warehouse to an unknown location. Jake and Anya's mission was to intercept it, to prevent it from falling into the wrong hands, and to eliminate the remaining threat Viktor's followers posed. The problem was the choice before them. These were not simply Viktor's henchmen; they were, until recently, members of the agency, agents who had once served alongside them. They were pawns, yes, but pawns who had made a conscious decision to side with Viktor, to betray everything they had sworn to protect. And now, Jake had to decide how to deal with them.

The ethical considerations gnawed at him. Kill them? Arrests could lead to information leaks. They were expendable in the grand scheme of things, but were they expendable in the realm of his conscience? He had seen firsthand the insidious nature of betrayal, the devastating consequences of misplaced loyalty. Sarah Walker's haunted eyes still burned behind his eyelids. He couldn't allow this cycle to repeat itself. Yet, letting these agents escape would compromise national security and potentially start another chain of events that would mirror the disastrous consequences of Viktor's actions.

His gaze drifted to Anya. She was observing the warehouse's layout, her expression a mixture of calculation and unease. They had run simulations, planned contingencies, but there was no accounting for the human element, for the unpredictable nature of desperate people fighting for their lives. This was not a clean fight. This was about survival, about choosing a side, not in a grand ideological battle, but in a gritty, brutal struggle for the soul of their agency.

"They know we're coming," Anya said, breaking the tense silence. "They're setting a trap."

Jake nodded, his mind racing. They couldn't storm the building head-on. They needed a plan, a subtle approach that would allow them to neutralize the threat without unnecessary bloodshed. He had to find a way to exploit their loyalty to Viktor, to use it against them, to turn the tables on their carefully laid trap.

He scanned the area, his eyes darting from the crumbling brick walls to the piles of discarded machinery. An idea sparked. A risky idea, but one that might just work. "Anya," he said, a glint in his eye, "I need you to play a part. You need to be Viktor's ghost."

Anya raised an eyebrow, her lips curving into a slight smirk. She understood. They would use the enemy's own desperation and beliefs against them. They would prey on their blind faith and twisted loyalty. They would become the phantom echo of Viktor himself, a terrifying specter rising from the ashes of his destruction.

The plan involved a carefully orchestrated deception. Anya would impersonate a high-ranking Viktor loyalist, delivering a cryptic message that would lead the agents to believe that Viktor had escaped and was coordinating a new operation. The message would contain false coordinates, drawing them to a different location – a pre-selected ambush point. Jake, meanwhile, would use his tactical skills to cut off their escape routes, sealing them in a deadly game of cat and mouse.

The tension was palpable as they executed their plan. Anya, shrouded in darkness and wearing a disguise that made her almost unrecognizable, delivered the message with chilling precision, her voice a low, hypnotic whisper that echoed the commanding tones of Viktor himself. The agents, clearly shaken by the events of the previous weeks, swallowed the bait without hesitation, their desperate loyalty overriding their instincts for self-preservation. They fell into their trap. The ambush was swift, brutal, but decisive. The loyalists were apprehended without loss of life on either side.

The transfer of the classified data was intercepted, securing a victory for the agency, preventing a potential international catastrophe. But the victory felt hollow, tinged with the bitter taste of betrayal and the weight of the difficult choices they had made. They had saved the agency, but at a price. The lines between right and wrong, friend and foe, had become increasingly blurred, leaving Jake questioning the very foundations of his profession.

The warehouse stood silent once more, its empty shell echoing the aftermath of their battle. As Jake and Anya left the scene, walking through the cold November night, the full weight of their actions settled upon them. They had chosen a side, a difficult side, one born from necessity and fraught with moral complexities. The war was over for now, but the battles within had only just begun. The fight for the soul of the agency, the fight for the principles they were sworn to uphold, was far from finished, the shadows still remained, ever-present, threatening to swallow them whole. They would never forget the decisions they made in that cold, dark warehouse. The cost of loyalty, the price of betrayal, the haunting echo of choices made in the face of overwhelming odds—they carried the burden of these realities, knowing that the fight would continue, even in the shadows.

Unraveling the Conspiracy

The adrenaline had barely begun to recede when the first unsettling piece of the puzzle fell into place. During the debriefing, a seemingly innocuous detail—a discarded data chip found near one of the apprehended agents—caught Anya's attention. It contained encrypted files, fragments of code that hinted at a network far larger, far more sinister, than Viktor's operation. It wasn't just about stealing classified data; it was about something far more insidious, a meticulously planned infiltration stretching back decades. The implications chilled Jake to the bone.

Anya, her fingers flying across the keyboard, managed to crack the encryption. The data revealed a pattern of carefully orchestrated events, a cascade of seemingly unrelated incidents that, when viewed through this new lens, painted a disturbing picture. Compromised government officials, leaked intelligence reports, even a series of seemingly random assassinations – all were pieces of a larger, more terrifying game. The conspiracy was a hydra, with many heads and tangled roots reaching into the highest echelons of power.

Jake felt the familiar tightening in his chest, a physical manifestation of the growing unease. This was beyond anything he had anticipated. This wasn't just about stopping a rogue operative; this was about unraveling a deep-seated conspiracy that threatened to shatter the very foundations of the agency, and perhaps the nation itself. The man they had just apprehended was just a pawn in a much bigger game, a game orchestrated by a mastermind who remained hidden in the shadows. Viktor, it seemed, was just a player, a relatively minor one at that.

The hunt for answers began in the dusty stacks of the National Archives. Days blurred into weeks as Jake and Anya immersed themselves in declassified documents, microfiche records, and forgotten files. The research was tedious, demanding, a slow and methodical piecing together of disparate clues. They spent hours hunched over microfilm readers, their eyes straining to decipher faded ink and blurred photographs, piecing together a narrative that hinted at betrayals, compromises, and a level of corruption that was simply staggering. The weight of history pressed down on them, the ghosts of past failures whispering warnings in their ears.

They discovered that the conspiracy wasn't new; it had been evolving, adapting, for decades. Its tentacles reached into every aspect of the government, twisting and turning, making it almost impossible to trace its origin. They found evidence suggesting the involvement of former agency operatives, high-ranking military officials, even members of the presidential cabinet. The scale of the deceit was breathtaking, a web of interconnected lies and betrayals so intricate that it was difficult to believe it was real.

Their search led them to forgotten libraries, tucked away in quiet corners of the city, each holding a piece of the puzzle. They combed through obscure journals, academic papers, and seemingly irrelevant historical records, meticulously cross-referencing data, searching for links and patterns. The hours spent hunched over books and documents took their toll, but the growing sense of urgency propelled them forward, pushing them beyond their limits of exhaustion. The discovery of each new piece of information was like finding a new key to unlock a previously hidden door, revealing a deeper level of deception.

One particularly revealing document, unearthed in a long-forgotten archive, hinted at a clandestine organization, an invisible hand that had been pulling the strings for generations. Its members operated in the shadows, manipulating events from behind the scenes, influencing policy, controlling narratives, and ensuring their continued power and influence. The organization was known only by a single, chilling codename: "The Obsidian Circle."

The name sent a shiver down Jake's spine. He had heard whispers of it during his training, hushed conversations between seasoned operatives, legends spoken in hushed tones. It was a myth, a bogeyman used to scare recruits, a warning of the darker side of espionage, a reminder of the risks associated with their profession. Now, the myth had become reality.

Their investigation shifted, taking them to less conventional locations. They traced the Obsidian Circle's influence through a labyrinth of clandestine meeting places, coded messages hidden within seemingly innocuous publications, and secret communication networks using encrypted channels that were nearly impossible to detect. They found themselves navigating a world of shadows, where identities were fluid, loyalties were questionable, and trust was a dangerous commodity. Every contact felt like a gamble, every meeting a potential trap.

The closer they got to the truth, the greater the risks became. They were being watched, followed, their every move monitored. Their phones tapped, their communications intercepted. They had to adapt, improvise, constantly changing their plans, their routes, their methods of communication. They were playing a dangerous game of cat and mouse with an unseen enemy, an enemy with resources beyond their comprehension.

One evening, amidst the cacophony of a bustling city street, Jake and Anya were ambushed. The attackers were efficient, ruthless, highly trained professionals, their movements practiced and precise. A furious gun battle erupted, the city's night turning into a blur of gunfire and shattered glass. Jake's instincts took over, his training kicking in, as he and Anya fought their way through the chaos, their movements fluid and deadly. They managed to escape, but not without casualties. The attack left Jake shaken, realizing they had underestimated the resources and power of the Obsidian Circle.

The ambush served as a stark reminder of their precarious position. They were treading on dangerous ground, challenging a force far more powerful than they had initially imagined. But the stakes were too high, the consequences too severe, to back down. The nation's security, perhaps the very fabric of democracy itself, hung in the balance.

Their investigation led them to a hidden underground facility, a subterranean lair teeming with sophisticated technology and advanced weaponry. It was here that they finally began to unravel the full extent of the Obsidian Circle's plans. They had been manipulating global events for their own gain, creating conflicts, destabilizing governments, all to accumulate wealth and power. The scale of their ambition was staggering, their reach extending to every corner of the globe.

The discovery was both terrifying and exhilarating. They were on the verge of exposing a conspiracy that had been operating in the shadows for decades. But the Obsidian Circle would not go down without a fight. They knew that their cover was blown and that time was running out. The fight for the soul of the agency, and perhaps the nation itself, was far from over. The confrontation would be epic. They had to prepare. The consequences of failure were too dire to contemplate. The shadows were closing in.

Following the Clues

The discarded SIM card, recovered from the debris of Viktor's ill-fated operation, proved to be the Rosetta Stone of their investigation. Its contents, painstakingly decrypted by Anya, revealed a series of coded messages, each a cryptic breadcrumb in a trail leading to the heart of the Obsidian Circle. The messages weren't sent directly; they were embedded within seemingly innocuous online interactions, disguised as casual conversations, hidden within encrypted images, and even subtly altered metadata of otherwise mundane files. It was the digital equivalent of a spy's invisible ink, only detectable to those with the right key.

Their first clue led them to a seemingly abandoned warehouse district on the outskirts of the city. The warehouse itself was nondescript, its exterior marked only by peeling paint and a faded shipping label. Inside, however, it was a different story. The space was meticulously organized, filled with rows of server racks humming with activity, and sophisticated monitoring equipment that hinted at a clandestine operation. They found no physical evidence connecting the location directly to the Obsidian Circle, but the sheer sophistication of the tech suggested a significant operation was being conducted here. More importantly, the server logs, painstakingly extracted by Anya, revealed a hidden network of encrypted communications, stretching across the globe.

This digital labyrinth led them to a series of dead drops, locations scattered across the country where information and operatives exchanged coded messages and physical artifacts. Each drop was more carefully planned and executed than the last, leaving almost no trace of its existence. They ranged from seemingly innocuous locations like a public park bench to more clandestine spots, like a forgotten subway tunnel. The meticulous planning reflected the organization's attention to detail and its commitment to remaining undetected.

Following one such trail led them to a secluded island off the coast of Maine, a place shrouded in mist and secrecy. The island, privately owned and rarely visited, was a perfect haven for clandestine activities. They found evidence of a hidden bunker, concealed beneath a seemingly ordinary lighthouse. The bunker, accessed through a cleverly disguised entrance, was surprisingly large, containing a network of interconnected rooms. Inside, they discovered an extensive library, filled with rare books, historical documents, and coded journals that hinted at the organization's long and shadowy history.

These documents revealed that the Obsidian Circle wasn't merely a modern organization; it had deep historical roots, dating back to the Cold War era. They were not simply accumulating wealth and power, but actively shaping global events to their benefit, orchestrating conflicts and influencing political leaders for generations. The scale of their influence was staggering, far beyond what Jake and Anya had initially imagined. They uncovered evidence of collaborations with former heads of state, disgraced military officials, and powerful corporations, all seemingly unaware of each other's involvement, yet all playing their part in a grand, decades-long scheme.

The island bunker also contained advanced encryption technology, far beyond what was available commercially. The sophistication of their technology hinted at a level of technological expertise that could only be acquired through clandestine government research or highly skilled individuals operating outside normal frameworks. They discovered several prototype weapons, advanced surveillance devices, and tools designed for covert operations. The sheer arsenal they uncovered was alarming, a testament to the Obsidian Circle's extensive resources and dangerous capabilities.

As they delved deeper, they encountered more resistance. The island became a virtual fortress. Their every move was tracked, every communication monitored. They engaged in a series of close-quarters skirmishes with the organization's highly trained security personnel – individuals clearly capable of engaging in lethal force, showing no hesitation. Jake's training became paramount in these moments; he found himself relying on instincts honed over years of intense preparation and combat scenarios.

One harrowing encounter found them cornered in a narrow corridor within the bunker. Anya, using her hacking expertise, disabled the security cameras and remotely triggered a diversion, creating a momentary window of escape. Jake, using hand-to-hand combat skills, neutralized two of their pursuers, buying time for Anya to secure a back route. They barely escaped, the sounds of their pursuers echoing behind them as they fled the island in a stolen fishing boat, a fierce storm brewing overhead, reflecting the tempestuous nature of their situation.

From the island, their investigation led them to a network of seemingly unconnected individuals – academics, journalists, and business executives – all subtly linked to the Obsidian Circle. They were not necessarily members, but useful pawns in the organization's larger game, unknowingly disseminating information or creating opportunities for the organization to further its influence. They were essentially unwitting accomplices in a global conspiracy.

Unraveling these seemingly disparate connections was akin to untangling a Gordian knot. Anya's skill with technology, coupled with Jake's intuitive grasp of human behavior, was crucial to the investigation. They used a combination of traditional investigative techniques and advanced digital forensics, sifting through mountains of data, identifying patterns and relationships.

Their journey took them from the bustling streets of New York City to the quiet, secluded corners of the Swiss Alps, from the opulent casinos of Monte Carlo to the dusty archives of forgotten libraries across Europe. The trail constantly led them to unexpected locations and startling revelations. They even uncovered evidence linking the Obsidian Circle to international terrorist organizations, suggesting that their reach extended far beyond financial gain or political manipulation. Their goals were far more ambitious, potentially encompassing global domination.

Throughout the investigation, the threat of exposure was constant. They were being monitored, watched, their communications intercepted. The stakes were raised significantly; failure was not an option. They had to be careful and precise in their actions; they were essentially walking a tightrope over a chasm. Each step could lead to their exposure, and potentially, their death.

They were constantly adapting their strategies, changing their communication methods, and learning to trust their instincts. They understood that every contact was a potential risk, every meeting a possible trap. They were no longer simply investigating a conspiracy; they were engaged in a dangerous game of cat and mouse with a shadowy enemy that possessed vast resources and seemingly limitless influence.

The closer they got to the truth, the more dangerous the game became. But Jake and Anya were determined to continue, to expose the Obsidian Circle and bring its leaders to justice, no matter the cost. The fate of the agency and potentially the nation, hung precariously in the balance. The final confrontation loomed. The shadows were closing in.

Dangerous Liaisons

The stolen fishing boat, battered by the relentless Maine storm, deposited Jake and Anya on the mainland, leaving them shivering and soaked, but alive. The immediate danger had passed, but the long shadow of the Obsidian Circle still loomed. Their investigation, far from over, had just entered a new, even more treacherous phase. The island raid had yielded crucial information, but it had also alerted the organization to their presence. They were now playing a high-stakes game of evasion, relying on their wits and skills to stay one step ahead of their powerful and ruthless adversary.

Their next lead came from a seemingly innocuous source: a seemingly forgotten footnote in one of the journals discovered in the island bunker. It mentioned a "Professor Armand Dubois," a renowned historian specializing in Cold War espionage, currently residing in Geneva. Dubois wasn't a name readily associated with clandestine activities, but the footnote hinted at a connection, a potentially valuable source of information. Jake and Anya knew they had to tread carefully; approaching Dubois directly was too risky. They needed a different approach, a way to extract information without revealing their true identities or intentions.

They decided to use a trusted contact, an old friend of Anya's from her days in university – a brilliant but eccentric cryptographer named Dr. Elias Thorne. Thorne, a recluse with a penchant for conspiracy theories and a remarkable ability to infiltrate secure systems, was uniquely equipped to help them. He agreed to investigate Dubois discreetly, gaining access to his research and personal communications without alerting the professor to their interest.

Thorne's findings were alarming. Dubois, it turned out, had been subtly manipulating historical records for decades, subtly rewriting narratives and shaping public perception to serve the Obsidian Circle's agenda. He wasn't a member, not in the traditional sense, but a highly valued collaborator, a master of subtle influence. He had been subtly changing narratives about events to help legitimize past actions of the Obsidian Circle and lay the groundwork for their future goals. He held considerable influence within academic circles, his reputation untarnished, his actions imperceptible to casual observers.

Their investigation now took a new turn, veering into the treacherous world of academic politics and historical revisionism. They discovered Dubois was involved in a clandestine network of historians and researchers, all seemingly independent but all subtly working to create a false historical narrative that advanced the interests of the Obsidian Circle. These were dangerous liaisons, each interaction fraught with risk.

The next person they decided to approach was a former KGB agent, now living under a assumed identity in a small village in the Swiss Alps. This agent, known only as "The Nightingale," was a shadowy figure, his past shrouded in mystery. He was notorious for his ruthlessness and his uncanny ability to survive the brutal world of espionage. Contacting him was a high-risk gamble, yet the information he held about the Obsidian Circle's early days, particularly its operations during the Cold War, could be invaluable. He was a known associate of Dubois, which meant that he could potentially offer more insight into his collaboration with the Obsidian Circle.

Reaching The Nightingale required navigating a complex web of informants, carefully vetting each contact to avoid a double cross. It took weeks of meticulous planning, numerous coded messages passed through layers of intermediaries, before they finally established contact. The meeting was fraught with tension. The Nightingale, a wizened old man with piercing blue eyes that seemed to see straight through you, was skeptical, his trust hard-earned.

He eventually agreed to talk, but only in exchange for a substantial sum of money, and even more importantly, for an assurance of his continued anonymity. He recounted tales of clandestine meetings, covert operations, and double-crosses, painting a picture of a organization far more cunning and dangerous than they had initially imagined. He described a highly structured organization, divided into cells operating independently, their connections masked through layers of secrecy.

The Nightingale's stories confirmed their suspicions regarding the Obsidian Circle's reach and influence. He revealed the organization's sophisticated network of informants, embedded within governments and corporations worldwide. They were not merely manipulating events, they were actively creating them, orchestrating crises, and exploiting opportunities to further their own agenda. He confirmed that the Obsidian Circle's ambitions extended far beyond simple financial gain or political power; they sought nothing less than global control.

His information confirmed that Dubois was one of the key players, tasked with shaping global narratives to create a more favorable environment for the organization. He offered more insights into Dubois' connections and revealed the names of other historians and academics who were colluding with the Obsidian Circle. He mentioned that these individuals were not all aware of the full scope of the organization's activities. Many were simply useful tools in the larger scheme.

However, The Nightingale's collaboration came at a price. He provided information that indirectly implicated a powerful European businessman, a supposed philanthropist, heavily involved in the Obsidian Circle's financial dealings. This businessman, Baron Von Hess, was not just a money launderer but a key operative, using his vast wealth and connections to fund the organization's operations and protect its members. He was extremely powerful and connected to a vast network of politicians and intelligence officials.

Exposing Von Hess would be incredibly dangerous. He possessed vast resources and was surrounded by a network of highly trained security personnel. But his exposure could be the key to dismantling the Obsidian Circle's financial infrastructure and cripple the entire organization. This was a decision fraught with danger, a gamble that could make or break their entire mission.

The next stage of their investigation required a different approach. Instead of relying on direct confrontation, they needed to work through indirect channels. They decided to target Von Hess's network, using a combination of infiltration, manipulation, and disinformation. They would need to work with new allies, and some of them could be more dangerous than their enemies.

Their first step was to establish contact with a former journalist, now working as a private investigator. He was known for his investigative prowess and his connections within the European underworld. His name was Marcel Dubois – no relation to the historian, but a man with a talent for uncovering secrets and an appetite for risk. He was skeptical initially, but after a careful vetting process, he agreed to help, drawn by the potential of exposing a global conspiracy and earning a hefty fee.

The partnership was fraught with tension. Marcel was pragmatic, only interested in the reward. He had no interest in the moral implications of the mission, he was simply driven by profit. Jake and Anya found themselves in an uncomfortable alliance, working alongside someone who was less concerned with saving the world and more interested in lining his own pockets. This was one of the most dangerous liaisons of all, as the line between ally and adversary started to blur.

Marcel's expertise in tracking financial flows and uncovering offshore accounts proved invaluable. He traced Von Hess's financial activities back to a series of shell corporations and offshore bank accounts scattered across the globe. It was a tangled web, carefully designed to conceal the organization's true wealth and power. He exposed a network of offshore banks and shell companies, all intricately linked to the Obsidian Circle's illicit activities. He showed how Von Hess utilized these entities to funnel money into the organization, supporting its operations and maintaining its secrecy.

Through Marcel, Jake and Anya discovered an additional layer of the Obsidian Circle's operation. The organization did not just operate through money laundering; it was actively involved in a sophisticated international arms dealing network, trading advanced weaponry and technology with various terrorist groups and rogue governments. This raised the stakes considerably; they weren't just dealing with a financial conspiracy, but a group with the potential to unleash chaos on a global scale. This was a discovery that could unravel the entire organization and would change the trajectory of the entire mission. The weight of the consequences was heavy, and the stakes were higher than ever before. The mission was far from over. The shadows were still closing in.

Facing the Mastermind

The information gleaned from Marcel painted a terrifying picture. The Obsidian Circle wasn't just a collection of ambitious criminals; they were a sophisticated, globally connected network capable of manipulating markets, orchestrating conflicts, and arming dangerous actors. Their reach was staggering, their influence far-reaching. And at the center of it all was Baron Von Hess, the seemingly benevolent philanthropist who was, in reality, the organization's financial engine, shielding its operations from the prying eyes of the world.

Jake and Anya knew that confronting Von Hess directly would be suicidal. He was protected by layers of security, surrounded by loyalists, and backed by a vast network of corrupt officials. They needed a different approach, a way to expose him without putting themselves directly in harm's way. Their plan involved exploiting the very network Von Hess used to protect himself – a network Marcel had painstakingly mapped out.

Their next move was daring, even reckless. They decided to use the information gathered from Marcel to create a controlled leak to a select group of journalists, carefully chosen for their integrity and investigative skills. This wasn't a haphazard leak; it was a meticulously orchestrated operation designed to send shockwaves through Von Hess's world without revealing their involvement. They needed to create enough chaos to force Von Hess to reveal himself, to make a mistake that they could exploit.

The leak consisted of carefully selected documents, evidence of Von Hess's financial dealings, his connections to the

Obsidian Circle, and the organization's involvement in international arms trafficking. The information was enough to topple Von Hess's empire and unravel the web of deceit he had meticulously woven. The leak was delivered through a secure, untraceable channel, a digital ghost in the machine.

The reaction was immediate and chaotic. The world's financial markets reacted with a shudder, sensing the turmoil brewing beneath the surface. Von Hess's carefully crafted reputation began to crumble as news of the leak spread. He was forced into damage control, desperately trying to contain the fallout. His denials were weak, his explanations unconvincing, as the evidence mounted against him.

The leak, however, had an unintended consequence. It brought the Obsidian Circle's full wrath down upon them. They knew they were close to being exposed, and their desperation grew. The pursuit intensified, the danger escalating exponentially. Jake and Anya found themselves constantly one step ahead of their pursuers, dodging attacks, changing locations, and relying on their wits and training to survive.

Their next encounter with the Obsidian Circle was far more brutal than anything they'd experienced before. They were ambushed in a secluded mountain village in the Austrian Alps, where they had sought refuge. The attack was swift and violent; a highly trained team of mercenaries, clearly professionals, descended upon them. The ensuing firefight was intense and left Jake and Anya on the verge of being overwhelmed. Anya suffered a significant injury during the attack, leaving her vulnerable. It became a desperate fight for survival.

Despite the odds, they managed to escape, aided by a timely intervention from an unexpected source – a former member of the Obsidian Circle who had grown disillusioned with the organization's brutality. This informant, a woman known only as "Seraphina," provided critical information about Von Hess's movements and his plans to escape the growing scrutiny. She also alerted them to the existence of a secret underground facility where Von Hess was hiding, where he was meeting with the organization's leadership.

This facility was a heavily fortified bunker, located deep beneath the Swiss Alps, shielded from satellite surveillance and defended by a state-of-the-art security system. Reaching it would be an enormous challenge, requiring meticulous planning and precise execution. But it was their only chance to confront the mastermind behind the conspiracy and dismantle the Obsidian Circle. The time for evasion was over; they needed to go on the offensive.

Using Seraphina's information, they planned their infiltration carefully. They used their combined skills to study the facility's layout, its security protocols, and the movements of its guards. They learned that the facility was guarded by advanced technology, including surveillance systems, motion detectors, and armed guards, all overseen by a sophisticated AI security system.

Their infiltration plan was risky, almost impossibly so. They had to bypass the security systems, evade the guards, and reach Von Hess without being detected. The slightest mistake could cost them their lives. It was a suicide mission, but they had to try. They had come too far, sacrificed too much to give up now.

The infiltration was nerve-wracking. They navigated through dark corridors, avoiding laser grids, pressure plates, and cameras. They moved with the precision of trained operatives, their movements synchronized, their actions perfectly executed. The tension was palpable, each breath a potential betrayal. It was a carefully orchestrated dance of stealth and precision.

After several hours of tense maneuvering, they managed to reach Von Hess's private quarters, just as he was preparing to leave the facility. The confrontation was swift and brutal. Jake engaged Von Hess's security team while Anya disabled the security systems, creating a diversion and buying them some time. The fight was fierce, a desperate struggle for survival against highly trained mercenaries.

Finally, they cornered Von Hess in his office. The confrontation was intense, a clash of wills between two highly intelligent and capable opponents. Von Hess, however, had underestimated Jake and Anya. He was captured without significant bloodshed, his elaborate web of deception falling apart around him.

With Von Hess in custody, the Obsidian Circle's leadership structure was severely weakened. The organization's financial infrastructure was crippled, and its operations disrupted. The global conspiracy began to unravel, its threads unwinding one by one. The mission was not quite over, but the most dangerous part was done. The victory was hard-won, achieved through courage, skill, and a carefully orchestrated series of calculated risks. The world was a safer place, thanks to the tireless work of Jake Riley and Anya Petrova, two agents who stared into the abyss and emerged victorious. The shadows receded, replaced by the faint light of justice. However, the lingering threat of other cells still operating under the Obsidian Circle's banner remained, and their future remained uncertain. The fight was far from over.

A HighStakes Gamble

The helicopter shuddered, buffeted by the ferocious winds whipping across the jagged peaks of the Himalayas. Below, the landscape was a brutal tapestry of snow and ice, a stark contrast to the opulent warmth of Von Hess's Swiss bunker. Anya, her arm still throbbing from the Austrian ambush, gripped the side of the aircraft, her gaze fixed on the swirling vortex of clouds obscuring their destination. Jake, his face grim, checked his weapon, the metallic click echoing in the confined space. Their mission wasn't over; it was merely entering its most perilous phase.

Their informant, Seraphina, had provided them with coordinates to a remote, almost mythical, monastery nestled high in the mountains. It wasn't just a religious retreat; according to Seraphina, it served as a clandestine meeting place for the Obsidian Circle's highest-ranking members, a place where they planned their next moves, consolidated their power, and laundered their ill-gotten gains. Von Hess, she'd claimed, was headed there to finalize a deal that would solidify the Circle's control over a significant portion of the global opium trade. Stopping him here, in this remote sanctuary, was their only chance to cripple the organization for good.

The helicopter dipped lower, the sheer drop below a stomach-churning reminder of the risks they were taking. The monastery, a collection of weathered stone buildings clinging precariously to the mountainside, appeared before them, a testament to both human resilience and the enduring power of faith. However, this façade of serenity masked a dark heart of treachery and deceit. The air crackled with anticipation; this was it – the high-stakes gamble. Failure wasn't an option. Success, however, was far from guaranteed.

Their infiltration plan, conceived during the harrowing flight, was a masterpiece of improvisation and daring. They would exploit the monastery's reliance on its remote location, a feature that both protected and isolated it. Jake, using his mountaineering skills honed during his covert training, would scale the sheer cliff face, while Anya would use her expertise in electronic warfare to disable the monastery's limited surveillance system. They relied on the assumption that the Circle's focus would be on external threats, not an infiltration from the near-vertical cliff face.

The climb was grueling, a battle against the elements and the sheer force of gravity. The biting wind threatened to rip them from the rock, the icy surface treacherous beneath their boots. Jake, his muscles burning, relied on his instincts and training, his movements fluid and precise. He made his way upwards inch by agonizing inch, the monastery slowly but surely coming into closer view.

Meanwhile, Anya, concealed in a crevice, worked tirelessly at her laptop. Her fingers danced across the keyboard, a symphony of keystrokes that was gradually dismantling the monastery's security network. The task was complex and demanding, but she had to succeed. Their lives, and potentially the stability of several nations, rested on her ability to circumvent the monastery's digital defenses.

Hours later, under the cover of a swirling blizzard, Jake reached the monastery wall. He moved with the silent grace of a phantom, his movements almost imperceptible. He found a weak point, a small gap between two stones that he could exploit. Using his specialized tools, he bypassed the monastery's alarms and slipped inside, a ghost in the hallowed halls.

Inside, the monastery's layout was a labyrinthine maze of corridors and chambers. The air was thick with the scent of incense and the weight of centuries of prayer. Jake made his way cautiously through the silent passages, his senses heightened, his every step measured. He eventually found Anya, who had successfully neutralized the monastery's external and internal security networks. They were in.

Their next challenge was locating Von Hess and the other Circle members. They knew that time was of the essence, that the window of opportunity was rapidly closing. The monastery's upper levels housed the monks' quarters; the lower levels, according to Seraphina's intel, contained the secret chambers where the Circle conducted its clandestine meetings. They descended into the darkness.

The lower levels were a stark contrast to the serene upper levels. The air was cold and damp, heavy with the musty smell of stone and decay. They navigated through a maze of dimly lit corridors, passing cryptic symbols and ancient murals that seemed to whisper of dark secrets and forgotten rituals. The silence was unnerving, broken only by the occasional drip of water and the faint sounds of their own breathing.

Finally, they reached a large chamber, its walls adorned with elaborate carvings and tapestries depicting scenes of violence and betrayal. In the center of the chamber, a long table was set for a feast, with lavish platters of food and fine wines. Around the table sat several figures, their faces shrouded in shadow. Von Hess was amongst them.

The tension in the room was palpable, the atmosphere thick with the expectation of violence. Jake and Anya knew that this was it; the moment of truth had arrived. They had to act swiftly and decisively. They had to gamble everything on this single, desperate move.

Jake moved first. He launched a series of perfectly timed attacks, disrupting the clandestine meeting. The mercenaries guarding the chamber reacted swiftly, but they were no match for Jake's superior training and skill. Anya disabled any remaining security systems, cutting off any possibility of outside assistance for Von Hess and his associates.

The ensuing melee was a whirlwind of motion, a chaotic ballet of death. Jake moved like a phantom, his strikes precise and deadly. Anya neutralized the guards with her specialized combat skills, a whirlwind of calculated movements. The chamber echoed with the sounds of gunfire, broken furniture, and the desperate cries of the wounded.

Finally, Jake cornered Von Hess, the mastermind behind the Obsidian Circle. The Baron, his face pale and contorted with fear, made a last, desperate attempt to escape, but Jake moved faster, stopping him. Von Hess's opulent world of power and influence had crumbled around him, leaving him vulnerable and exposed.

With Von Hess and several key members of the Obsidian Circle in custody, their mission was effectively accomplished. The remaining members were scattered and disoriented; the organization's intricate web of deceit was unraveling at last. The world, for now, was a little safer. The high-stakes gamble had paid off.

As the sun rose over the snow-covered peaks of the Himalayas, casting a golden light on the once-forbidding monastery, Jake and Anya stood on the helicopter's landing pad, the wind whipping through their hair. The fight was far from over. The Obsidian Circle's tentacles reached far and wide, but this was a crippling blow. They had won this battle, but the war continued. Their victory was a testament to their skill, their courage, and their unwavering commitment to justice – a victory hard-earned, bought with blood, sweat, and the sheer audacity to confront the darkness and emerge victorious. The journey was far from over.

Confronting the Past

The helicopter's rotors thrummed a steady beat against the crisp Himalayan air, a stark contrast to the echoing silence of the monastery they'd just left behind. Anya, her face pale but resolute, checked her gear one last time. The adrenaline had begun to fade, leaving behind a gnawing exhaustion that threatened to pull her under. Jake, however, seemed strangely detached, his gaze distant, lost in a world beyond the snow-capped peaks. The successful takedown of Von Hess and the dismantling of the Obsidian Circle's immediate operation should have brought a sense of relief, a triumphant exhale after holding their breath for so long. But Jake's silence was heavier than any mountain wind.

Later, back at their safe house – a secluded cabin nestled deep within a remote valley – the tension remained. The celebratory mood expected after such a perilous mission was absent. Anya, sensing something was amiss, broke the uncomfortable silence. "You alright, Jake?" she asked, her voice soft, laced with concern. He looked at her, his eyes holding a profound weariness that went beyond physical exhaustion. "It's…complicated," he mumbled, running a hand through his already disheveled hair. The crisp mountain air did little to refresh him.

The following days were a blur of debriefings and reports. The intel they'd gathered from the monastery was invaluable, revealing a web of corruption that extended far beyond their initial expectations. Jake participated, answering questions efficiently and precisely, but his responses lacked the usual sharp edge, the quick wit that had always been his trademark. He was present, yet absent. He was a ghost in his own life. He was a passenger watching his life pass him by. He'd done it before. Many times.

One evening, as Anya meticulously organized their recovered data, Jake retreated to the cabin's small library. He pulled out a worn leather-bound baseball glove, its stitching frayed and faded, a relic from a life he'd left behind. The scent of aged leather, of sun-baked diamonds, and freshly cut grass brought a rush of memories, sharp and sudden like a lightning strike. He hadn't touched this glove in years. He hadn't thought about his past in years. But now the ghost of his past was sitting right there on the table.

A flood of memories washed over him. The roar of the crowd, the crack of the bat, the thrill of the game – a life lived in the bright sunlight of public adoration, a stark contrast to the shadows he now inhabited. He saw himself, young and carefree, a rising star, his future seemingly limitless. He saw Coach Miller, his gruff but supportive mentor, his words of encouragement echoing in his mind. He saw Sarah, his girlfriend, her laughter ringing in his ears, the promise of a future together, now a distant, haunting melody. The memory of his father's disappointed sigh hung heavy in the air.

Then, the darkness crept in. The injury, the abrupt end of his career, the crushing disappointment, the gnawing self-doubt. He'd buried those emotions deep, pushing them away with relentless focus on his new life. But now, in the quiet solitude of the mountain cabin, they resurfaced, potent and painful. He'd sacrificed so much to become the man he was now – the ghost of Jake Riley – but at what cost? Had he traded one cage for another? A gilded cage of public praise for one of shadows and secrets?

He remembered the day he received the offer from the agency. The allure of a new challenge, a chance to use his skills and intelligence in a different arena, had seemed like a lifeline. But now, he questioned his motivations. Had he run from the pain, seeking refuge in danger? Had he subconsciously chosen a life of risk and deception to avoid confronting his past failures? Was this life he'd built on deceit any better than the life he'd left behind? The question lingered. It burned. It scorched his soul. It felt like a million tiny cuts, all bleeding out at once.

The weight of his choices pressed down on him, crushing him under its burden. He hadn't just abandoned his baseball career; he'd abandoned a part of himself, a part he hadn't fully realized until now. He had shed his identity to become something else entirely. And he was tired of the charade. He was tired of living a lie.

He picked up his phone and dialed a number he hadn't dialed in years. The line rang, the sound echoing the uncertainty in his own heart. He heard a familiar voice answer. It was Sarah. He hadn't been ready to talk before now. But now he was.

Their conversation was halting at first, filled with awkward silences and unspoken regrets. The years had passed, both of them had moved on, but the bond they'd shared was still there, a resilient ember in the ashes of a forgotten past. He listened as she talked about her life, her career, her new family. He listened, truly listened. For the first time in years, he allowed himself to be vulnerable, to acknowledge the pain and regret he'd been suppressing. The weight of his choices seemed less crushing now.

The next day, Jake approached Anya. He explained his struggles, the turmoil he had been wrestling with. Anya listened patiently, her understanding evident in her eyes. She'd seen him fight through life-threatening situations with ice in his veins, but she'd never seen him confront his demons in this manner. She saw the pain. She saw the guilt. She saw the fragility of a man who had spent his entire life protecting his armor. Now the armor was gone, revealing a wounded man. But it was a wounded man ready to heal.

She shared her own experiences, the challenges she had overcome, the sacrifices she'd made. They found solace in shared vulnerability, a mutual understanding that transcended their professional relationship. They had faced death together. They could face this now, together.

Their bond strengthened, forged in the crucible of shared experience and mutual support. The mission in the Himalayas hadn't just been about stopping Von Hess; it had been about confronting the ghosts of their past, both individually and together. Jake realized that true redemption wasn't about erasing the past; it was about accepting it, learning from it, and moving forward with a renewed sense of purpose. He realized that the shadows he'd inhabited weren't solely defined by deceit and espionage. They were also shaped by his own heart, his own past, and his own quest for redemption.

He learned that true strength lay not in suppressing his emotions, but in embracing them, allowing himself to feel the pain, the regret, the guilt, and using it as fuel for growth and change. The road ahead was still uncertain, the challenges still immense, but he was no longer running. He was facing them head-on. He had found a path towards redemption, not by escaping his past but by confronting it, and in doing so, he found a peace that transcended the violence and chaos of his profession. He was Jake Riley, a man who had lost and found himself, a man who had accepted the darkness and chosen to fight back against it, not with bullets and knives, but with the very core of his soul. He was finally at peace. Finally.

Reconciliation and Forgiveness

The phone call to Sarah had been the first domino. Its fall triggered a chain reaction, a cascade of long-overdue conversations and difficult confrontations. He started small, reaching out to his estranged father, a man whose disappointment had been a silent, ever-present weight on Jake's shoulders. The initial conversation was stilted, filled with awkward pauses and carefully chosen words, a cautious dance around unspoken resentments. But beneath the surface, Jake sensed a shift, a thawing of the icy distance that had separated them for years. His father's voice, gruff but laced with a hint of vulnerability, revealed a regret mirroring his own. They didn't magically erase the past, the years of missed birthdays and unspoken feelings, but they began to build a bridge across the chasm of their fractured relationship, a bridge built on shared silence and hesitant forgiveness.

Next came Coach Miller. The old man, weathered and worn but still sharp-eyed and insightful, welcomed Jake with a gruff hug and a knowing smile. There were no grand pronouncements of forgiveness, no dramatic confessions. Instead, they sat on the porch of Coach Miller's modest home, watching the sunset paint the sky in hues of orange and purple, sharing memories of games won and lost, of triumphs and failures, of a time when life felt simpler, less burdened by the weight of secrets and lies. Coach Miller, a man who had always believed in Jake, saw past the spy, past the ghost, to the young man he had once mentored. He saw the pain in Jake's eyes. He listened patiently to Jake's confession. The old coach quietly admitted his own failures in not understanding the pressures Jake was facing. It was a quiet reconciliation, forged in shared understanding and a mutual respect born out of years of knowing each other.

These reconciliations weren't easy. Each conversation involved confronting painful truths, acknowledging mistakes, and accepting the consequences of past actions. There were tears, both shed and unspoken, moments of raw vulnerability that exposed the deep wounds that years of deception and self-imposed isolation had inflicted. But with each conversation, Jake felt a burden lifting, a sense of peace gradually replacing the gnawing anxiety that had haunted him for so long. He wasn't seeking absolution; he was seeking understanding, forgiveness, and the healing power of human connection. He realized that true redemption wasn't a destination, but a journey, a gradual process of healing and growth.

The most difficult reconciliation, however, was with himself. He had spent years running from his past, hiding from the pain of his failed baseball career, seeking solace in the adrenaline-fueled world of espionage. He had crafted a new identity, a new life, built on deception and secrets. But in the quiet solitude of his mountain cabin, surrounded by the remnants of his former life – the worn baseball glove, the faded photographs, the echoes of his old life – he finally confronted the truth. He acknowledged the pain, the regret, the self-doubt, the fear, the anger, and most importantly, the sadness. He had not escaped his old self. He had only buried his old self and was now forced to exhume him. He allowed himself to feel the full weight of his choices, the sacrifices he had made, and the losses he had endured. He was Jake Riley, and this was his reality. And he had to accept it. He had to forgive himself.

He started journaling. The act of writing, of pouring his thoughts and feelings onto paper, became a form of catharsis, a way to process his emotions and come to terms with his past. He wrote about his childhood dreams, his baseball aspirations, the crushing disappointment of his injury, the allure of his new life, and the profound loneliness that had accompanied his transformation into a ghost. The act of writing allowed him to see himself clearly. It allowed him to be honest with himself. It was painful but freeing. Through the act of writing, he was able to start healing. He started to become Jake Riley, the man he wanted to be.

His journey toward reconciliation extended beyond the personal realm. His work with the agency provided unexpected opportunities for redemption. He used his skills and knowledge to help those who had been harmed by the Obsidian Circle, working to dismantle their remaining networks and bring their leaders to justice. This work wasn't simply about fulfilling his duties; it was about making amends, about using his unique position to help repair the damage caused by the very organization he was a part of. It was a path towards healing, not through violence, but through the pursuit of justice. In his work, he found a kind of justice and peace. A sense of purpose he had been missing for a long time.

The process of reconciliation and forgiveness wasn't instantaneous. It wasn't a clean break. There were setbacks, moments of doubt and despair, times when he questioned whether he could truly atone for his past actions. But through it all, he held onto the hope of healing, the belief that he could find peace and redemption. He had built a new life on deceit and violence, a world of shadows and secrets. But now he was building a new life based on truth and reconciliation. A life based on love and forgiveness. A life free of the ghosts that had haunted him for so long. He was ready for a new chapter, a new beginning.

One evening, sitting by the fire in his cabin, he looked at the worn baseball glove, the faded photographs, and the journals filled with his confessions and reflections. They were reminders of his past, of the choices he had made and the mistakes he had committed, but they were also symbols of his journey toward redemption. He was no longer a ghost, haunted by the shadows of his past. He was a man at peace with himself and with the world around him. He had found his redemption not through escape, but through confrontation. Not through violence, but through reconciliation. Not through secrets, but through honesty and openness. He was Jake Riley, and he was finally at home.

Acceptance of Identity

The mountain air, crisp and clean, seemed to wash over him, carrying away the lingering residue of guilt and self-doubt. He'd spent weeks, months even, wrestling with the ghosts of his past, the specter of the man he'd been before the Agency, before the shadows and the secrets. He'd faced his father, his coach, and the painful truth of his own failures. But the truest battle, the one that had tested him to his very core, was the battle for his own self-acceptance.

It wasn't a dramatic, earth-shattering epiphany. There was no sudden rush of enlightenment, no dramatic moment of clarity. It was a slow, gradual process, a subtle shift in perspective, like the slow melting of snow on a mountainside, revealing the solid ground beneath. He started small. He began by simply acknowledging his past, not judging it, not denying it, but simply accepting it as a part of who he was. He understood now that his past didn't define him; it shaped him. It had forged him into the man he was today, a man capable of both great darkness and surprising light.

He found solace in the routine of his work, the precision of his movements, the satisfaction of a mission accomplished. The Agency, once a refuge from his shattered past, had become a surprising source of purpose. He discovered that he possessed a particular aptitude for identifying and neutralizing the Obsidian Circle's remaining cells. He excelled at dismantling their operations, not with brute force, but with meticulous planning and strategic thinking. His skills, honed through years of rigorous training, were now being used to dismantle the very organization he had once served. This irony was not lost on him. In fact, it became a driving force, a constant reminder of the path he'd walked, the mistakes he'd made, and the amends he was making.

His work extended beyond mere operations. He began to focus on preventative measures, developing strategies to identify and disrupt the Circle's recruitment efforts before they could take root. He immersed himself in the study of their tactics, their psychology, their vulnerabilities. He analyzed their propaganda, their recruitment strategies, the subtle ways they exploited people's fears and insecurities. He became an expert in their methodology, a master of their own game. He learned to see them not as faceless enemies but as individuals, driven by their own motivations, their own desires, their own flaws. This understanding helped him find new ways to counter their influence.

His new perspective wasn't just about dismantling the Obsidian Circle; it was about preventing others from falling prey to their insidious manipulation. He found a deep satisfaction in this work, a sense of purpose that transcended the thrill of the chase. He was no longer running from his past; he was using his past to shape his future, to create something meaningful, something positive.

The nights were quieter now. The shadows that had once haunted him seemed to recede, replaced by a sense of calm, a quiet contentment. The journals remained, a testament to his struggle, a chronicle of his transformation. He continued to write, but the tone had shifted. The raw anguish and self-recrimination were gradually giving way to a newfound self-acceptance, a cautious optimism. His words now reflected a journey towards peace, a journey towards the integration of his past and present selves.

He rediscovered a love for baseball, but not in the way he'd known it before. He no longer chased the glory or the fame.

He found joy in simply playing catch with a local boy, sharing his love for the game, imparting the lessons he'd learned on the field and in life. This simple act, this sharing of something he loved, brought him a deep sense of connection, a reminder that his past didn't have to define him.

He allowed himself to build new relationships, cautiously at first, then with increasing openness. He learned to trust again, to allow himself to be vulnerable, to share his true self with others. He formed a bond with a local wildlife biologist, sharing his quiet evenings around a campfire, exchanging stories and perspectives. He found companionship without succumbing to loneliness. He had learned to be alone, but now he chose connection.

The Agency recognized his transformation. His superiors observed his change. They saw his growth and his commitment. They saw the shift from a man consumed by shadows to one who embraced the light. They appreciated his new understanding of strategy and the impact he was having on the Circle's operations. He was no longer just an operative; he was becoming an asset, a mentor. He was guiding younger agents, sharing his experiences, helping them navigate the treacherous world of espionage while also reminding them of the importance of preserving their humanity.

He found an unexpected kinship with his colleagues. The bonds forged in shared experiences, in moments of life-threatening danger and quiet camaraderie, were stronger now, deeper than ever before. They respected his journey, his honesty, his resilience. They saw his redemption, not as a weakness, but as a strength.

One day, he received a letter from Sarah. It wasn't an apology, nor a confession, but a simple, heartfelt expression of understanding. It spoke of acceptance, of forgiveness, and of the enduring strength of the human spirit. It was a small act, a simple gesture, yet it carried immense weight, a symbol of the closure he had sought for so long. It was a testament to the healing power of time, of acceptance, and of forgiveness. He responded with a letter of his own, a letter filled with hope and gratitude, a letter that acknowledged the pain of the past and affirmed the possibility of a future built on truth and understanding.

His journey of self-acceptance wasn't a destination; it was a continuous process, a lifelong commitment to self-reflection and growth. He knew there would always be moments of doubt, of uncertainty, of temptation. But now, he had the tools to confront those challenges, the resilience to overcome them. He had found his redemption, not in forgetting his past, but in embracing it, in transforming it into a source of strength and purpose. He was Jake Riley, and he was at peace. He was home. He was finally, truly, himself. The shadows were gone, replaced by the clear light of self-acceptance, and the quiet understanding that true redemption lay not in escaping the past, but in embracing it, learning from it, and finally, accepting it as a part of who he was.

Renewed Purpose

The desert sun beat down on Jake's face as he squinted, studying the intricate network of irrigation canals snaking across the arid landscape. This wasn't the clandestine world of shadowy alleyways and clandestine meetings he'd grown accustomed to. This was something different, something… peaceful, yet strangely exhilarating. He was in Arizona, working with a small team on a seemingly innocuous project: identifying and disrupting the Obsidian Circle's attempts to infiltrate agricultural supply chains. It was a far cry from his previous missions, the adrenaline-fueled chases and high-stakes confrontations. But this, he discovered, held a different kind of thrill. This was the satisfaction of preventative action, of stopping the rot before it could spread.

He found himself drawn to the methodical nature of the work, the meticulous detail required to trace the Circle's operations through seemingly mundane transactions and seemingly insignificant individuals. He learned to read the subtle clues hidden in shipping manifests, invoices, and fertilizer orders. His sharp mind, once honed on the baseball diamond, now dissected complex supply chains with an almost surgical precision. He was no longer reacting to events; he was anticipating them, preventing them. This proactive approach provided a unique sense of satisfaction, a feeling of control that was entirely new to him.

He spent hours poring over satellite imagery, identifying anomalies in crop yields, patterns in transportation routes, and inconsistencies in water usage. He collaborated with agricultural experts, learning about soil composition, crop rotation, and the intricacies of irrigation systems. He even found himself enjoying the quiet rhythm of rural life, the slow pace, the connection to the land. He spent evenings stargazing with his team, sharing stories and laughs under the vast expanse of the desert sky. The camaraderie was genuine, forged not in the crucible of danger, but in the shared pursuit of a common goal.

The contrast between this and his previous life was striking. The sterile, impersonal environment of the Agency's headquarters was replaced by the vastness of the desert landscape. The constant pressure, the ever-present danger, were replaced by a sense of calm purpose. He was still working in the shadows, but the shadows now held a different hue. They were no longer the dark, menacing shadows of his past; they were the softer, more subtle shadows of a dawn breaking on a new day.

His work extended beyond the immediate investigation. He began to develop training modules for other agents, sharing his knowledge and experience in identifying and countering the Circle's infiltration techniques. He found a profound sense of purpose in mentoring younger agents, guiding them through the complexities of their work while emphasizing the importance of ethical conduct and human compassion. His empathy, once buried under layers of guilt and self-doubt, now served as a powerful tool in shaping the next generation of operatives. He taught them not just to identify the enemy, but to understand the underlying motivations that drove them. He stressed the importance of preserving their humanity, even in the face of overwhelming darkness.

Weekends often found him volunteering at a local community center, coaching underprivileged children in baseball. The familiar rhythm of the game, the crack of the bat, the thrill of a well-executed play, brought him a surprising sense of peace. He discovered he could share his passion for the game without the pressure of professional competition. It was a way to connect with others, to mentor young people, to give back to a community that had welcomed him. He found genuine joy in their enthusiasm, their energy, their unwavering belief in themselves.

He continued to write in his journals, but the tone had changed. The raw, visceral accounts of his past struggles were gradually replaced by reflections on his present experiences, his newfound sense of purpose, and his evolving understanding of himself. His writing became a testament to his transformation, a chronicle of his journey from self-destruction to self-acceptance. The entries were still personal, but they now carried a thread of hope, of optimism, of faith in the human capacity for redemption.

One evening, as the desert sun dipped below the horizon, painting the sky in a blaze of vibrant colors, Jake received a call from his former handler, a seasoned veteran named Marcus Thorne. Thorne's voice, usually clipped and businesslike, carried a hint of warmth. He offered Jake a new assignment, one that would test his skills in a different way. It involved infiltrating a seemingly legitimate philanthropic organization suspected of laundering money for the Obsidian Circle. This was not an operation involving guns and explosives, but it required his unique blend of investigative skills, strategic thinking, and interpersonal acumen.

The mission presented a new set of challenges, but Jake was ready. He had honed his skills, developed his perspective, and found his renewed sense of purpose. He approached the task with a confidence and clarity he hadn't felt before. He embraced the complexity of the mission, the intricate web of relationships he needed to navigate. He approached each individual not as an enemy, but as a person with their own motives and ambitions, and he learned to exploit those weaknesses, not through violence, but through subtle manipulation and strategic alliances.

He moved through the opulent world of high-society fundraisers, exclusive galas, and private dinners, using his charm and wit to build relationships, gather information, and gather evidence against those involved in the conspiracy. His past experiences, the lessons learned in darkness, illuminated his path through this new maze. He found he could utilize his deceptive skills without becoming consumed by them. His experience had given him a depth of understanding, and his newfound self-acceptance gave him a moral compass he never thought he'd possess. He had found a way to leverage his skills for good, to use the darkness to expose the darkness.

As the weeks passed, Jake felt a growing sense of accomplishment. He wasn't just dismantling the Obsidian Circle's operations; he was exposing its intricate network, unraveling its hidden connections, and bringing those responsible to justice. This was more than just catching criminals; it was about preventing future atrocities, protecting the vulnerable, and making the world a safer place.

His success on this mission solidified his position within the Agency. He wasn't just a spy anymore; he was a leader, a mentor, an example. He had become a symbol of redemption, proving that even those who stumble, even those who make terrible mistakes, can find a path to redemption, a path to a renewed purpose. He was living proof that second chances are not only possible, but essential. And as he stood under the clear night sky of the Arizona desert, watching the stars shimmer above, he knew that he was finally, and truly, home. The shadows of his past were behind him, and the light of his future was bright.

A New Beginning

The Arizona desert, once a harsh and unforgiving landscape, now held a different meaning for Jake. It had been the crucible in which he'd forged his new identity, a place where he'd shed the ghosts of his past and embraced a future he hadn't dared to imagine. He stood on a windswept mesa overlooking a valley bathed in the golden light of a setting sun, a panorama that mirrored the transformation within him. He'd completed his assignment, dismantling a significant portion of the Obsidian Circle's network, exposing their intricate money laundering scheme and bringing several key players to justice. The sense of accomplishment was profound, a deep satisfaction that went beyond the simple closure of a case. This was about more than just catching criminals; it was about leaving a legacy, a ripple effect of positive change in a world that often seemed irrevocably scarred.

His phone buzzed, breaking the quiet contemplation. It was Marcus Thorne, his handler, his voice as gravelly and reassuring as the desert rocks. "Riley," Thorne began, his tone both formal and familiar, "You've exceeded expectations. The Director wants to meet with you." A meeting with the Director wasn't routine. It signified a significant step, a recognition of his value, his potential. It was an invitation to a new level, a new playing field.

The meeting took place in a secluded compound nestled deep within the Appalachian Mountains, a stark contrast to the arid landscape of Arizona. The air was thick with the scent of pine and damp earth, a world away from the sterile environments of Agency headquarters. The Director, a woman named Evelyn Reed, was a study in controlled power, her sharp eyes missing nothing. She didn't offer platitudes or empty praise. She simply stated, "You've proven your worth, Riley. You're more than just a skilled operative; you're a strategic thinker. We have a new program, a more…proactive approach to global threats. We're looking for individuals with your unique skillset."

The details were vague, shrouded in the typical Agency secrecy. It involved a new breed of threats, sophisticated networks operating outside the traditional frameworks of espionage. It required a different type of intelligence, a deeper understanding of human psychology, a capacity for empathy as well as deception. Jake listened intently, his mind already working, anticipating challenges, formulating strategies. He knew this wasn't just about thwarting immediate threats; it was about shaping the future.

"Think of it, Riley," Reed continued, her voice low and compelling, "as preventing the fire before the spark ignites. We're building a team, a vanguard, to operate in the grey areas, the spaces between nations, the cracks in the system. We need agents who can anticipate, who can influence, who can shape events before they escalate into crises."

He spent the next several weeks in intensive training, honing his skills in psychological manipulation, strategic forecasting, and international relations. He learned to identify subtle shifts in geopolitical landscapes, to read between the lines of diplomatic pronouncements, to understand the undercurrents of power struggles. He immersed himself in complex scenarios, navigating simulations designed to push him to his limits, testing his ability to adapt and improvise.

The training wasn't just about honing his skills; it was about developing his intuition, sharpening his instincts. He learned to trust his gut feeling, to recognize patterns and anomalies that others might miss. He discovered a new level of self-awareness, an understanding of his own strengths and weaknesses that had eluded him in his earlier, more impulsive years.

His new assignment took him to Geneva, Switzerland, the heart of international diplomacy. He worked undercover, embedded within a multinational corporation with suspected ties to a clandestine organization involved in bioweapon research. This was a far cry from the high-stakes confrontations of his past, but the pressure was just as intense, the stakes just as high. It demanded a different kind of courage, a different type of strength. He had to navigate complex power dynamics, forge alliances with unlikely allies, and maintain his cover amidst constant scrutiny.

He spent months immersed in the world of high finance, political maneuvering, and international intrigue. He learned to blend into the opulent world of lavish parties and exclusive gatherings, using his charm and intelligence to gather information, build trust, and identify vulnerabilities. He was no longer just a spy; he was a chameleon, adapting to his surroundings, morphing into different personas as needed. He was becoming more than he ever thought possible.

His success in Geneva cemented his position as a rising star within the Agency. He became a key player in shaping the Agency's strategy, his insights and foresight proving invaluable in preventing several potential crises. He was no longer reacting to events; he was shaping them, proactively mitigating risks and influencing outcomes.

His journey was far from over. He knew that the shadows would always be a part of his life, but they no longer held the same power over him. He had found a purpose, a path to redemption, a way to use his skills for good, to make a difference in the world. As he stood on the shores of Lake Geneva, the Alps rising majestically in the distance, he looked towards the future, embracing the unknown with a newfound confidence and a sense of purpose that burned brighter than any sunset he'd ever seen. He was Jake Riley, and this was just the beginning. The future held more challenges, more risks, more adventures, but he was ready. He was ready for anything. He had earned his redemption, not just in the eyes of the Agency, but in his own. He had found his home, not in a place, but in a purpose. The quiet hum of the city, the gentle lapping of the waves against the shore, all whispered a promise of what was to come, of a new dawn, a new beginning, a new chapter. The world, with all its shadows and complexities, was his oyster.

Unwavering Commitment

The Geneva assignment had been a masterclass in subtle manipulation, a ballet of deception played out amidst the gilded cages of international high society. He'd walked a tightrope between his cover identity as a financial analyst and his true purpose: uncovering the clandestine bioweapons research. The pressure had been immense, the stakes impossibly high. One wrong move, one misplaced word, could unravel months of painstaking work, exposing not only himself but potentially jeopardizing the entire operation. Yet, he'd thrived under the pressure, proving his adaptability and resilience.

His success wasn't just a matter of skill; it was a testament to the unwavering loyalty he fostered with his team. He relied on his network – a diverse group of individuals from different backgrounds, each with unique skills and perspectives. There was Anya Petrova, a former Russian intelligence officer with an encyclopedic knowledge of the organization they were targeting; Jean-Luc Dubois, a seasoned Swiss banker who provided crucial financial insights; and Dr. Kenji Tanaka, a biochemist whose expertise helped them decipher the complex scientific data. These weren't just colleagues; they were his family, bound together by a shared mission and a deep sense of mutual respect.

Jake's loyalty extended beyond his immediate team. He understood that the success of any operation, no matter how intricate, relied on the trust and collaboration of numerous unseen hands. The analysts who tirelessly sifted through mountains of data, the tech specialists who ensured secure communication, the field support personnel who maintained a watchful eye from the shadows – each played a crucial role. He acknowledged their contributions, understanding that their commitment was as vital as his own.

His next mission took him to the bustling streets of Hong Kong, a city pulsating with energy and intrigue. The target this time was a notorious arms dealer known only as "The Serpent," a shadowy figure who supplied weapons to terrorist organizations across the globe. This was a far cry from the sophisticated world of international finance; it was raw, dangerous, and unpredictable. But Jake was ready. He had honed his skills, sharpened his instincts, and strengthened his resolve.

Operating in the densely populated city, Jake relied on his street smarts, blending seamlessly into the crowded marketplaces and vibrant nightlife. He developed a network of informants, cultivating trust with seemingly ordinary individuals – street vendors, taxi drivers, bar owners – who provided crucial snippets of information. Each piece of intelligence was a fragment of a larger puzzle, and Jake's ability to assemble those fragments, to see the bigger picture, was crucial.

In Hong Kong, he faced a test of loyalty unlike any other. His contact, a seasoned informant named Li Wei, was betrayed, his cover blown by a double agent within the Serpent's organization. Li Wei, caught in a desperate situation, was forced to make a choice – betray Jake or face certain death. He chose loyalty, sacrificing himself to protect Jake and the operation. This loss deeply affected Jake. He mourned the loss of a friend and comrade, but Li Wei's sacrifice strengthened his resolve, underscoring the immense risks involved in the life he had chosen.

The weight of that sacrifice spurred Jake forward, fueling his determination to bring The Serpent to justice. He pursued the arms dealer with relentless intensity, relying on his wit, his skills, and the unwavering support of his team back in Geneva. The final confrontation was a tense standoff, a test of nerves and skill, played out against the backdrop of a stormy night. The Serpent, a cunning and ruthless adversary, fought back fiercely, but Jake's training, his experience, and his determination prevailed.

The arrest of The Serpent wasn't a solitary victory. It was a testament to the collective effort, the shared commitment, the unwavering loyalty within the Agency. It was a recognition of the sacrifices made by countless individuals who worked tirelessly in the shadows, risking everything for the greater good. This mission reinforced Jake's understanding of the profound nature of loyalty: it was not merely an abstract ideal, but a cornerstone of survival and success in his chosen profession.

Jake's commitment extended beyond his operational duties. He consistently championed the values of justice and fairness, even within the morally ambiguous world of espionage. He refused to compromise his principles, even under immense pressure. He understood that the fight against injustice was a continuous battle, one that required patience, resilience, and unwavering dedication.

His dedication extended to mentorship. As his profile grew within the Agency, he found himself taking on junior agents under his wing. He shared his knowledge and experience, guiding them through the complexities of the profession, instilling in them the same values of loyalty and integrity that had shaped his own career. He saw it as his responsibility to ensure that the next generation of operatives upheld the highest standards, maintaining the Agency's reputation for excellence and ethical conduct.

The price of loyalty wasn't merely the physical and emotional risks he faced daily. It was also the sacrifices he made in his personal life. He knew that his chosen path would forever limit his connections with the outside world, the possibility of a stable family life, and the luxury of a conventional existence. Yet, he accepted these limitations, realizing that his commitment to a greater cause outweighed any personal longing. His life was a constant negotiation between duty and desire, commitment and sacrifice, and he accepted that uneasy balance as the price of unwavering loyalty.

His next assignment tested his loyalty in a different way. He was sent to a war-torn nation, a region teeming with political instability and armed conflict. His mission was to extract a key witness who held crucial information about a series of atrocities committed by a powerful warlord. This wasn't just about gathering intelligence; it was about protecting an innocent life, ensuring that the truth was brought to light. In this dangerous environment, he worked with local resistance fighters, individuals who shared his ideals of justice and his unwavering commitment to protecting the vulnerable. He forged bonds with these unlikely allies, respecting their courage and resilience, earning their trust through his actions and his unwavering loyalty to their shared cause.

The extraction mission was fraught with peril, fraught with the potential for betrayal. But through strategic planning, skillful negotiation, and an unwavering reliance on his team, Jake succeeded. The witness was safely extracted, their testimony instrumental in bringing the warlord to justice. It was a victory not only for the Agency, but for the countless victims whose suffering had gone unaddressed for too long. This success underscored his belief that his commitment and dedication brought real change, a profound impact on the world. His loyalty wasn't just a virtue, it was a tool, a driving force for making the world a better place, one mission at a time. He had accepted the price of loyalty; the risks, the sacrifices, the loneliness. But for Jake Riley, the rewards were far greater than the costs, for he had discovered that true purpose lay not in personal glory, but in unwavering commitment to a cause greater than himself. The quiet satisfaction he felt was far deeper than any fleeting sense of accomplishment – it was the quiet hum of a life lived with purpose, a life devoted to a higher calling. And that, he knew, was a victory worth fighting for.

Sacrifice and Duty

The humid air hung heavy, thick with the scent of diesel fumes and desperation. Jake stood on a crumbling rooftop in Mogadishu, the Somali capital, a city perpetually teetering on the brink of chaos. Below him, the streets throbbed with a nervous energy, a cacophony of car horns, shouting vendors, and the distant crackle of gunfire. This wasn't the polished world of Geneva or the neon-drenched streets of Hong Kong. This was a warzone, raw and unforgiving. His mission: to extract Dr. Farah Omar, a renowned physician who had been secretly documenting the atrocities committed by a ruthless warlord, known only as "The Jackal." The Jackal controlled vast swathes of the country, his reign marked by unspeakable violence and systematic oppression. Dr. Omar held the evidence that could finally bring him to justice, but she was in grave danger.

The extraction plan was intricate, a carefully choreographed dance of deception and precision. Jake had assembled a small, highly skilled team comprised of individuals whose commitment to justice mirrored his own. Among them was Aisha, a fierce and resourceful Somali operative with an intimate understanding of the city's labyrinthine underbelly; and Marcus, a former US Special Forces medic whose expertise was as crucial as his unwavering courage. Trust was paramount; in this environment, betrayal was a constant threat. Each member of the team had to be completely reliable, their loyalty absolute.

Days blurred into weeks as Jake and his team navigated the treacherous landscape of Mogadishu. They moved like shadows, their movements meticulously planned, each step calculated to minimize their risk. They relied on a network of informants – courageous individuals who risked their lives to help them, driven by a shared desire for justice and a deep-seated hatred for The Jackal. These were not paid informants; they were individuals deeply committed to their cause, fueled by patriotism and a desperate hope for a better future. Their sacrifices were monumental, their commitment unquestionable.

One night, while meeting with a key informant in a dimly lit cafe, a sudden barrage of gunfire shattered the fragile calm. The cafe erupted into chaos as armed men stormed in, indiscriminately firing their weapons. Jake and his team found themselves trapped in a deadly crossfire. Aisha, ever vigilant, reacted swiftly, pushing Jake to safety as she engaged the attackers in a fierce firefight. Her combat skills were extraordinary, honed over years of fighting for survival. But the odds were stacked against them. They were outnumbered and surrounded.

During the ensuing chaos, Marcus was struck by a stray bullet. Jake, without hesitation, dragged him to safety, administering emergency first aid under the relentless gunfire. Their escape was a desperate scramble, a harrowing flight through the city's war-torn streets. They finally reached their safehouse, a dilapidated building nestled in the heart of a crowded slum, only after intense fighting and narrowly avoiding capture. Marcus, gravely wounded, received immediate medical attention. His survival was a testament to Jake's skill, and his unwavering loyalty to his team.

The incident underscored the brutal reality of their mission. The price of loyalty was not just measured in sweat and sleepless nights; it was paid in blood and sacrifice. The lives hanging in the balance weren't just their own; they were the lives of the people they were working to protect, of the people who, without their intervention, would be left at the mercy of The Jackal's reign of terror.

The extraction of Dr. Omar proved to be far more challenging than they had anticipated. The Jackal's network was vast and deeply entrenched; his informants were everywhere. Jake had to employ all his skills – his wit, his cunning, his ability to blend into any environment – to evade detection. He even had to navigate a complex web of political allegiances, balancing the needs of his mission with the delicate realities of the local power dynamics. This was a game of chess played on a battlefield, where every move carried the potential for catastrophic consequences.

The final extraction was a daring nighttime operation, fraught with peril. They moved with the precision of a well-oiled machine, navigating through the maze-like alleyways and deserted streets of Mogadishu. At one point, Jake had to single-handedly hold off a patrol of The Jackal's heavily armed soldiers, providing cover for Aisha and Dr. Omar to reach their extraction point. His training, his reflexes, and his sheer determination allowed him to prevail.

As they finally made their escape, heading towards the rendezvous point, the weight of the mission bore down on Jake. He reflected on the sacrifices made – the near-death experiences, the physical toll, the emotional strain. The cost of loyalty was profound, a relentless erosion of his personal life and well-being. Yet, as he looked at Dr. Omar, her face etched with relief and gratitude, he knew that it was a price worth paying. He had not only protected a life, but he had secured vital evidence that would bring a ruthless warlord to justice, potentially saving countless others from suffering and death.

The return to the Agency wasn't a triumphant homecoming. It was a quiet acknowledgment of a job well done, a recognition of the immense risks undertaken and the sacrifices made. There were no parades, no medals, only the quiet satisfaction of a mission accomplished. Jake understood this was the nature of his work; the rewards often went unseen, unacknowledged. His reward was the knowledge that he had made a difference, that his loyalty, his dedication, and his willingness to sacrifice had brought about a measure of justice in a world desperately in need of it. The price of loyalty was high, but for Jake Riley, it was a price he would willingly pay again and again, for the sake of a world that desperately needed his skills and his unyielding commitment to justice. The quiet hum of a life lived with purpose resonated within him, a constant reminder of the path he had chosen and the sacrifices he had made, and would continue to make, in the name of duty and loyalty. The mission in Mogadishu was a stark reminder that in the shadows of global conflicts, the truest victories are often quiet, unseen, and paid for in the currency of sacrifice.

Difficult Choices

The debriefing was less a celebratory affair and more a sterile interrogation. General Petrov, a man whose face seemed permanently etched with the weariness of a thousand sleepless nights, stared at Jake across a polished mahogany desk. The air in the room was thick with unspoken tension, the silence punctuated only by the rhythmic ticking of a grandfather clock in the corner. "The Jackal's network is far deeper than we initially assessed," Petrov stated, his voice low and gravelly. "Your actions, while effective, have inadvertently exposed certain… vulnerabilities."

Jake remained silent, his gaze unwavering. He knew what Petrov meant. Saving Dr. Omar had come at a cost. Several of their informants, individuals who had risked their lives for the mission's success, were now compromised. Their identities were potentially exposed, leaving them vulnerable to The Jackal's brutal retribution. The weight of those lives, those sacrifices, pressed down on him, a heavy cloak of guilt.

"We have reason to believe The Jackal is aware of our involvement," Petrov continued, his eyes piercing. "He's retaliating. We've seen increased activity in the region, a tightening of security. He's hunting. And he's hunting us." Petrov leaned forward, his gaze intense. "Your next mission is to neutralize a known associate of The Jackal – a man called 'The Serpent.' He's crucial to The Jackal's operations, his logistics man, his shadow. Taking him down is our best chance of disrupting his network and limiting the damage."

Jake felt a cold dread grip his heart. This wasn't just another extraction. This was a mission that demanded a different kind of loyalty, a more profound sacrifice. The Serpent operated in the heart of a heavily fortified compound in the remote mountains of Afghanistan, surrounded by mercenaries and heavily armed guards. Infiltration seemed impossible. But more unsettling was the information that accompanied the mission briefing. The Serpent wasn't just a logistical operator; he was a former colleague, a fellow recruit from Jake's training class, a man named Dimitri.

Dimitri, unlike Jake, had chosen a different path. He'd been seduced by the allure of power, the intoxicating promise of wealth and influence. He'd betrayed the Agency, embracing the darkness instead of fighting it. The news hit Jake like a physical blow. He'd shared grueling training sessions with Dimitri, had shared laughter, sweat, and near-death experiences. He'd trusted him, respected him. Now he was tasked with killing him.

The moral dilemma was agonizing. He wrestled with the conflicting demands of his duty and his conscience. Could he kill a man he once called a friend? Could he reconcile the unwavering loyalty to the Agency with the personal bond he had once shared with Dimitri? The mission parameters were clear: eliminate the threat. But the human cost felt unbearable.

The Agency's response to his internal struggle was swift and uncompromising. They presented him with an alternative: a covert operation to expose Dimitri, gather evidence of his crimes, and bring him to justice through legal channels. This approach carried its own set of risks, though less violent. A prolonged investigation could expose more agents, give The Jackal time to consolidate his power and further his atrocities. The successful execution of this course of action was uncertain, with far-reaching consequences either way.

Jake spent sleepless nights weighing the options, the choices echoing in his mind like a relentless drumbeat. He revisited his training, the rigorous moral philosophy instilled in him. They had taught him that loyalty meant more than blind obedience; it demanded moral integrity. It meant weighing the consequences of his actions, understanding the ripple effects of his choices. He sought the counsel of Aisha, whose own experiences in the tumultuous landscape of Somalia had forged a steely resolve and a deep understanding of ethical ambiguities.

Aisha listened intently, her dark eyes reflecting the weight of Jake's dilemma. "You face the hardest kind of choice, Jake," she finally said, her voice low. "The kind that leaves no easy answers. You are caught between the cold logic of the mission and the fire of your conscience. There is no perfect outcome here, only less imperfect options." Her words weren't comforting, but they were true.

He decided that a direct confrontation would likely end with both him and Dimitri dead, offering no resolution. He needed to find a way to expose Dimitri without resorting to outright violence. He opted for the covert operation, devising a plan that involved deep penetration into The Jackal's organization. He required a carefully calibrated infiltration using subterfuge and deception.

His team, now augmented by a skilled hacker named Lena, whose skills were as deadly as any weapon, began to gather intelligence. They pieced together Dimitri's movements, his communications, his financial dealings. They discovered evidence of far-reaching corruption, implicating not only Dimitri but also several high-ranking officials within the Afghan government. The stakes were now higher than ever before. Their investigation was uncovering a conspiracy of international proportions.

The final confrontation wasn't in a blazing gunfight, but in a dimly lit backroom of a Kabul casino. Dimitri, oblivious to the Agency's operation, was engaged in a high-stakes poker game with a shadowy figure who was, unbeknownst to him, one of Jake's operatives. The evidence was presented, irrefutable. Dimitri, caught in the web of his own deceit, was left with no option but to surrender. The arrest was swift and efficient. The sense of victory was bittersweet. Justice had been served, but at a considerable cost. The information they had gathered was far-reaching, and its revelation would cause significant political ripples. The potential loss of life associated with a violent conflict had been avoided, but it had come at the price of prolonged tension and vulnerability.

The aftermath left Jake grappling with the profound moral implications of his choices. He had chosen the path of compassion and justice, but that path had been equally fraught with danger and sacrifice. The quiet moments, the ones where he wasn't actively engaged in missions or debriefings, brought home the weight of his actions. He would never forget Dimitri, the friend lost to the darkness, a poignant reminder of the price of loyalty, and the ever-present cost of difficult choices. The world of espionage, he realized, was not a black-and-white affair, but a gray expanse of ethical ambiguities, where the truest battles were fought not on the battlefield but within the confines of one's own conscience. The price of loyalty was not simply a matter of life and death, but also a matter of the soul.

Standing for Justice

The arrest of Dimitri sent shockwaves through the Agency. His connections ran deeper than anyone anticipated, extending into the highest echelons of the Afghan government. The information gleaned from his interrogation, coupled with the evidence Lena's team had meticulously compiled, painted a grim picture of systemic corruption, a network of bribery and collusion that stretched from Kabul to Washington D.C. The Jackal, it seemed, was not just a ruthless mercenary; he was a puppeteer, manipulating political levers from the shadows.

The ensuing investigation was a delicate dance on a tightrope. Each revelation threatened to unravel a carefully constructed web of alliances, triggering a domino effect of political upheaval. Jake found himself thrust into the heart of the maelstrom, working with a hand-picked team of legal experts and intelligence analysts to unravel the complex threads of the conspiracy. He was no longer just a field operative; he was a key witness, his testimony crucial in bringing down a network that had operated in the shadows for decades.

The pressure mounted. Anonymous threats arrived, veiled warnings delivered through cryptic messages and coded emails. Jake's apartment was placed under 24/7 surveillance, and his movements were meticulously tracked. He felt the chilling breath of The Jackal on his neck, a constant reminder that justice was a two-edged sword. The fight for truth had transformed into a fight for survival.

His days were consumed by endless briefings, interrogations, and the painstaking process of verifying evidence. He spent hours poring over financial records, deciphering encrypted communications, and piecing together the fragments of a vast conspiracy. The work was tedious, draining, yet vital. Every document, every piece of intelligence, was a step closer to exposing the truth. He felt the weight of responsibility, the knowledge that his efforts could have significant consequences, not just for the Agency but for the geopolitical landscape of the region.

The trial was a spectacle. Dimitri, his face etched with a mixture of regret and defiance, pleaded guilty to a reduced charge in exchange for his cooperation. His testimony, however, was not what the prosecution had anticipated. Dimitri, now facing a life sentence, revealed a hidden layer of the operation, a detail that shocked even Jake and his team. It transpired that The Jackal had been working with a mole within the Agency itself – someone deeply embedded within the organization, manipulating events from within.

The search for the mole became Jake's new obsession. It was a race against time, a desperate hunt for a phantom within their midst. The Agency was fractured, suspicion festering amongst the ranks. Trust was a commodity in short supply, and old alliances were tested to their breaking point. Jake, despite the risk to himself, was determined to expose the traitor, to cleanse the Agency of the insidious corruption that had festered for so long.

He delved into the Agency's history, poring over personnel files, scrutinizing past missions, looking for any anomalies, any inconsistencies. He interrogated former colleagues, re-examining past relationships, searching for signs of betrayal. The pressure was immense, the stakes impossibly high. The mole, skilled and cunning, was leaving no trace, their actions carefully orchestrated, their motives deliberately obscured.

The trail led to an unexpected source – a seemingly insignificant administrative clerk who had access to sensitive information. The evidence, initially subtle, gradually accumulated, forming a compelling case against the clerk. It was a betrayal that shook Jake to his core, someone he had considered a friend, a colleague, a confidante.

The subsequent arrest of the mole brought about a period of soul-searching within the Agency. A sweeping internal investigation was launched, purging the organization of those compromised by The Jackal's network. The fallout was significant, careers ruined, reputations tarnished. But the operation, despite its internal turmoil, had succeeded. The Jackal's network had been dismantled, his operations disrupted, his reach significantly curtailed.

However, Jake's journey didn't end there. The exposure of Dimitri and the Agency mole had merely scratched the surface of a much deeper, more insidious conspiracy. The investigation revealed a far-reaching web of international arms dealing, money laundering, and political corruption that extended to several global powers. The hunt for The Jackal, now a far more elusive and dangerous adversary than ever before, resumed. Jake found himself confronting a shadowy network that spanned continents, wielding vast influence and untold resources.

The Jackal, unlike his associates, was an enigma, a ghost in the machine. He remained faceless, nameless, his true identity shrouded in mystery. Jake's pursuit led him from the bustling souks of Marrakech to the frozen landscapes of Siberia, a relentless chase that pushed him to the very limits of his physical and mental endurance. The world of espionage he inhabited was a dangerous place, a realm where loyalty was a fickle commodity and trust was a luxury few could afford.

His relentless pursuit ultimately led him to a hidden base in the Himalayas. It was a fortress, impenetrable from the outside and camouflaged perfectly into the mountainous terrain. Getting in was a harrowing experience, requiring Jake to utilize every ounce of his training and ingenuity. The final confrontation with The Jackal wasn't a dramatic gunfight, but rather a battle of wits, a game of chess played with lives as pawns. It was a tense standoff, a silent duel between two masters of deception. The Jackal, cornered and exposed, attempted one last desperate gambit to escape, but Jake's vigilance and cunning thwarted his plan. The Jackal's arrest was not a triumph, but a conclusion, a chapter in an ongoing war against shadow organizations and their influence.

The victory felt hollow. While justice had been served, a profound sense of unease remained. He knew, with chilling certainty, that the world of espionage, the fight for justice and truth, was far from over. The shadows lingered, and new threats would inevitably emerge. Jake, weary but resolute, understood that his fight was a lifelong commitment, a never-ending quest for truth in a world saturated in lies. The price of loyalty, he knew, was eternal vigilance, a relentless commitment to the fight, even when the odds seemed insurmountable, even when the cost was personal and profound. The shadow war continued, and so did his commitment. The fight for justice, he knew, was an endless journey.

Consequences of Actions

The Himalayan air bit at Jake's lungs, thin and icy even at midday. The victory, the capture of The Jackal, felt distant, a phantom echo in the vast, echoing silence of the mountain fortress. He sat on a jagged outcropping of rock, the wind whipping his hair across his face, the panoramic view of snow-capped peaks offering no solace. The adrenaline had drained away, leaving behind a bone-deep weariness that settled in his soul like a shroud.

He ran a hand over his stubbled jaw, the rough texture a familiar comfort in the unsettling stillness. The trial had been a whirlwind, a media circus fueled by leaked information and breathless speculation. Dimitri's confession, followed by the shocking revelation of the mole within the Agency, had sent shockwaves through the political and intelligence communities. The public outcry had been deafening, a demand for accountability that reverberated through the halls of power.

The Agency, fractured and reeling from the betrayal, had undergone a radical transformation. A massive purge had removed those compromised by The Jackal's network, a brutal culling that had left a trail of shattered careers and broken lives. The faces of former colleagues, once friendly and familiar, now haunted his dreams – a constant reminder of the collateral damage of his actions. He had played a pivotal role in dismantling a vast criminal enterprise, but the victory tasted like ash in his mouth.

A memory flickered, a vivid flashback to his baseball days. The roar of the crowd, the crack of the bat, the exhilaration of the game – a simpler time, a simpler life. He remembered the camaraderie, the shared dreams, the unwavering loyalty amongst his teammates. That world felt a million miles away, a distant dream from the harsh realities of espionage. He missed the uncomplicated nature of the game, the clear-cut rules and predictable outcomes. The world of shadows offered no such comforts.

He closed his eyes, the icy wind a stark contrast to the warmth of the memories. He thought of Lena, her sharp intelligence and unwavering dedication. Their collaboration had been crucial in exposing The Jackal's network, their partnership forged in the crucible of danger and shared sacrifice. But even the bond they had forged felt strained now, tested by the weight of their shared experiences. The emotional toll of their work, the constant threat to their lives, had created an invisible chasm between them.

The consequences of his actions were far-reaching and unpredictable. He had been instrumental in bringing down a network of international criminals, but at what cost? The lives disrupted, the trust betrayed, the careers destroyed – these were the shadows that clung to his victory, a constant reminder of the human cost of war, even a war fought in the shadows.

He thought of the administrative clerk, the seemingly insignificant figure who had betrayed the Agency. It had been a betrayal that cut deep, the violation of trust a wound that festered. The clerk, once a friend, was now a symbol of the pervasive corruption that had infiltrated the very heart of the organization. It was a painful lesson learned, a stark reminder of the fragility of human relationships in a world where deception and betrayal were commonplace.

Jake traced the outline of a distant mountain peak with his finger. He was not immune to the mistakes he had made. He had risked everything, jeopardized his life and the lives of those closest to him, to pursue justice. But justice, he was beginning to realize, was a slippery concept, a relentless pursuit that rarely offered definitive closure.

The weight of responsibility pressed down on him. The revelation of the mole had shaken his confidence, not just in the Agency, but in himself. He had been manipulated, used, his judgment clouded by the exigencies of the mission. He had lost sight of the ethical boundaries that had once defined his actions.

He stood up, the wind whipping his clothes around him. The cold air cleared his head, sharpening his focus. The past could not be undone, but it could be learned from. The mistakes he had made were etched into his soul, harsh lessons that would forever shape his understanding of the world. He could not erase the past, but he could control his future.

He was no longer the naive recruit who had entered the Agency's shadowy world. He had grown, hardened, and learned the brutal realities of power and betrayal. He understood that loyalty had a price, and that price could be exacted in many ways. He had lost friends, allies, and even a part of himself in the process.

The journey had been arduous, his spirit tested to its limits. The constant threat of death, the betrayals, the moral dilemmas – these had all left their mark. He had confronted his own mortality, the fragility of life, and the ever-present shadow of death.

But amidst the darkness, a flicker of resolve remained. The fight for justice, he knew, would continue. The shadow war, with its intricate web of deceit and treachery, was far from over. New threats would emerge, new challenges would arise.

He descended the mountain, the setting sun casting long, dramatic shadows across the snow-covered landscape. The air was growing colder, and a sense of foreboding clung to him like a second skin. The Jackal was gone, but the war was far from over. He was a changed man, scarred but unbroken, ready to face whatever challenges lay ahead. The price of loyalty had been high, but he was prepared to pay it, again and again, for as long as the fight for truth continued. His path was unclear, the future uncertain, but one thing remained constant: his unwavering commitment to the fight against the shadows. The world needed men like him, men who were willing to stand in the darkness and fight for the light, even if it meant facing the darkness within themselves. The shadow war had changed him, but it had not broken him. He would carry the scars, the lessons, and the resolve to keep fighting. The price of loyalty, he knew, was a lifelong commitment.

Testing Alliances

The opulence of the Geneva hotel suite felt like a cruel joke. Crystal chandeliers glittered, reflecting the nervous sweat beading on Dimitri's forehead. He'd been cooperative, almost eager, to spill the Jackal's secrets, but the genuine remorse in his eyes had been replaced by a calculating coolness. Jake felt it instinctively, a shift in the tectonic plates of their uneasy alliance. Dimitri's confession had been a carefully constructed narrative, leaving out crucial details, conveniently omitting names and precise locations. It was a calculated risk, a gamble on Jake's trust.

"The information you provided... it's incomplete," Jake stated, his voice low and even, masking the simmering anger. He watched Dimitri carefully, noting the slight twitch of his left eye, a telltale sign of deception he'd learned to recognize during his intensive training.

Dimitri sighed, a theatrical display of weariness. "My cooperation has its limits, Mr. Riley. I've already risked more than my freedom. My family... they are still vulnerable." He spoke with an almost childlike vulnerability, a carefully crafted shield of innocence.

Jake knew better. The price of loyalty, he'd learned, was always higher than it seemed. The Agency had paid a steep price for Dimitri's initial cooperation, and Jake suspected the full cost hadn't yet been tallied. This carefully orchestrated show of vulnerability was a way to protect himself, to safeguard his remaining assets and future options.

Their meeting was a delicate dance of suspicion, a silent war fought with words and unspoken threats. Dimitri played the role of the repentant informant, offering tantalizing bits of information while carefully guarding his secrets. Jake, in turn, employed his honed skills of observation and deduction, attempting to unravel the carefully constructed facade. He saw the subtle cues, the fleeting expressions, the nervous twitches – all the tiny cracks in Dimitri's carefully constructed story.

Later that evening, Jake met with Lena in a secluded café, the aroma of strong coffee doing little to mask the tension between them. Their partnership, once forged in the fires of a shared mission, now felt brittle, frayed by the weight of secrets and unanswered questions.

"He's holding something back," Jake said, his voice barely a whisper. He recounted his meeting with Dimitri, detailing the subtle inconsistencies and carefully crafted deceptions.

Lena's sharp eyes narrowed. "I suspected as much. Dimitri's always been a pragmatist, a survivor. He'll cooperate only to the extent that it benefits him."

"But who is he protecting?" Jake pressed, his frustration mounting. "And what other players are in this game?"

Lena leaned forward, her voice dropping to a conspiratorial murmur. "There are whispers of a larger network, something beyond The Jackal's operation. A shadow organization pulling the strings, controlling the players." She spoke of shadowy figures operating in the background, of clandestine meetings in neutral territories, of anonymous bank accounts and untraceable funds.

Jake felt a chill run down his spine. This was beyond his experience, venturing into a world of intrigue and manipulation that seemed to defy even the Agency's reach.

The following days were a blur of clandestine meetings, covert surveillance, and perilous chases across continents. Jake and Lena, each working independently but sharing information through encrypted channels, started to unravel the threads of this larger conspiracy. They navigated a treacherous landscape of shifting alliances, uncovering hidden agendas and betrayals at every turn.

In Rome, Jake encountered Marco, a former colleague whose loyalty had been questioned during the Agency's purge. Marco, haunted by the ghosts of his past, offered cryptic information about a shadowy organization known only as "The Syndicate." He claimed they were the puppet masters behind The Jackal and Dimitri, funding their operations and orchestrating their moves.

The information was scarce, fragmented, like pieces of a jigsaw puzzle scattered across a vast, dark landscape. Each piece, when fitted into place, revealed a more terrifying picture of the Syndicate's reach and power. They operated in the shadows, their existence shrouded in secrecy, their influence stretching across continents and impacting global politics.

In Moscow, Lena discovered evidence of a secret collaboration between The Syndicate and a rogue faction within the Russian intelligence service. The documents she acquired revealed financial transactions, coded messages, and the names of individuals involved in the illicit activities. She knew that her life was in grave danger.

The stakes continued to rise. Each step forward brought Jake and Lena closer to the truth, but also closer to the heart of a dangerous and ruthless network. They were playing a deadly game of cat and mouse, with the lives of countless individuals hanging in the balance.

The pressure mounted, the risk escalated, and their own trust, already fragile, was tested to its limits. Jake found himself questioning not only Dimitri's allegiance but also Lena's. The Syndicate's reach extended its tendrils into their own world, casting suspicion on every contact, every alliance. Was Lena herself compromised? Was she acting independently, or was she a pawn in someone else's game?

One rainy night in London, Jake received an anonymous message—a cryptic note left in a seemingly empty safe deposit box. The message contained a single piece of information: a code name—"Nightingale." It sent shivers down his spine. Nightingale was a legend, a ghost story whispered among seasoned agents. A master manipulator who had been presumed dead for decades, someone whose existence was a mere myth.

The information triggered a frantic search, leading Jake into a labyrinthine world of hidden identities and false trails. The investigation strained his resources and tested his resolve. He began to see parallels between Nightingale's methods and the actions of Lena. Her strategic moves, her calculated risks, the seemingly impossible access she had—it all pointed to a dangerous possibility. Could Lena be Nightingale?

The realization hit him like a physical blow. The suspicion, the careful observations, the nagging doubts—they all culminated in a terrifying truth. It was too close to home, too dangerous. Could his closest ally be the enemy all along? The weight of this revelation, the stark reality of his situation, made his breath catch in his throat.

The next few hours were a battle against time, against doubt, and against the encroaching darkness. He had to know, he had to confirm or deny this devastating revelation before it was too late. The line between trust and betrayal had blurred into an indistinguishable grey, leaving Jake alone in the chilling uncertainty. He had to decide who he could trust, before the Syndicate's web of deceit destroyed him and everything he had fought for. The shadows were closing in, and the truth, he suspected, was far more sinister than he could ever have imagined. The game had changed. He was no longer just hunting the enemy; he had to determine if he had already been captured.

Navigating Deception

The anonymous message, a single word – Nightingale – echoed in Jake's mind, a discordant note in the symphony of suspicion that had become his life. He'd spent days chasing shadows, piecing together fragments of a vast conspiracy, only to find the most dangerous threat lurking within his own circle of trust. Lena. The thought was a bitter pill, hard to swallow, yet the evidence, however circumstantial, pointed undeniably in her direction.

His investigation took him to a forgotten archive in Prague, a labyrinthine repository of dusty files and forgotten secrets. He spent days sifting through microfilm, deciphering coded messages, and piecing together the fragmented history of Nightingale. The legend was more than just a ghost story; it was a meticulously crafted narrative, a carefully constructed illusion designed to protect a clandestine network. Nightingale wasn't just a single person, it was a mantle, passed down through generations of skilled operatives, each inheriting the mantle and continuing the network's shadowy operations.

The archive yielded a treasure trove of information, but it was the subtle details that were the most revealing. He found references to operational techniques mirrored in Lena's recent actions, her seemingly impossible access to secure locations, her uncanny ability to anticipate their enemies' moves. Each discovery strengthened the unsettling conclusion. The more he learned about Nightingale, the more he saw a chilling reflection in Lena's actions.

His next move was a calculated risk. He needed to test his suspicions, to confirm or deny the terrifying possibility that the woman he trusted implicitly was the enemy. He arranged a clandestine meeting, a seemingly innocuous rendezvous in a quiet Parisian square. The air hung heavy with anticipation, the silence punctuated only by the distant sounds of the city. He used a coded phrase, a subtle probe designed to gauge Lena's reaction.

Her response was immediate, a flicker of something in her eyes – a fleeting expression that betrayed a hidden knowledge, a subconscious acknowledgment of the code. It wasn't proof, but it was enough to confirm his darkest fears. He pressed further, leading the conversation towards Nightingale, dropping carefully chosen words, watching her reactions with hawk-like intensity. Her responses were too quick, too precise, revealing a familiarity with the details that she shouldn't possess unless she was Nightingale herself. He saw the mask of her composure slip, the carefully constructed facade crumbling under the pressure of his carefully orchestrated interrogation.

The confrontation was inevitable, a clash of wills in a dimly lit backroom of a Prague pub. He laid out his evidence, a carefully curated collection of facts and observations, meticulously assembled to paint an undeniable picture. He accused her directly, watching her face for any sign of denial, any hesitation, any telltale sign of deception. He had anticipated her responses, her counterarguments, even her attempts at manipulation. He'd trained for this moment, prepared for this betrayal, and his training paid off. He saw the flicker of fear behind her eyes, the slight tremor in her voice – cracks in the carefully constructed facade of her composure.

Lena's response was not denial, but a confession of sorts. She admitted to being a part of the network, a player in the larger game. However, her explanation was convoluted, a web of half-truths and calculated omissions, designed to protect her own interests and those she was sworn to protect. She spoke of loyalty, of a higher purpose, a grand scheme that transcended national boundaries and personal ambitions.

"The Syndicate isn't just about money or power, Jake," she said, her voice low and intense. "It's about survival, about safeguarding a legacy that extends far beyond our lifetimes. We are protecting the world from a far greater threat, a darkness that operates beyond the comprehension of ordinary men."

Her words were a mixture of truth and deception, a carefully constructed narrative designed to sway him, to elicit sympathy and understanding. He listened carefully, dissecting her words, searching for the truth hidden beneath the layers of carefully constructed deception. He knew he couldn't trust her, not completely, but he also knew that she possessed valuable information, information that could unravel the Syndicate's web of deceit and expose the true threat.

He faced a difficult decision. Should he betray her, handing her over to the Agency and potentially destroying the only link he had to the heart of the Syndicate? Or could he trust her, however reluctantly, and use her knowledge to destroy the organization from within? The stakes were immense, the risks insurmountable. One wrong move could destroy everything he'd worked for, leading to his own death or the death of countless others.

The days that followed were a precarious dance on the edge of a knife. He and Lena, bound together by a shared understanding of the danger, navigated a treacherous landscape of shifting alliances and unpredictable betrayals. They worked in tandem, albeit warily, using their respective skills and knowledge to dismantle the Syndicate piece by piece. They discovered the organization's global reach, its deep penetration into the highest echelons of power, and its shadowy control over global events.

In their pursuit, they encountered unexpected allies and dangerous enemies. Old ghosts from Jake's past resurfaced, offering cryptic clues and warnings. Each encounter brought them closer to the heart of the conspiracy, but also exposed them to greater danger. They uncovered a network of sleeper agents, embedded in key positions of influence across the globe. They were infiltrating governments, manipulating markets, and sowing discord across continents.

The final confrontation took place amidst the chaos of a major international summit. The Syndicate's leaders, cloaked in anonymity and protected by layers of security, were revealed. Their plan was ambitious, a calculated attempt to reshape the world order, to seize control of global resources and consolidate power under their command.

Jake and Lena, working in concert, orchestrated a carefully planned takedown, using their combined skills and knowledge to expose the Syndicate's operations to the world. The climax was a whirlwind of action, betrayal, and suspense. They faced life-threatening situations, narrowly escaping capture, engaging in deadly firefights, and surviving treacherous betrayals from within their own ranks.

In the aftermath, the world was stunned by the revelation of the Syndicate's existence and its audacious plot. Jake and Lena, their identities protected by the Agency, slipped back into the shadows, their roles in the operation forever shrouded in secrecy. Their success came at a heavy cost, leaving both of them forever marked by the experience. The line between trust and betrayal would always remain a haunting memory, a reminder of the price they paid to protect the world from the darkness they had confronted. The shadows remained, but they were no longer in control.

Unmasking the Enemy

The Parisian rendezvous had been a calculated gamble, and it had paid off handsomely, albeit chillingly. Lena's subtle reactions, the fleeting expressions that betrayed her carefully constructed facade, confirmed Jake's worst fears. She was Nightingale, the elusive leader of a clandestine network operating in the shadows. But her confession wasn't a simple admission of guilt; it was a carefully woven tapestry of half-truths and calculated omissions, a performance designed to manipulate and confuse.

Her narrative spoke of a higher purpose, a desperate struggle to protect the world from a nameless, faceless enemy—a shadowy organization even more powerful and dangerous than the Syndicate itself. She painted a picture of a global threat, one that extended beyond national borders and traditional power structures. This new enemy, she claimed, manipulated world events from the shadows, pulling strings from hidden control points scattered across the globe. It was a dangerous game of chess, played on a global scale, with humanity's future hanging in the balance.

Jake knew he couldn't fully trust her, but he also recognized the chilling possibility that she might be telling the truth. Her knowledge of the Syndicate's inner workings was undeniable. Her insights into their intricate network of sleeper agents, their penetration into various governments, and their covert influence on international events were simply too detailed to be fabricated. This was far beyond the typical information gleaned from casual observation or basic intelligence gathering. This was intimate knowledge, the kind possessed only by someone who had been at the very heart of the organization.

Their uneasy alliance continued, a fragile partnership forged in the crucible of shared danger. They navigated the treacherous landscape of the Syndicate's global network, each step forward carrying the potential for deadly repercussions. Their investigation led them to a remote island in the South Pacific, a seemingly idyllic paradise that masked a highly sophisticated technological facility. Here, hidden beneath the tranquil surface of the ocean, was the Syndicate's command center, a fortress of steel and secrets.

The facility was a marvel of technological innovation, a testament to the Syndicate's vast resources and engineering prowess. Sophisticated surveillance systems monitored every corner, biometric scanners guarded access points, and redundant power systems ensured uninterrupted operation. Navigating this high-tech labyrinth was a test of their skills, requiring precise timing and flawless execution. They bypassed laser grids, disabled motion sensors, and evaded pressure plates, their movements fluid and synchronized.

Inside, they discovered the true scope of the Syndicate's ambition. They uncovered evidence of a catastrophic bioweapon, capable of wiping out millions. The weapon wasn't just a theoretical concept; it was fully functional, ready for deployment. Data logs revealed plans for its use – a coordinated, multi-pronged attack designed to cripple nations and destabilize global economies, thus allowing the Syndicate to seize control in the ensuing chaos.

The suspense ratcheted up as they delved deeper into the heart of the facility, their every move tracked by the Syndicate's all-seeing eyes. They faced near misses, narrowly avoiding detection, their hearts pounding with every tense moment. The facility was a maze of corridors and hidden chambers, each turn potentially leading to a deadly trap. They relied on their training, their intuition, and their combined skills to overcome the formidable security systems.

One particularly harrowing encounter involved navigating a room filled with pressure-sensitive floors, each step triggering a cascade of alarms. Jake, using his athletic agility and quick thinking, devised a daring plan that involved using shadows and a carefully calculated leap to bypass the sensors. Lena, meanwhile, expertly disabled a remote surveillance system, creating a temporary blind spot that allowed them to proceed without being detected.

Their efforts weren't without cost. During a tense moment, they encountered a heavily armed security detail. Jake, using his honed combat skills, neutralized the guards, his movements a blur of precision and speed, leaving them incapacitated but unharmed. The incident underscored the lethal nature of their mission and the ever-present threat of discovery.

The climax arrived when they reached the heart of the facility, a vault containing the bioweapon itself. They faced the Syndicate's most elite operatives, highly trained soldiers armed with state-of-the-art weaponry. The ensuing confrontation was a deadly ballet of precision strikes and tactical maneuvers, a terrifying dance with death.

Jake used his superior hand-to-hand combat skills and precise marksmanship, while Lena used her tactical expertise and technology prowess to overcome their adversaries. They fought their way through wave after wave of attackers, their movements honed to perfection, a testament to their years of training. The battle was brutal, brutal, the air thick with the sounds of gunfire and the cries of the dying.

Finally, cornered and outnumbered, they activated a self-destruct sequence for the facility, destroying all evidence of the Syndicate's bioweapon and crippling their operational capabilities. Their escape was a harrowing race against time, a desperate sprint through the collapsing facility. They survived, their bodies battered, but their resolve unbroken. In the end, they had destroyed a significant threat to global security, exposing the Syndicate to the world and dismantling a global conspiracy.

The aftermath was a chaotic blend of apprehension and relief. Governments scrambled to address the implications of the Syndicate's exposure. Jake and Lena, their identities carefully shrouded in secrecy by the agency, faded back into the shadows, leaving behind the wreckage of their mission and the chilling legacy of their close brush with global catastrophe. The world may have been safe, but the experience left both of them permanently scarred. The line between trust and betrayal had been tested, and the wounds it had inflicted would heal slowly, if at all. The echoes of the past would haunt them for years to come, a constant reminder of the price they paid to safeguard the world from a darkness they had barely begun to understand. The silence that followed the storm was deafening, a stark contrast to the chaos they had just survived. Their work was done, but the shadows lingered, a constant reminder of the ever-present dangers lurking just beneath the surface.

Confronting Treachery

The escape from the island facility had been a harrowing experience, a blur of collapsing concrete and desperate maneuvers. But the fight wasn't over. The Syndicate, though crippled, was far from defeated. Their network, vast and insidious, still held pockets of power, loyalists who would stop at nothing to avenge their fallen comrades and resurrect their operation. Jake and Lena knew this, and as they debriefed with their handlers, the grim reality settled in: the confrontation wasn't over; it was just beginning.

Their first target was Petrov, a high-ranking Syndicate operative who had orchestrated Lena's initial recruitment into the organization, twisting her loyalty and using her skills for his nefarious purposes. Petrov, a man of immense wealth and influence, had been instrumental in the creation of the bioweapon, and his network of contacts stretched into the highest echelons of power across several nations. His capture was crucial, not just for bringing him to justice, but for dismantling the remaining threads of the Syndicate's intricate web.

Their handler, a stern-faced woman named Agent Thorne, laid out the plan. A discreet operation, cloaked in secrecy and conducted far from prying eyes. Petrov resided in a luxurious villa nestled amidst the rolling hills of Tuscany, guarded by a team of highly skilled mercenaries. The villa itself was a fortress, equipped with state-of-the-art security systems. Their mission was simple: infiltrate the villa, neutralize the guards, and extract Petrov without raising the alarm. Failure would have significant repercussions.

The Tuscan countryside, bathed in the golden hues of a late summer sunset, provided a deceptively tranquil backdrop for their operation. As Jake and Lena approached the villa, shrouded in the twilight, the palpable tension was almost suffocating. The villa stood as a symbol of Petrov's wealth and power, a testament to his corruption and cruelty. He had betrayed many, and now he would pay the price.

Their infiltration was a masterpiece of stealth and precision. Jake, using his exceptional agility, scaled the villa walls, his movements fluid and silent. Lena, meanwhile, bypassed the perimeter security systems, disabling alarms and cameras with her technological expertise. They moved like shadows, their every step calculated, their senses heightened.

Once inside, the villa's opulent interior was a stark contrast to the shadows they inhabited. Chandeliers cast dancing lights across marble floors, priceless artwork adorned the walls, and the air hummed with the quiet luxury of wealth. It was a world of excess, a stark reminder of the inequality they fought to dismantle. But their focus remained unwavering. They navigated the labyrinthine corridors, their senses alert for any sign of danger.

The guards, clad in black tactical gear, were strategically positioned throughout the villa. Jake neutralized them swiftly and silently, using a combination of martial arts skills and non-lethal weaponry. Lena, using her advanced electronic gadgetry, disabled security cameras and communication systems, ensuring their movements remained undetected. They worked as a well-oiled machine, their movements perfectly synchronized, their skills perfectly complemented.

They finally confronted Petrov in his lavish study, a room filled with the symbols of his ill-gotten gains. The confrontation was not a brutal fight, but a tense standoff, a clash of wills. Petrov, though surprised, remained defiant, his eyes glinting with a chilling mix of arrogance and fear. He knew his time was over, yet he refused to submit without a struggle. He tried to bargain, to offer information, to plead for mercy. But Jake and Lena were unwavering, their resolve hardened by the countless lives ruined by his actions.

Petrov's attempts at manipulation were met with cold indifference. Jake reminded him of the victims of his greed and cruelty, the lives destroyed by his insatiable ambition. Lena presented irrefutable evidence of his crimes, his involvement in the bioweapon conspiracy, and his extensive network of corruption. There was no escape; the weight of his actions pressed down on him like an inescapable burden. He was a broken man, his veneer of power stripped away, his arrogance replaced by a hollow despair.

The extraction was swift and efficient. Petrov, subdued but not harmed, was taken into custody, his reign of terror brought to an abrupt end. As they left the villa, the Tuscan hills seemed to sigh in relief, the weight of his presence lifted from the land. Their work was done, but the journey was far from over. The Syndicate's reach extended far and wide, and many more betrayals remained to be avenged, many more battles to be fought. The fight for justice was a relentless pursuit, a long and arduous path that required unwavering commitment and courage. The weight of their mission pressed heavily upon them, but their resolve remained unshaken. The world might never know their names, but their impact would reverberate through history, a silent testament to the unwavering fight against treachery and deceit. The shadows would always lurk, but they were ready.

The next target was a man known only as "The Architect," a brilliant but ruthless computer programmer who had designed the security systems for the Syndicate's global network. He was a ghost, a phantom who operated from the shadows, his location constantly shifting, his movements unpredictable. Tracking him was like chasing a phantom, a futile exercise in frustration. But Lena, with her unparalleled technological prowess, had managed to trace him to a secluded research facility in the heart of the Siberian wilderness.

The Siberian landscape was a harsh and unforgiving mistress, a landscape of snow and ice, where survival was a constant struggle. The research facility, buried deep within the frozen tundra, was a fortress of steel and concrete, designed to withstand the harshest conditions and the most determined attackers. Infiltrating it would be a challenge that would test their skills and their resilience to their very limits.

Their journey to the facility was treacherous, a grueling trek across the snow-covered plains, facing blizzards and sub-zero temperatures. Their bodies were pushed to the limit, but their spirits remained unbroken. The weight of their mission drove them forward, fueled by their commitment to justice.

The facility, when they finally reached it, was a chilling monument to human ambition, a testament to the depths of human depravity. It was a sterile environment, devoid of warmth and life, where experiments were conducted on unsuspecting subjects. The Architect, with his cold, calculating demeanor, was the mastermind behind the horrors conducted within its walls.

The infiltration was a complex affair, requiring a blend of stealth, skill and precise timing. Jake used his knowledge of close-quarters combat to neutralize the guards while Lena bypassed the sophisticated security systems. The Architect, however, was not easily surprised. He had anticipated their arrival, and he had prepared accordingly.

The confrontation was intellectual, a chess match of wits and intelligence. The Architect, entrenched in his technological fortress, believed himself invulnerable, his ego inflated by his brilliance. He underestimated Jake and Lena, underestimating their resolve and their unwavering determination to bring him to justice. They exploited his arrogance and his overconfidence, exploiting weaknesses in his systems to gain the upper hand.

The battle was a terrifying dance of light and shadow, the flickering screens of computers reflecting the intensity of the confrontation. The Architect's clever traps were countered by Jake's tactical brilliance and Lena's technological mastery. The cold, sterile environment seemed to amplify the tension. The final confrontation involved a complex hacking sequence, a digital duel of minds, a fight for control of the facility's systems and ultimately the Architect's downfall. Lena, with her superior skill and knowledge, prevailed, disabling his defenses and exposing his operations.

The Architect, beaten but not broken, accepted his defeat with a chilling resignation. His brilliance had been turned against him, his ingenuity used as a weapon of his destruction. He knew his time was over, that his reign of terror was at an end. He was taken into custody, his chilling genius transformed into a tool of justice. He was one piece in the larger game but an important one. With the Architect's capture, another major component of the Syndicate's operations was destroyed, their infrastructure weakened, their capabilities diminished.

The final confrontation took place in a bustling metropolis, a stark contrast to the isolated settings of the previous encounters. This was a confrontation not with a single individual but with a network, a conspiracy that stretched across continents and penetrated the highest levels of power. The network, in the aftermath of Petrov's arrest and the Architect's capture, was desperate, their reach waning. They made a last desperate gamble, a final, violent attempt to assert their dominance.

Their handler, Agent Thorne, had anticipated this move, and she had laid out a comprehensive plan, a trap meticulously designed to catch the Syndicate in its own web of deceit. The trap was set in a heavily populated area, requiring precision and skill, as they had to ensure that they neutralized the threat without causing harm to innocent civilians. The final act of the play was a carefully orchestrated ballet of deception, a game of cat and mouse played out on the world stage.

The confrontation was explosive, a chaotic blend of gunfire, explosions, and close-quarters combat. Jake and Lena, utilizing their years of training and experience, navigated the chaos, their movements fluid and precise, their actions a testament to their exceptional skills and unwavering resolve. The streets were turned into a battleground and they had to use the environment to their advantage. The resulting chaos provided excellent cover for their operations.

In the end, the Syndicate's remaining forces were dismantled, their plot exposed, their network destroyed. Jake and Lena, battered but unbowed, watched as the final vestiges of the Syndicate crumbled, their power finally broken. Justice, though hard-won, had prevailed. The victory was bittersweet, however, a reminder of the sacrifices made and the lives lost. The shadows had retreated, but their presence lingered, a silent reminder of the constant struggle against darkness. The fight was over, at least for now.

Restoring Trust

The dust had settled, the immediate threat neutralized. But the victory felt hollow, a bitter taste lingering on Jake's tongue. The mission's success hadn't erased the cracks that had appeared in his relationships with his colleagues. The intense pressure, the constant deception, the near-death experiences – they had taken their toll. Trust, once a cornerstone of their operations, had crumbled under the weight of suspicion and betrayal. He felt the sting of their unspoken doubts, the icy distance in their gazes. Restoring that trust, rebuilding the fractured bonds, was now as critical as any future mission.

His first step was Lena. Their partnership had been forged in the fires of combat, a symbiotic relationship built on mutual respect and unwavering loyalty. Yet, even with Lena, a subtle shift had occurred. The shared trauma, the unspoken fears, had created a chasm between them, a silence that hummed with unspoken anxieties. He found her in the agency's quiet observation room, her usual sharp focus softened by a weariness that mirrored his own. She was reviewing data from the final confrontation, her fingers flying across the keyboard, but her eyes held a haunted look.

"Lena," he began, his voice low, "we need to talk."

She looked up, her gaze meeting his. The years of shared experiences, the unspoken understanding, flickered briefly before being extinguished again by a wall of reserve. "About what, Jake?" she asked, her tone guarded.

He hesitated, unsure how to breach the invisible barrier that had sprung up between them. "About us. About what happened."

He recounted the events of the last few weeks, his voice raw with honesty. He spoke of his doubts, his fears, the agonizing decisions he'd made under pressure. He acknowledged his mistakes, his lapses in judgment. He didn't expect absolution, only understanding. He needed to show her that he valued their partnership, that he valued her.

Lena listened, her expression unreadable. When he finished, silence hung heavy in the air. Then, she spoke, her voice quiet but firm. "I know things haven't been easy, Jake. The Syndicate... they messed with our heads. We saw things... we did things..." Her voice trailed off, a flicker of vulnerability in her eyes. "But we survived. Together."

The simple statement was a breakthrough, a crack in the ice that had formed between them. They spent the next few hours talking, unpacking their shared experiences, acknowledging the trauma, and reaffirming their commitment to each other. It wasn't a magical fix, but it was a start. The restoration of trust wasn't just a matter of words; it required action.

He approached Agent Thorne next. Their relationship had always been professional, even distant. Thorne, a woman who valued efficiency above all else, had rarely shown emotion, her demeanor consistently cool and calculated. Yet, even her impenetrable façade had shown signs of strain in the aftermath of the operation. He sought her out in her office, a stark, minimalist space reflecting her personality.

"Agent Thorne," he began, his voice respectful but firm, "I know things haven't been easy for anyone. I owe you an apology."

She looked up from her files, her gaze sharp and assessing. "For what, Riley?"

He explained the events leading to the near-compromise of their operation, accepting responsibility for his part in the incident. He laid bare his self-doubts and admitted his mistakes. He didn't try to justify his actions but to explain them, to show that he understood the gravity of the situation.

Thorne listened patiently, her expression unchanged. When he finished, she simply nodded. "Your actions had consequences, Riley. But you corrected them. The mission was a success, and that's what matters." It was not a warm endorsement, but it was an acknowledgement, a tacit acceptance of his apology. The absence of her usual cold disapproval spoke volumes.

The next few weeks were dedicated to restoring his relationships with the rest of the team. He made a concerted effort to be more open, more communicative, more willing to share his burdens and his concerns. He participated in team-building exercises, pushing himself beyond his comfort zone to foster camaraderie. He spent time getting to know his colleagues on a personal level, learning about their lives, their aspirations, their fears. He organized a small gathering, a casual dinner, as a gesture of reconciliation. It wasn't a grand gesture, but it was sincere. The team responded positively, the atmosphere easing, the cracks gradually healing. The awkward silences dissipated, replaced by genuine camaraderie.

The process wasn't easy. There were setbacks, moments of doubt, periods where old wounds reopened. But Jake persisted, his commitment unwavering. He knew that trust, once broken, required careful cultivation. It demanded honesty, empathy, and a genuine desire to connect. The process wasn't about erasing the past, but about acknowledging it, learning from it, and building a stronger foundation for the future. The shared experience of almost losing everything had created a stronger bond between the operatives. They respected each other's skills and dedication, understanding that their lives depended on each other.

Ultimately, the restoration of trust was not a single event, but a continuous process, a gradual weaving together of broken threads. It required time, patience, and a relentless commitment to transparency and accountability. The journey wasn't easy, but it brought an important result. His actions didn't magically erase the past, but they demonstrated a willingness to atone and move forward. The trust rebuilt wasn't just about their working relationships; it was about their shared humanity, their shared understanding of the sacrifices they made, and the consequences of their actions. The trust they re-established forged an unbreakable bond, a foundation upon which they would face future challenges with strength and resilience, a testament to their resilience and the strength of the human spirit. The shadows remained, but they were no longer alone in confronting them. The team was stronger, more unified, and ready for whatever the future held.

The Chase

The sleek black sedan, its tires screaming in protest against the asphalt, fishtailed around a corner, narrowly avoiding a collision with a sputtering taxi. Inside, Jake gripped the steering wheel, his knuckles white, the city a blur of neon lights and fleeting shadows. The adrenaline coursed through him, a potent cocktail of fear and exhilaration. He glanced at the rearview mirror; the pursuing vehicles, a pack of relentless wolves, were gaining ground. Their headlights, twin malevolent eyes, pierced the darkness. He pushed the accelerator harder, the engine roaring in response, a desperate plea for more speed.

This wasn't some carefully orchestrated operation; this was a chaotic, high-octane chase, a desperate flight from an unknown pursuer. The mission, a seemingly simple extraction, had gone horribly wrong. The target, a high-ranking official with sensitive information, had been compromised. Now, they were running, not toward a planned rendezvous point, but simply toward survival.

The streets of the city became a twisted labyrinth, each turn a gamble, each intersection a potential death trap. Jake weaved through traffic, his driving a reckless ballet of near misses and hair-raising maneuvers. He used his knowledge of the city's back alleys and hidden routes, the skills honed during his rigorous training, to evade his pursuers. The chase stretched on, an endless game of cat and mouse played at breakneck speed.

He caught a glimpse of Lena in the passenger seat, her face grim, her hands firmly gripping the dashboard. Her eyes, usually sharp and observant, were wide with alarm, but her expression betrayed nothing of her fear. She was a soldier, a veteran of countless covert operations, but even her steely resolve was tested by the relentless pressure of the chase. She was monitoring the comms, her fingers flying across the small, rugged device as she tried to get a sense of what exactly was going on behind them. Yet, every channel was jammed.

The city lights blurred into streaks of color, the sounds of the chase a deafening symphony of screeching tires, blaring horns, and the pounding of his own heart. Each block was a battle, each intersection a perilous gamble. He relied on instinct, on years of honed reflexes, pushing the car and himself to their absolute limits. He wasn't just driving a car; he was conducting a desperate symphony of evasion, his every move a calculated risk in a deadly game of chance.

The chase took them through the city's vibrant heart, then into its quieter, more sinister underbelly. They dodged through narrow alleyways, their tires spitting gravel, past crumbling buildings that whispered tales of forgotten lives. The shadows seemed to deepen, the darkness pressing in, as if the city itself was conspiring against them. They passed deserted docks, shrouded in mist, the silence amplified by the constant, throbbing pursuit.

Then, a sudden change of pace. The pursuers, who had been relentlessly close, inexplicably fell back. A fleeting moment of reprieve, a sliver of hope in the overwhelming darkness. Jake seized the opportunity, executing a sharp turn onto a deserted highway leading out of the city. The escape was short lived, as a helicopter appeared overhead, its searchlight piercing through the night.

The helicopter was a different ballgame. On the ground, he could use the city's labyrinthine streets to his advantage. But in the open expanse of the highway, he was a sitting duck. He had to find a way to lose the helicopter. Lena called for support, but the comms were useless.

The landscape shifted from the urban sprawl to open country, the road twisting and turning through dark, unfamiliar terrain. The helicopter continued its relentless pursuit, its shadow a menacing presence above them. The car was taking a beating, each bump and pothole a sharp reminder of their precarious situation. The suspension was failing.

Suddenly, Jake spotted it – a series of abandoned rail lines cutting through the countryside. A long shot, but it might offer a way to lose the helicopter, to break the line of sight. He swerved sharply, the car's tires protesting as they left the main road, and took the chance. The rail lines provided cover, a temporary shield against the relentless pursuit from above. The change in terrain, the bumps and the dips, were slowing the car down, but they were also confusing the helicopter.

The helicopter was still circling overhead, its searchlight a constant, menacing threat, but it was losing altitude, indicating it was running low on fuel or was struggling to maintain its position. Jake knew it was a temporary reprieve, but every second counted. Their escape was far from over; the race for survival was far from won.

They continued their dangerous journey along the abandoned tracks, each turn, each bump, filled with anxiety and anticipation. The darkness was their ally, the shadows their cloak of invisibility. Yet, a persistent feeling of being watched clung to them, as though the very air was heavy with unseen eyes. The sense of impending doom was overwhelming.

As the helicopter's rotor blades began to whine in protest, indicating their own limitations, they knew the end of the chase was not yet certain. There could be additional forces deployed, even if this helicopter disappeared, it may very well be a temporary retreat, not the end of their pursuit. The shadows still lurked, both in the dark countryside and in their own minds. The game was far from over. The hunt was still on, and their lives remained precariously balanced on a knife's edge.

The car sputtered, its engine coughing and wheezing, a testament to its battered condition. They'd driven hard, pushed the car to its limits, and it had finally responded. Jake pulled over to the side of the road, and they sat in silence, listening to the engine slowly cool. The sound of crickets chirping in the distance offered a false sense of peace, a temporary illusion in their stressful situation. The tension was palpable, the silence broken only by the rhythmic sounds of their breaths and the occasional moan from the stressed engine.

Lena finally spoke, her voice low and tight, "We need to find another way. This…this isn't sustainable." Her assessment was brutally honest, reflecting the dire reality of their situation. The car was beyond repair, at least in the field. They were stranded, vulnerable, and surrounded by an unknown enemy.

Jake nodded, his gaze fixed on the dark expanse of the countryside. He knew Lena was right. Their escape had bought them time, a precious commodity in their current predicament, but it wasn't a solution. The chase had shown them that they were being hunted relentlessly, and the situation was far from over. The question remained; what would their next move be? How would they survive? The answers lay hidden somewhere in the deep shadows, a challenge that could define their survival, and ultimately, their lives. The hunt had given way to a new and more formidable challenge: survival. The night remained fraught with danger, and the shadows held their breath. The next chapter of their desperate escape was just beginning.

Evasive Maneuvers

The battered sedan, its engine wheezing like a dying man, shuddered to a halt. The silence that followed was a stark contrast to the cacophony of the chase, a heavy blanket suffocating the already tense atmosphere. Stars, cold and indifferent, glittered overhead, offering no comfort in the oppressive darkness. Lena's breath hitched, a short, sharp intake of air, the only sound for a long, agonizing moment.

Jake ran a hand over his face, feeling the grime and sweat, the residue of their frantic escape. His mind raced, a whirlwind of strategies and contingencies, each one as desperate as the last. The abandoned rail line had bought them time, a precious commodity, but it had also left them stranded, vulnerable, miles from civilization, with a damaged vehicle and an unknown, relentless enemy.

"We need to ditch the car," Lena said, her voice devoid of emotion, a stark reflection of the situation. "It's a beacon." She was right. The car, once a tool of escape, was now a liability, a glaring signal in the vast, dark expanse. Leaving it behind was a painful decision – it was their only means of transport, their only shield against the elements. But clinging to it would be suicide.

Jake nodded, the decision already made. He was a soldier, a spy, trained to adapt, to improvise, to survive. Sentimentality was a luxury he couldn't afford. He retrieved a small, lightweight backpack from the trunk, containing supplies they'd stashed there. It held essentials: water, energy bars, a first-aid kit, and most importantly, a satellite phone, its signal hopefully strong enough to pierce the rural isolation.

They moved swiftly, silently, under the watchful gaze of the stars. They left the car where it sat, a metallic corpse in the silent landscape, and melted into the shadows, walking parallel to the abandoned rail lines, hoping to use them for cover and direction. Their objective was simple: reach a point with better cell reception, and call for extraction. The hope was fragile, the reality brutal.

Their progress was slow, hampered by the rough terrain. The darkness, once their ally, was now a constant threat, hiding unseen dangers, potential ambush points, every rustle of leaves a potential enemy. Lena, with her years of experience in clandestine operations, moved with an uncanny grace, her senses heightened, alert to any sign of pursuit. She scanned their surroundings constantly, her eyes like a hawk's, missing nothing.

They encountered a small, derelict farmhouse, its windows dark, its walls crumbling. It offered meager shelter, a momentary respite from the cold night air. Jake carefully checked the structure for signs of habitation, ensuring it was safe. They entered cautiously, the air heavy with the smell of dust and decay. The interior was desolate, nothing of value, but it provided essential concealment.

Inside, using a small, waterproof map tucked into Lena's boot, they plotted their course. The map revealed a network of secondary roads and trails, possibly leading to a nearby town. They knew it was a gamble, but it was a calculated risk, a necessary step toward survival.

They rested for a few hours, rationing their water and energy bars. Sleep was out of the question, the tension too high, the danger too real. Their conversation was minimal, exchanging only essential information, saving their energy, both physical and mental.

The satellite phone remained stubbornly silent, no signal. Their pleas for help were unanswered echoes in the vast emptiness of the countryside. Their hopes began to dwindle, replaced by a stark and chilling realization: they were on their own.

As dawn broke, painting the sky in hues of grey and orange, they set off again, following the mapped trails. The landscape changed as they moved, from the abandoned rail lines to the undulating terrain of the countryside. They passed fields of dormant crops, silent witnesses to their desperate flight. The sense of isolation was overwhelming.

They encountered several obstacles along the way, testing their resourcefulness and resilience. A swiftly flowing creek forced them to detour, adding miles to their journey. A barbed wire fence, remnant of a forgotten farm, required careful maneuvering to avoid injury. Each challenge was a test, a reminder of the harsh reality of their situation.

At one point, they heard the distant drone of a vehicle. Their hearts pounded in their chests, adrenaline surging through their bodies. They dropped to the ground, concealing themselves in the tall grass, their bodies tense, ready for action. They waited, their breath held, until the sound faded into the distance. The respite was fleeting, the tension never relenting.

The landscape changed again as they continued. The open fields gave way to a dense forest, its trees gnarled and ancient, their branches clawing at the sky. The forest offered a new set of challenges—thick undergrowth, unpredictable terrain, and the ever-present fear of being ambushed.

Their progress was slow, agonizingly slow, each step a struggle against fatigue, hunger, and the relentless pressure of their pursuers, who, they were convinced, were still out there, somewhere, unseen, their patience as endless as the countryside. The hope of rescue dwindled with each passing hour. Yet, they pressed on, driven by the instinct to survive, a primal force that pushed them to their limits.

As they emerged from the forest, they saw it—a small, barely visible road, a thread of hope in the vast emptiness. They followed the road, their weary bodies driven by a renewed sense of purpose, knowing that civilization, or at least a semblance of it, was near. They were closer to escape, but their journey was far from over. The hunt might have slowed, but it hadn't ended. The shadows still stretched long and menacing, and the end remained uncertain. Their escape remained tenuous, their survival a constant, brutal struggle against the odds. The relentless pursuit was still a shadow hanging over them, a chilling reminder that the hunt was far from over.

HighOctane Action

The road, a barely discernible ribbon of asphalt, offered little comfort. It was merely a change in the landscape, not a guarantee of safety. The exhaustion gnawed at them, a relentless predator feeding on their dwindling strength. Jake, despite his rigorous training, felt the strain. His muscles screamed in protest, his lungs burned with each labored breath. Lena, however, showed little outward sign of fatigue, her movements as precise and economical as ever. She was a machine, honed to perfection by years of brutal training and countless missions.

Rounding a bend, they spotted it – a dilapidated gas station, clinging precariously to the edge of the road like a forgotten relic. It offered a glimmer of hope, a chance to replenish their supplies and perhaps, most importantly, make contact with the outside world. But caution dictated their approach. They moved slowly, their senses heightened, scanning the area for any sign of danger. The silence, broken only by the whisper of the wind through the dried grasses, was unsettling, a stark contrast to the adrenaline-fueled chase that had preceded their arrival.

As they crept closer, Jake spotted a figure lurking behind a rusted fuel pump, his silhouette barely visible in the dim light. Instinct took over. He signaled Lena to take cover, his hand instinctively reaching for the concealed weapon holstered at his hip. Lena, ever vigilant, was already in a defensive position, her gaze fixed on the shadowy figure. The air crackled with anticipation, the silence thick with unspoken tension.

The figure moved, and Jake reacted, sprinting towards cover, his body low to the ground, using the terrain to his advantage. Lena followed, her movements fluid and effortless. They exchanged glances, a silent communication passing between them, a shared understanding of the imminent threat. They were in the heart of enemy territory.

The shadowy figure, realizing he'd been spotted, lunged from behind the pump, revealing a hulking silhouette, his weapon raised. A brief, brutal firefight erupted. The roar of gunfire shattered the pre-dawn stillness, the bullets tearing through the air. Jake, his training kicking in, returned fire with precision, each shot calculated, each movement deliberate. Lena, utilizing her superior tactical skills, provided covering fire, effectively neutralizing the adversary's position.

The confrontation was short, sharp, and incredibly violent. The figure, outnumbered and outmaneuvered, fell silent, his weapon clattering to the ground. The gas station stood as a silent testament to their close call. They moved quickly, securing the area, their senses alert for any other potential threats. The adrenaline coursed through them, a potent mix of fear and exhilaration.

Inside the gas station, they found a dusty payphone, a relic of a bygone era. The hope for a reliable signal was slim, but it was their best shot. Jake frantically dialed the number they'd been given, his heart pounding in his chest, each ring a nail-biting moment. Finally, a voice answered, a gruff, authoritative voice that cut through the tension. It was their contact, the one who could orchestrate their extraction.

"Riley? It's about time," the voice crackled over the line. Relief washed over Jake, a wave of intense gratitude. He relayed their location, their situation, the details of the encounter. The response was immediate, crisp, and devoid of emotion: "ETA fifteen minutes. Stay put." The line went dead.

They waited, the silence now a welcome reprieve, the tension significantly eased, replaced by a growing anticipation of rescue. They used the time to assess their injuries and replenish their supplies, their earlier frantic rush replaced by a controlled calmness, a professional efficiency that was second nature to them.

Fifteen minutes later, a low hum resonated in the distance. A black SUV, unmarked and nondescript, pulled up to the gas station, its presence a beacon of hope in the oppressive darkness. It was the promised extraction. Two figures emerged, their faces obscured by shadows, but their movements spoke volumes of their training and competence.

Without a word, they led Jake and Lena to the vehicle. They were whisked away from the gas station, the dilapidated building fading rapidly into the background. They were headed towards a safe house, a place where they could finally rest and recover, where the immediate threat would no longer dictate their every move. But the brief respite would soon come to an end, their reprieve from danger short-lived. The mission wasn't over; it had simply entered a new phase.

The journey was punctuated by bursts of speed, sharp turns, and tactical maneuvers that suggested their pursuers were still close behind. The chase was far from over, even if the immediate danger had abated. The SUV navigated a series of backroads and winding country lanes, each turn a testament to the driver's skill and the team's desperate need for speed. They were being hunted, and every moment was critical. The weight of the situation hung heavy in the air, the possibility of capture a chilling undercurrent in their desperate flight.

During the tense ride, they were filled in on the details of their pursuers. It was a well-organized, ruthless group with significant resources. Their escape had been a close call, and their current success merely a temporary reprieve from the relentless pursuit. The information solidified the urgency of their mission, the importance of their next steps.

Finally, they arrived at their destination, a secluded farmhouse tucked away deep within a wooded area, far removed from the prying eyes of their pursuers. The house, while seemingly innocuous from the outside, was a well-guarded sanctuary, equipped with state-of-the-art security systems and trained personnel. It was a place where they could regroup, reassess their situation, and plan their next moves. The temporary safety of the safe house, however, was merely a fleeting moment of respite. The shadows stretched long and dark, hinting at the continued threat, the constant reminder that the hunt was far from over. The game was still on.

The relief of reaching the safe house was palpable, but it was quickly replaced by a grim determination. They had escaped a deadly ambush, but the threat remained, lurking just beyond the edges of their newly found safety. The sense of urgency underscored every conversation, every decision. The next steps in the mission were crucial, and the pressure was immense. Their temporary respite was not an end in itself, but a crucial stepping stone in their continued struggle for survival and the success of their mission. Their escape was only a small victory in a larger, more dangerous war. The shadows still lingered, the hunt still pursued, and the end remained uncertain.

Strategic Advantage

The farmhouse, nestled deep within the whispering pines, offered a deceptive sense of peace. The crackling fire in the hearth cast dancing shadows on the rough-hewn walls, a stark contrast to the chilling reality of their situation. While the immediate threat of capture had receded, the weight of their mission pressed heavily upon them. This wasn't a time for rest; it was a time for strategic planning, for leveraging every advantage they could glean from their precarious position.

Jake, his body still humming with the adrenaline of the near-death experience, sat at the worn wooden table, a map spread before him. The flickering firelight illuminated the intricate details, revealing a network of roads, forests, and small towns – their potential escape routes, their potential battlegrounds. Lena, ever watchful, stood by the window, her gaze sweeping across the landscape, scanning for any sign of movement, any hint of their pursuers. She was a sentinel, her senses honed to a razor's edge, ever vigilant against the invisible threat that surrounded them.

"They know we're here," Lena stated, her voice low and measured, breaking the tense silence. "They're resourceful, and they're persistent. We can't count on our current advantage lasting for long."

Jake nodded, his eyes never leaving the map. "We need a strategic advantage," he murmured, tracing a route with his finger. "Something that will level the playing field, something that will turn the hunt into a chase on our terms."

He began to analyze their situation with clinical precision. Their current location, while secure for the moment, was isolated. Resupply was difficult, and escape routes were limited. Their pursuers, on the other hand, likely possessed superior resources and intelligence. The odds were stacked against them, but Jake was not one to surrender to adversity. He thrived on challenges, and this one promised to be his most formidable yet.

"They're expecting us to attempt a direct escape," he said, finally looking up at Lena. "They'll be watching the main roads, anticipating a conventional getaway. We need to exploit their expectations, use their assumptions against them."

His plan began to form, a tapestry woven from threads of deception and calculated risk. He proposed a daring maneuver, one that played upon the assumptions of their pursuers, turning their perceived strength into a vulnerability. They would not simply flee; they would manipulate their enemies into chasing shadows, while they slipped away unseen.

He detailed the plan to Lena, explaining every intricate step, every calculated risk. Lena, ever the pragmatist, questioned every detail, scrutinizing every potential weakness, every possibility of failure. Her scrutiny was invaluable, a necessary check on his ambition. Together, they refined the plan, honing it to a razor's edge, mitigating risks, and maximizing their chances of success.

The first element of their strategy involved a series of carefully planned diversions. They would create a series of false leads, leaving behind a trail of misleading clues to throw their pursuers off their scent. This would involve a combination of technology and old-fashioned deception, a blend of sophisticated gadgets and well-placed misdirection.

Jake utilized his knowledge of electronics to create a series of false signals, mimicking their movements, leading their pursuers on a merry chase across the countryside. Lena, meanwhile, focused on physical misdirection, leaving behind a trail of cleverly planted false clues that would lead their pursuers away from their true escape route.

Their second element hinged upon exploiting the terrain. They would utilize the natural cover of the surrounding forests and mountains, leveraging the landscape to conceal their movements and slow their pursuers down. Their knowledge of the terrain, gleaned from the map and Lena's keen observation, provided them with a significant advantage. They knew the hidden paths, the blind spots, the places where their pursuers would be most vulnerable.

The third and most crucial element involved a risky maneuver—infiltrating their pursuers' supply chain. Using their past intelligence contacts, they were able to gather information about their adversaries' logistics, their resupply points, and their communication networks. They identified a weakness, a point of vulnerability in their enemy's network that could be exploited for a decisive advantage.

This risky move involved a daring infiltration of a clandestine warehouse, a move that required impeccable timing and coordination. It was a gamble, a calculated risk that could either cripple their pursuers or lead to their own capture. But Jake, ever the gambler, believed the potential rewards outweighed the risks. The warehouse held not just supplies but also critical communication equipment – equipment that, in the right hands, could turn the tide of the hunt.

The operation was executed with surgical precision. They moved like shadows, unseen and unheard, exploiting their knowledge of the warehouse layout, navigating the maze of corridors and storage rooms. They disabled security systems, intercepted communications, and planted their own devices, subtly altering the flow of information. Their act of sabotage was subtle, yet its impact was likely to be catastrophic to their adversaries.

The final act of their strategic masterpiece involved a carefully planned escape. Having significantly hampered their pursuers' capabilities and created a diversion, they utilized a network of hidden trails and waterways, moving through the landscape with the grace and skill of seasoned professionals. They used their understanding of the terrain, the natural cover, to slip away from their pursuers, leaving them hopelessly lost, their resources depleted, their communication disrupted, effectively turning the tables on their pursuers.

They emerged from the woods, battered but not broken, their mission accomplished, their pursuers left far behind, their temporary sanctuary now a distant memory. The hunt had ended, but the mission had only just begun. They had gained a crucial strategic advantage, transforming themselves from hunted prey into hunters, a metamorphosis born from intelligence, skill, and sheer grit. The game was theirs to play, and the stakes were impossibly high.

Narrow Escape

The biting wind whipped at Jake's face as he scrambled over the jagged rocks, the icy grip of the mountain threatening to pull him down into the chasm. Below, the churning river roared a constant, ominous symphony, a stark reminder of the fate that awaited a single misstep. He risked a glance over his shoulder, the fading light painting the snow-covered peaks in shades of grey and purple. No sign of pursuit yet. Not yet.

He pressed onward, the adrenaline a potent cocktail fueling his aching muscles. This wasn't some Hollywood-style chase; this was raw, brutal survival. He was playing a game of inches, a deadly game where one wrong move meant the end. His escape route was a treacherous labyrinth of icy paths and sheer cliffs, a path chosen not for its ease, but for its inaccessibility.

He remembered Lena's words, echoing in his mind, a grim reminder of the stakes. "They won't give up easily, Jake. They're relentless. This isn't over until they're dead or we are."

He'd chosen this route, this brutal climb, precisely because it was the most difficult. His pursuers, assuming he'd take a faster, more conventional route, would be focusing their efforts elsewhere. It was a gamble, a high-stakes bet on his own endurance and their predictable habits.

The cold seeped into his bones, numbing his fingers and toes. He could feel the sting of frostbite creeping in, a silent enemy as deadly as any human pursuer. Each breath was a labored effort, his lungs burning with the thin mountain air.

He paused briefly, huddled against a rocky outcrop, attempting to regain his breath and assess his situation.

He checked his supplies: a half-empty water bottle, a dwindling supply of energy bars, and a first-aid kit – already partially depleted. He had pushed himself to the absolute limit; his body screamed in protest, but his mind was clear, focused on the task at hand. He had to reach the rendezvous point. He had to meet Lena.

The rendezvous point was a dilapidated shepherd's hut, nestled precariously on a remote hillside, a forgotten relic of a bygone era. It offered little in terms of comfort or security, but it provided a crucial element: concealment. It was a place where he could rest, regroup, and await Lena's arrival.

As he continued his ascent, he noticed subtle signs that his pursuers were not far behind. A broken branch, displaced snow, a faint track in the freshly fallen powder – all whispering tales of a relentless pursuit. They were closing in. He had to accelerate his pace, pushing himself beyond his limits.

He stumbled, his foot slipping on a patch of ice. He felt a sharp pain in his ankle as he fell, the icy ground meeting his face with a jarring impact. He scrambled to his feet, adrenaline masking the pain, his heart pounding in his chest like a war drum. He couldn't afford to stop. He couldn't afford to be caught.

He pressed on, his resolve strengthened by a grim determination. He imagined their faces, the faces of his pursuers, their relentless determination, their unwavering focus. They were relentless, but he was more so. He was fueled by a burning need to survive, to outwit his adversaries, to win this deadly game.

He finally reached the shepherd's hut, his body screaming in pain, his lungs burning, his vision blurring. He collapsed inside, the rough-hewn walls offering a meager respite from the elements. He drank the last of his water, consumed a meager energy bar, and tried to tend to his injured ankle.

The wait was agonizing, each passing moment feeling like an eternity. He strained his ears, listening for any sign of his pursuers, for any hint of their approach. The silence was broken only by the howling wind and the occasional screech of a distant bird.

Then, he heard it – the faint crack of a twig, the sound of footsteps crunching through the snow. His heart lurched in his chest. They were coming.

He grabbed his weapon, a small but deadly knife, his only defense against the imminent threat. He positioned himself strategically, his back against the wall, ready to defend himself. The sounds grew louder, closer.

The door creaked open, and a figure emerged, silhouetted against the pale moonlight. He held his breath, his senses on high alert. The figure stepped inside, the faint scent of woodsmoke clinging to their clothes. It wasn't one of his pursuers.

It was Lena.

Relief washed over him, a wave of exhaustion and gratitude. Lena looked battered but unharmed, her eyes reflecting the fierce intensity of a warrior. She had made it. They had both made it.

"They're close," Lena whispered, her voice barely audible above the wind. "We need to move, now."

They left the hut, slipping away into the shadows, leaving behind the fragile safety of their temporary refuge. They were still in danger, still hunted, but now they were together. Their escape was far from over. But for now, they had a fleeting moment to catch their breath, to plan their next move, to regroup and refocus their energies on survival. The hunt continued, but for the first time, Jake felt a flicker of hope, a spark of optimism amidst the unrelenting darkness. The game was far from over, but it was far from lost.

Urgent Mission

Lena's words, sharp and urgent, sliced through the lingering relief. "They're not after us anymore, Jake. Not directly, at least. This is something… bigger." She pulled a crumpled data chip from her pocket, its surface scratched and marred. "This came from inside. A leak from within the Agency itself."

The information contained within the chip was breathtaking in its scope. It detailed a plot to destabilize a volatile region in the Middle East, a plan so audacious and dangerous it could ignite a global conflict. A rogue faction within the Agency, it seemed, was playing a deadly game of international chess, using a series of carefully orchestrated events to spark a war. The collateral damage – millions of lives, global economic chaos – was a horrifying prospect.

Jake felt a cold dread wash over him, a chilling wave of responsibility. He had faced down assassins, outwitted ruthless operatives, and survived treacherous escapes, but this… this was different. This wasn't about individual survival; it was about preventing a catastrophe of unimaginable proportions.

Lena explained the plan: a series of seemingly unrelated attacks on key infrastructure targets – power grids, oil pipelines, communication networks – designed to create chaos and destabilize the region. The attacks, subtle and carefully planned, would be blamed on a militant group, escalating tensions and ultimately triggering a wider conflict. The Agency's rogue element was masterfully manipulating events, using the very tools of their trade to bring about their nefarious aims.

Their target was a shadowy figure known only as "The Architect," the mastermind behind the plot. The Architect was a ghost, a phantom who operated from the shadows, leaving no trace but devastation. Intelligence on the Architect was scarce, fragmented, and often contradictory. His true identity remained shrouded in mystery.

"We have a window," Lena said, her voice strained. "Forty-eight hours, maybe less. We need to stop him before he initiates the next phase of his plan."

Their mission was to infiltrate a high-security compound in Prague, a heavily fortified facility believed to be The Architect's command center. The compound was a technological marvel, protected by state-of-the-art security systems, armed guards, and sophisticated surveillance equipment. Getting in was akin to walking through a minefield.

The journey to Prague was a blur of hurried flights, clandestine meetings, and coded messages. They moved like shadows, constantly looking over their shoulders, their every move calculated and precise. They relied on a network of trusted contacts, a shadowy underworld of informants and double agents who were equally adept at deception. They exchanged information in hushed tones, their conversations cryptic and filled with coded language.

Jake felt the weight of the world on his shoulders. This wasn't just another mission; this was a race against time, a desperate struggle to prevent a global catastrophe. The stakes were higher than anything he'd ever encountered, the consequences far-reaching and devastating. The fate of millions rested on their shoulders.

The Prague compound was an imposing fortress, a monolithic structure of steel and glass that dominated the city's skyline. Its defenses were formidable, a testament to the meticulous planning and vast resources at the disposal of The Architect. Lena had procured blueprints of the facility, but even with these, the task seemed almost impossible.

Their plan was audacious, risky, and relied on a precise sequence of events. They would utilize a combination of deception, infiltration, and brute force to penetrate the compound's defenses. Jake, with his athleticism and combat skills, would serve as the primary point of entry, while Lena, with her technical expertise and intelligence network, would handle the inside operations.

They spent hours studying the blueprints, analyzing security systems, and planning their approach. Every detail was critical, every move had to be calculated with deadly precision. Failure was not an option. The thought of failure was not just unacceptable; it was unimaginable. The potential ramifications were too terrible to contemplate.

The night of the infiltration was cold and damp, the air thick with anticipation. They moved like phantoms through the city's shadows, their movements precise and almost silent. Jake, using a combination of grappling hooks and agility, scaled the compound's exterior wall, his movements fluid and effortless. Lena, meanwhile, remotely disabled the facility's external security cameras. Their coordinated effort was flawless.

Inside, they navigated a maze of corridors and security checkpoints, each step measured, every sound echoing in the vast expanse of the building. Jake used his training to disable security systems, while Lena expertly bypassed the surveillance equipment. They moved swiftly, silently, their progress a dance of evasion and precision.

They finally reached the command center, a heart of the facility, the nerve center of The Architect's operation. Inside, they found a sophisticated control room filled with monitors displaying a real-time map of the planned attacks. The evidence was undeniable; the plan was not just theoretical; it was about to be executed.

The Architect himself was not there. Instead, they found a heavily encrypted data terminal, containing the final details of the plan. Lena, with her expertise, managed to crack the encryption. The information confirmed their worst fears: the next phase of the attacks was imminent. The world was on the brink of chaos.

Just as they were about to transmit the information to their Agency contact – an ally who remained loyal – an alarm blared. The compound was on lockdown. They had been discovered. Their window of opportunity was closing.

Armed guards swarmed the corridor, their weapons trained on Jake and Lena. A firefight erupted, a desperate struggle for survival. Jake, using his combat training, fought with ferocious intensity, clearing a path through the guards. Lena, meanwhile, fought alongside him, her technical expertise proving useful in disabling the guard's weapons.

They fought their way through wave after wave of security personnel, their movements coordinated and deadly. The entire compound seemed to be against them, the building itself becoming their enemy. Every corridor was a gauntlet, every room a battlefield. They were outnumbered, outgunned, but not outmaneuvered.

Finally, after a brutal and exhausting battle, they reached a hidden exit, a secret passageway leading to the city's sewer system. They escaped the compound, leaving behind the chaos and destruction they had caused in their wake.

They emerged from the sewers, battered, bruised, and exhausted, but alive. They had successfully obtained the data and disrupted The Architect's plan, buying the world precious time. The urgency was not gone, but their work was far from over. The battle was won, but the war, the fight to unravel the entire conspiracy, was far from finished. The hunt for The Architect continued. The race against time continued. The world was safe, for now.

Time Constraints

The adrenaline coursing through Jake's veins was a tangible thing, a physical manifestation of the ticking clock. Forty-eight hours. Lena had said forty-eight hours, maybe less. Less felt more likely now, with every echoing gunshot, every flashing light in the Prague night, every strained breath they took as they navigated the labyrinthine sewer system. The escape from the compound had been brutal, a desperate scramble for survival against overwhelming odds. But even as they splashed through the fetid water, the chilling reality of their predicament settled in: they had bought time, precious time, but not enough.

The Architect's plan, as revealed in the stolen data, was a masterpiece of calculated chaos. It wasn't just about triggering a conflict; it was about engineering a specific outcome, manipulating the geopolitical landscape to suit a hidden agenda. The data revealed intricate details: specific targets, precise timing, and contingency plans that demonstrated a terrifying level of foresight. The Architect hadn't just planned for success; he had meticulously anticipated every possible setback, every potential countermeasure. This wasn't a desperate gamble; this was a meticulously crafted strategy spanning years, even decades, of patient manipulation.

They reached their pre-arranged extraction point, a nondescript alleyway near the Vltava River. A battered black sedan, driven by a woman whose face remained obscured by shadows, waited for them. Lena, her face pale but determined, collapsed onto the back seat, her breath coming in ragged gasps. Jake, despite his physical exhaustion, felt a surge of grim determination. They had accomplished something monumental, but their work was far from over. The Architect was still out there, his plan still unfolding. They had merely slowed him down, bought the world a few more precious hours.

The drive to their safe house was a blur of speeding cars and nervous glances. Lena, using a secure communication device, relayed the acquired data to their contact within the Agency, a man known only as "Sentinel." Sentinel's response was terse but reassuring: they had managed to avert an immediate catastrophe, but the threat remained. The next phase of the Architect's plan was still unknown, and the clock was still ticking.

The safe house was a spartan affair, devoid of any personal touches, its walls cold and sterile. Yet, it offered a crucial respite, a haven in the swirling storm of their mission. They immediately began deciphering the remaining encrypted data, working tirelessly to glean any clues that might lead them to the Architect's identity or his next move. The information was fragmented, deliberately obscured, a jigsaw puzzle with crucial pieces missing. Yet, there were hints, bread crumbs, subtle clues that hinted at the Architect's grand scheme.

Hours melted into a whirlwind of analysis and speculation. Jake, using his honed observational skills, noticed patterns in the data that Lena had initially overlooked. He meticulously cross-referenced information, piecing together fragmented intelligence, his mind working like a finely tuned machine. Lena, meanwhile, utilized her technological expertise to decipher complex algorithms and break through security protocols. They worked in tandem, a perfectly synchronized team, their combined expertise proving invaluable.

The pattern that emerged was chilling. The Architect's targets weren't random. They were interconnected, part of a larger strategy designed to destabilize the global financial system. The Architect wasn't just aiming for regional conflict; he was aiming for global economic collapse, a controlled implosion that would reshape the world order according to his twisted vision.

The pressure mounted with each passing hour. The time constraint wasn't just a matter of urgency; it was a matter of survival. The longer they waited, the greater the risk that the Architect would execute his plan, unleashing a catastrophic chain of events. The world was teetering on the brink, and Jake and Lena were the only ones who could stop it.

They needed more information, more pieces of the puzzle. Their initial contact, Sentinel, proved invaluable, providing additional intelligence that helped them refine their understanding of the Architect's motives and methodology. He supplied them with a list of potential associates, individuals who had been linked to suspicious financial transactions and other activities that could be related to the Architect's network. This expanded their investigation, offering new avenues of inquiry.

Sleep was a luxury they couldn't afford. They worked on instinct, fueled by adrenaline and black coffee. Each piece of information they uncovered added to their understanding, but also multiplied the pressure. The gravity of the situation was immense; they were staring into the abyss, wrestling with the very fate of the world. The world hung in the balance, its stability predicated on their success. Failure meant unimaginable global chaos.

As the final hours of their deadline approached, they made a crucial breakthrough. They identified a hidden offshore account, linked to a shell corporation registered in the Cayman Islands. This account, they realized, was the Architect's central repository for his operations. The transactions revealed a network of seemingly unrelated individuals and organizations, all connected through a complex web of coded communication and clandestine meetings.

Their next move was audacious, a high-stakes gamble based on intuition and incomplete information. They had to infiltrate the offshore account, uncover the Architect's true identity, and alert the appropriate authorities before it was too late. Time was running out. The pressure was immense, a suffocating weight on their shoulders. They had to act, and they had to act now. The world held its breath. They were racing against a shadow, a phantom, a mastermind whose plan threatened to unravel the very fabric of global civilization. This wasn't just a mission anymore; it was a desperate, life-or-death struggle against the forces of chaos. The final countdown had begun.

Risky Choices

The Cayman Islands shimmered under the tropical sun, a deceptive paradise masking a nest of viperous finance. Jake stared at the coordinates on the encrypted map, a tiny pinprick on a vast, azure canvas. This was it: the heart of the Architect's empire, a digital fortress guarded by layers of encryption and impenetrable security protocols. Lena, her face etched with a mixture of apprehension and grim determination, reviewed the plan one last time.

"The chances of success are…slim," she admitted, her voice barely a whisper. "The firewalls are formidable, the surveillance is omnipresent. One wrong move, and we're exposed."

Jake nodded, his gaze unwavering. "Slim is all we have. We can't afford to wait. The longer we delay, the more time the Architect has to solidify his position, to make his move." He tapped a finger on the screen, highlighting a specific data point. "This is our entry point. We exploit a vulnerability in their system, a backdoor left open by a careless programmer. It's risky, but it's our best shot."

The risk wasn't just theoretical; it was palpable, a suffocating presence in the air. They were operating outside the established protocols, venturing into uncharted territory. The Agency, while providing support, had explicitly warned against this level of direct confrontation. This was a rogue operation, a gamble fueled by desperation and the sheer weight of their responsibility.

Their chosen method involved a sophisticated social engineering attack, a digital infiltration disguised as a routine security audit. Lena, using her mastery of disguise and deception, impersonated a highly credentialed cybersecurity expert from a reputable firm. She fabricated a compelling backstory, complete with forged credentials and a convincing personality, creating a believable façade to gain access.

The infiltration was a nail-biting exercise in patience and precision. Hours bled into each other as Lena navigated the labyrinthine network, skillfully bypassing security measures and leaving no digital footprints. She moved with the grace of a phantom, unseen, unheard, her every keystroke a silent whisper in the digital ether. Jake, meanwhile, monitored the operation from a remote location, providing real-time support and analyzing the data streams for anomalies.

The tension was unbearable. Every ping of the server, every flicker of the screen, sent a jolt of adrenaline through them. They could feel the Architect's invisible gaze, a silent sentinel watching their every move, waiting for the slightest slip-up. The air crackled with the palpable tension of a thousand ticking clocks.

As Lena delved deeper, she discovered a network of encrypted files, a digital vault containing the Architect's innermost secrets. The encryption was formidable, far beyond anything they had anticipated. It would take hours, maybe days, to crack it using conventional methods. Time, however, was their most precious and dwindling asset.

Jake suggested a radical solution. They would use a brute-force algorithm, a digital hammer that would shatter the encryption through sheer computational power. It was a high-risk strategy, consuming massive resources and potentially triggering alerts within the system. It was the digital equivalent of throwing a grenade into a room filled with explosives.

Lena, initially hesitant, recognized the urgency. They had reached a critical juncture; delay was synonymous with failure. She initiated the brute-force attack, a digital storm unleashed upon the Architect's fortress. The process was agonizingly slow, each increment measured in agonizing minutes.

Then, as if in answer to their desperate prayer, a breakthrough. A sliver of information, a fragment of the Architect's master plan, a cryptic message embedded within the encrypted data. The message confirmed their suspicions: the Architect wasn't just aiming for financial chaos; he was aiming for global conflict. He had been manipulating events, using cleverly concealed operations, orchestrating disasters to create a world ripe for a devastating conflict between major global powers.

The data also revealed the Architect's identity: a name that sent a chill down Jake's spine – a name that echoed through the halls of power, a name that had been whispered in the corridors of government for decades. It was the name of a man thought to be dead, a man whose influence extended far beyond the realm of finance. It was the name of a ghost, now revealed as the puppet master pulling the strings of global chaos.

The revelation was stunning, almost unbearable. They had uncovered the identity of a ghost, a master manipulator, who had woven a web of deceit that stretched across continents and spanned decades. They had stared into the abyss and glimpsed the face of chaos.

Armed with this knowledge, Lena immediately initiated the final phase of their operation: alerting the appropriate authorities. They had taken a colossal risk, a gamble on a razor's edge, and against all odds, they had succeeded. Their actions would trigger a global response, bringing the Architect's carefully constructed plan crashing down.

The escape was as perilous as the infiltration. They had to cover their tracks, destroy any evidence of their intrusion, and vanish before the security systems alerted their quarry to the breach. The escape was a blur of digital maneuvers, a delicate dance in the shadows of cyberspace, a high-wire act played out on a global stage.

As the digital dust settled, they were left with a chilling realization. They had stopped a global catastrophe, averted a war, and exposed a conspiracy that had spanned decades. They had stared into the heart of darkness and emerged victorious, battered, bruised, and forever changed by the perilous choices they had made. The world remained unaware of the brink it had stood on, oblivious to the averted cataclysm. But Jake and Lena knew. They had risked everything, and they had won. The victory, however, was bittersweet. The shadows they had encountered, the darkness they had witnessed, would forever linger in their memory. The race against time had been won, but the echoes of the battle would resonate for years to come. They had faced impossible odds, made impossible choices, and survived to tell the tale. Yet, the weight of their secret, the responsibility they now carried, was a burden they would bear for the rest of their lives.

Unexpected Challenges

The Cayman Islands' idyllic façade shattered as reality intruded. The encrypted files, while revealing the Architect's identity and nefarious plan, presented a new, unforeseen hurdle. The brute-force attack, while successful in cracking the encryption, had left a digital trail, a faint but detectable disturbance in the system's activity logs. The Architect, despite his apparent obliviousness, possessed advanced monitoring capabilities; a delayed response from a seemingly minor server function was enough to raise an alert in his sophisticated security infrastructure.

Lena, her face pale but resolute, studied the escalating alerts on her console. "They're on to us," she whispered, her voice strained. The initial success felt like a distant memory, the euphoria replaced by a chilling sense of urgency. Their escape, once a carefully planned maneuver, was now a desperate race against an increasingly sophisticated adversary.

Jake, monitoring the situation from a remote server farm in Iceland, cursed under his breath. Their contingency plans, meticulously crafted during weeks of intense preparation, were rendered obsolete by this unexpected development. The Architect's security was far more resilient and adaptive than they had anticipated. He wasn't merely a financial mastermind; he was a master of digital warfare, anticipating their moves with an unnerving prescience. His systems weren't just reactive; they were proactive, learning and adapting to their intrusion in real-time.

The initial plan for a clean getaway, involving a series of carefully orchestrated digital decoys and a meticulously crafted exit strategy, was now hopelessly compromised. They needed a new plan, and they needed it fast. The situation demanded improvisation, a reliance on instincts honed through years of rigorous training and countless simulations.

Jake suggested a daring, almost suicidal, alternative: a complete network meltdown. They would overload the Architect's system with a massive data flood, a digital tsunami designed to overwhelm his defenses and create enough chaos to mask their escape. It was a high-stakes gamble, a digital equivalent of setting the entire building ablaze to escape a single room. Failure meant complete exposure, likely leading to capture, or worse.

Lena, though initially hesitant given the inherent risks, recognized the desperate nature of their predicament. They were running out of time and options. The Architect's defenses were adapting faster than they could counter. This was their last, best hope.

The execution was a heart-stopping ballet of digital destruction. Lena unleashed a series of carefully crafted digital bombs, each designed to target a specific vulnerability, cascading through the system like a chain reaction. Jake, simultaneously, deployed a series of decoy attacks, misdirecting the Architect's attention and creating a smokescreen of digital chaos. The servers groaned under the strain, their cooling systems struggling to cope with the sudden surge in activity.

The digital landscape transformed into a maelstrom of data packets, a raging storm of digital debris. The Architect's defenses, momentarily overwhelmed, struggled to maintain control. The network was teetering on the brink of collapse, a chaotic digital wasteland. It was a breathtaking spectacle of destruction, a testament to their skills, but also a harbinger of potential failure.

Amidst the chaos, Lena executed their escape strategy, deleting their digital footprints and masking their activities with a series of sophisticated countermeasures. She worked with the precision of a surgeon, each keystroke deliberate and precise. The pressure was immense, the stakes impossibly high. One wrong move could unravel everything.

As they prepared to sever their connection, they received an unexpected communication from a previously unknown source, a cryptic message embedded within the digital debris they'd created. The message was short, blunt, and alarming: "The Architect knows. He's using the chaos to cover his tracks. He's already one step ahead."

This new information plunged them back into the heart of the crisis. Their escape was no longer a simple matter of evading digital security systems; it was now a high-stakes chase against a cunning opponent who had anticipated their every move. They were no longer just escaping a digital fortress; they were fleeing a carefully laid trap.

The ensuing escape was a chaotic blur. They navigated treacherous digital pathways, narrowly avoiding detection as the Architect's systems struggled to regain control. They employed every trick and tactic in their arsenal, leaving a trail of digital red herrings and deceptive countermeasures in their wake. They employed a series of virtual private networks (VPNs) to mask their IP addresses, hopping across servers and locations, leaving the Architect's digital hounds barking up the wrong trees. They used steganography to hide crucial data within seemingly innocuous files, concealing their escape route within a torrent of meaningless information.

The final leg of their escape involved physically escaping from the server farm. They had to move quickly, using a secondary escape route they had planned only as a remote contingency. This involved a daring nighttime escape over rugged terrain, evading surveillance and avoiding capture. They were exhausted, their nerves frayed, their minds exhausted from the constant pressure and adrenaline.

Finally, they were free. Safe, for now. They were alive, and they had managed to expose the Architect's plot. But the near-miss left a bitter taste. The experience had been a brutal lesson in adaptability, underlining the unpredictable nature of their profession. They had faced insurmountable odds, defied impossible expectations, yet the victory remained precarious, tinged with the ever-present knowledge that the Architect was still out there, plotting his next move, his shadow extending over a world teetering on the precipice. The race against time had been won, but the war was far from over. The unexpected challenges had been conquered, but the shadows remained, deeper and darker than before.

Success or Failure

The Icelandic wind howled a mournful dirge, mirroring the turmoil in Jake's gut. He'd never felt such a potent cocktail of adrenaline and exhaustion. Lena, her face smudged with grime and sweat, leaned against a battered Jeep, the rhythmic thump of its engine a fragile counterpoint to the storm raging outside. Their escape from the server farm had been a near-death experience, a frantic scramble across treacherous, snow-covered terrain, punctuated by the chilling crackle of branches underfoot and the distant, echoing howl of the wind. They'd managed to shake their pursuers, at least for now. The encrypted comms link to their handler, a woman only known as "Nightingale," remained stubbornly silent. Silence, in their line of work, was often the most deafening sound.

The initial euphoria of their seemingly successful digital assault had quickly evaporated. The Architect's response had been swift, brutal, and chillingly efficient. The network meltdown had provided the perfect cover, a cacophony of digital chaos that masked their actions, but it had also served as a smokescreen for the Architect's own maneuvers. He'd used the ensuing pandemonium to subtly shift assets, reroute funds, and erase incriminating data. He'd anticipated their every move, and counteracted them with surgical precision. It was like playing chess with a grandmaster who could see ten moves ahead.

The cryptic message, the one that had shattered their hard-won sense of security, reverberated in Jake's mind: "The Architect knows. He's using the chaos to cover his tracks. He's already one step ahead." It was a chilling testament to the Architect's foresight and strategic brilliance. He wasn't just a financial mastermind; he was a digital sorcerer, manipulating the very fabric of the internet to conceal his nefarious scheme. His reach extended far beyond the Cayman Islands; this was a global network of power, influence, and deception.

The Jeep lurched as Lena started the engine. The immediate danger might be behind them, but the long-term consequences remained unclear. The Architect's influence was vast, his reach insidious. They'd exposed a significant portion of his operation, but the core of his network, the heart of his operation, remained elusive. They had uncovered a vast money laundering scheme, a sophisticated web of offshore accounts and shell corporations, a clandestine operation that threatened global financial stability. But had they truly crippled him?

The drive to Reykjavik was a blur of icy roads and silent contemplation. The harsh Icelandic landscape mirrored the desolation in Jake's heart. He'd expected closure, a sense of accomplishment after their harrowing escape, but all he felt was a gnawing unease. The victory felt hollow, tainted by the knowledge that the Architect was still out there, plotting his next move, his shadow lengthening across the globe.

In Reykjavik, the safety of a secure house provided a brief respite. Lena, ever the pragmatist, began meticulously documenting their findings, meticulously cataloging the evidence they had gathered, the digital bread crumbs they had painstakingly collected. Jake, however, struggled to shake the sense of impending doom. His intuition, honed through years of training, screamed that they were far from out of the woods. The Architect's network was vast, a labyrinthine web of connections stretching across continents. He had underestimated his opponent.

Nightingale finally contacted them, her voice devoid of emotion, a professional mask concealing whatever turmoil might lie beneath. She confirmed their findings, acknowledging the scale of the Architect's operation. She also revealed a new layer of complexity: the Architect wasn't merely a criminal mastermind; he was connected to a shadowy organization, a network far more powerful and influential than they could have imagined. The mission had evolved from a simple financial crime investigation into a far larger, far more dangerous game. They were now playing in the big leagues.

The mission briefing was brief, stark, and alarming. The Architect had anticipated their moves, prepared for this contingency. He had already begun to rebuild his network, leveraging his vast resources and connections. Their initial success, however fleeting, had been a costly mistake. It had alerted the shadowy organization, pulling them into a conflict they were woefully unprepared for. This was no longer a cat-and-mouse game; it was a war, a high-stakes conflict with a far-reaching opponent whose capabilities dwarfed anything they'd previously encountered.

The ensuing days were a whirlwind of covert operations, clandestine meetings, and near-misses. They were forced to adapt, improvising on the fly, using a combination of digital espionage and old-fashioned fieldcraft. The Architect's countermeasures were relentless, his tactics constantly evolving. He was a phantom, a ghost in the machine, his presence felt but never seen.

The chase led them from the icy wastes of Iceland to the bustling streets of London, from the sun-drenched beaches of the Mediterranean to the shadowy alleys of Hong Kong. Each location presented a new challenge, a new set of obstacles, a new layer of complexity. The pressure was immense; the stakes were impossibly high. The threat was always lurking, just beneath the surface. They were always one step behind, constantly reacting, always playing catch-up.

The climax arrived in a seemingly innocuous location: a secluded villa overlooking the Mediterranean Sea. It was a seemingly idyllic setting, a stark contrast to the tension and uncertainty that hung heavy in the air. The Architect wasn't present, but his presence was felt. His meticulous planning, his intricate strategies, his unwavering foresight were all palpable. The villa was a trap, a beautifully orchestrated snare designed to capture them.

The ensuing confrontation was a ballet of deception, a deadly dance between predator and prey. They used every skill they possessed, every tactic they had learned, every ounce of their training to survive. The final confrontation was a blur of motion and reaction. There were near misses, heart-stopping escapes, and moments of sheer desperation. The outcome remained in doubt until the very end.

In the end, they emerged victorious, but the victory was hard-won, bittersweet. They had managed to disrupt the Architect's operation, to expose his connections, to prevent him from achieving his ultimate goal, but at a heavy price. The shadows of the conflict extended far beyond their immediate victory, and the ever-present knowledge of the shadowy organization's existence hung over them. They had won a battle, but the war, that much was clear, was far from over. The world was a far more dangerous place than they could have ever imagined. The race against time was won, but the long shadow of the Architect still stretched across the horizon, a reminder of the ever-present threat lurking just out of sight. The chilling whisper of "one step ahead" haunted them, a dark premonition of the battles yet to come.

Gathering Evidence

The Reykjavik safe house, while offering a temporary reprieve from the icy winds and relentless pursuit, felt claustrophobic. Lena, her usual efficiency tempered by exhaustion, meticulously organized the digital fragments they'd salvaged: encrypted emails, fragmented financial transactions, coded messages hinting at shell corporations and offshore accounts. Each piece of data, painstakingly extracted from the Architect's crumbling digital fortress, was a tiny shard of a much larger, terrifying puzzle.

Jake, however, felt the urgency of the situation pressing down on him like a physical weight. The digital evidence was crucial, but it wasn't enough. He needed something tangible, something that could stand up in a court of law, something that could expose the Architect's connections to the shadowy organization Nightingale had mentioned. He needed proof beyond a reasonable doubt.

His first lead came from a seemingly insignificant detail buried within the recovered data: a series of coded transactions linked to a Swiss bank, a bank known for its discretion and its clientele – the ultra-wealthy and the notoriously secretive. He needed access to their archives, and that meant navigating a labyrinthine bureaucracy, bypassing layers of security protocols, and working within an impossibly tight timeframe.

The next few weeks were a blur of discreet inquiries, whispered conversations in dimly lit bars, and clandestine meetings with contacts cultivated over years of covert operations. He learned about back channels, informants, and the shadowy world of private intelligence gathering. He discovered the existence of a retired Swiss banker, a man known only as "Monsieur Dubois," who possessed unique insights into the bank's operations and was rumored to have a penchant for lucrative side deals.

Contacting Dubois proved a delicate operation. Jake had to navigate a complex web of intermediaries, utilizing a network of encrypted messaging apps and secure communication channels. The information exchange was carefully orchestrated, shrouded in secrecy and layers of plausible deniability. The risk of exposure was ever-present, a constant, gnawing fear. One wrong move, one misplaced word, could unravel everything.

Dubois, when finally reached, proved to be a pragmatic mercenary, motivated primarily by money. He agreed to share information, but only for a substantial sum, delivered in untraceable cryptocurrency. The information he provided was a goldmine: details of accounts, names of key players, and even a physical address – a secluded villa on the outskirts of Geneva, belonging to a seemingly legitimate businessman, yet linked to several of the shell corporations identified in the digital evidence.

Armed with Dubois's information, Jake and Lena headed to Geneva. The city, a picture of elegant neutrality, concealed a world of hidden wealth and clandestine operations. The Swiss archives, a bastion of privacy and discretion, presented a formidable challenge. Gaining access required navigating a complex web of regulations and permissions, a process that threatened to consume precious time. Jake, however, leveraged his resources and contacts, employing a combination of legal maneuvering and covert operations to gain entry.

The archives themselves were a treasure trove of documents, meticulously organized and meticulously protected. Jake spent days poring over records, sifting through decades-worth of financial transactions, tracking down the paper trail that linked the Architect to his global network. He discovered documents proving the laundering of billions of dollars, traced the flow of funds through a maze of shell corporations and offshore accounts, and uncovered evidence of bribery and corruption at the highest levels.

The evidence was compelling, damning, and far-reaching. It extended beyond the initial scope of their investigation, implicating influential political figures, high-ranking government officials, and multinational corporations. The implications were staggering; the scale of the conspiracy far exceeded their initial expectations. They were dealing with a web of deceit that reached the highest echelons of power, a conspiracy capable of destabilizing global markets and undermining democratic institutions.

But the physical documents weren't enough. They needed irrefutable proof, something beyond suspicion and circumstantial evidence. They needed to tie the Architect directly to the shadowy organization. This led them to a series of research facilities, think tanks, and private intelligence agencies, each guarded closely and each holding a piece of the puzzle.

Their investigation led them to a seemingly innocuous academic institution, a think tank specializing in global economics and financial security. However, this seemingly legitimate façade masked a deeper involvement in the conspiracy. Through a contact within the institution, a disillusioned researcher who had grown weary of the organization's clandestine activities, they gained access to a hidden server room. The server room held the missing piece of the puzzle: a database containing encrypted communications between the Architect and the leadership of the shadowy organization.

The decryption of the communications proved to be the most challenging task yet. It required a combination of advanced cryptographic techniques, digital forensics, and a healthy dose of luck. They spent sleepless nights deciphering coded messages, working through layers of encryption and obfuscation. Finally, the fruits of their labor were revealed – a series of emails and chat logs detailing the Architect's role within the organization, his contributions to the money laundering scheme, and his plans for exploiting the global financial system. The evidence was concrete, irrefutable, and deadly.

The evidence, meticulously documented and securely stored, was now ready. It was time to deliver the final blow. The carefully compiled evidence, the digital fragments, the physical documents, the decrypted communications – all pointed to the same devastating truth. The Architect wasn't just a financial criminal; he was a key player in a far-reaching conspiracy, a pawn in a larger, far more dangerous game. The evidence pointed to a global network of power, influence, and corruption, a network far more powerful and insidious than anyone had ever imagined. The game, it seemed, was far from over. The pursuit of truth had led them down a rabbit hole, a treacherous descent into a world of shadows and deceit, a world where the line between right and wrong blurred, and the stakes were impossibly high. The Architect might be one step ahead, but they were closing in. The unraveling had begun.

Connecting the Dots

The Reykjavik safe house had yielded a treasure trove of digital debris, but the fragmented data felt like grasping at smoke. Lena, ever the pragmatist, had meticulously organized the digital shards, painstakingly piecing together the fractured narrative. Encrypted emails hinted at shell corporations, financial transactions danced around offshore accounts like phantoms, and coded messages whispered of shadowy figures pulling strings from the periphery. Yet, it remained a mosaic of tantalizing clues, lacking the cohesive narrative needed for a conviction. The Architect, it seemed, was a master of obfuscation, his digital footprints carefully erased, leaving behind only a trail of breadcrumbs leading to a labyrinthine conspiracy.

My gut told me the digital trail was just the tip of a much larger iceberg. I needed something tangible, something that could stand up in a court of law, something that would force the Architect out of the shadows and into the light. The fragmented data, however, pointed to something larger than just financial crimes; it hinted at a political conspiracy of immense scale. The pieces wouldn't fall into place until I understood the motives of those pulling the strings, their ultimate goals, and the method by which they sought to achieve them. The answer, I sensed, lay not just in the digital realm but in the real world, hidden within the carefully constructed facades of seemingly respectable institutions.

My first breakthrough came from an unexpected source: a seemingly innocuous news article detailing a series of suspicious land deals in the Cayman Islands. The names of companies involved mirrored some of the shell corporations we'd uncovered in the Architect's digital footprint. A deeper dive revealed a network of offshore accounts, cleverly disguised behind layers of anonymous trusts and shell companies. The trail led to a renowned tax haven, a place where secrecy was not just a privilege but a highly profitable business model.

The Cayman Islands were notoriously difficult to penetrate, a financial black hole where money flowed freely, untraceable and unregulated. My contacts in the region, a mix of former law enforcement officials and disgruntled insiders, proved invaluable. They provided me with local insights, navigating the labyrinthine bureaucracy and pointing me towards individuals who might be willing to cooperate in exchange for the right incentives. It was a dangerous game, operating in a jurisdiction known for its ruthlessness towards those who dared to expose its secrets.

One contact, a former Cayman Islands attorney disillusioned with the system, pointed me towards a specific individual – a seemingly unremarkable accountant working for a prestigious accounting firm. This accountant, however, was privy to the inner workings of some of the most secretive offshore trusts and shell companies. He had an unusual access to information, and after months of carefully cultivating a relationship, he finally agreed to meet. The meeting took place in a secluded beach bar, a carefully chosen location to maintain secrecy and plausible deniability.

The information the accountant revealed was explosive. He confirmed the suspicions I'd formed from the digital evidence and provided irrefutable documentation linking the Architect to several high-profile politicians and business tycoons. The accountant's records also revealed a series of coded transactions, which led me down another rabbit hole. These transactions, I discovered, were linked to a seemingly legitimate charitable foundation, a façade for a far more sinister operation. It was a money laundering scheme of immense proportions, channeling billions of dollars through a network of shell corporations and offshore accounts.

The charitable foundation, I learned, had a global reach, funding various projects under the guise of philanthropy. Yet, a closer examination revealed that many of these projects served as a cover for illegal activities, such as arms trafficking and political manipulation. The money flowed through a maze of shell companies and offshore accounts, making it virtually impossible to trace. I had to dismantle this complex network layer by layer, meticulously uncovering the links and tracing the flow of funds.

This involved a perilous journey across the globe – from the bustling financial centers of London and Hong Kong to the isolated tax havens of the British Virgin Islands and the Bahamas. Each location offered a new piece of the puzzle, each encounter a risky gamble. I relied on a network of informants, leveraging relationships cultivated over years of covert operations. Some were former colleagues, others were disgruntled insiders seeking revenge against the corrupt systems they'd served. They provided me with critical information, often at great personal risk.

In Hong Kong, I met with a former intelligence officer who had access to the internal workings of a major global bank. He provided me with details of a secret offshore account linked to the Architect, confirming the suspicions I'd previously held. The account, held under a false name, contained billions of dollars in illicit funds. The information he provided helped me piece together the financial puzzle, revealing a complex network of shell corporations and offshore accounts, carefully structured to conceal the true origins of the money.

My investigation also took me to Washington D.C., where I met with a disillusioned former government official. He had grown weary of the corruption he'd witnessed and decided to expose the Architect's connections to a group of powerful individuals in the government. The information he provided implicated a number of influential politicians, revealing a pattern of bribery and influence peddling. It was a breathtaking exposure of corruption, reaching the highest echelons of power.

The pieces of the puzzle, once scattered and seemingly unrelated, began to fall into place. The Architect wasn't merely a financial criminal; he was a key player in a far-reaching conspiracy, a pawn in a larger, far more dangerous game. I now understood the scale of his operation, the extent of his influence, and the sheer audacity of his ambition. He was pulling strings from the shadows, manipulating governments and global markets for his personal gain. And his network of allies was far larger and more powerful than I could have ever imagined.

The truth was a chilling revelation, a web of deceit and corruption that extended to the highest levels of power. It was time to expose them. The unraveling had begun, but the road ahead promised to be fraught with danger and uncertainty. I knew the Architect was powerful, well-connected, and ruthless. He would fight back with every resource at his disposal. But I was ready. The game was far from over.

Unforeseen Consequences

The exposure of the Architect's sprawling network didn't come without a price. My meticulously crafted plan, built on years of experience and countless sleepless nights, began to unravel with the publication of the first article in the *Guardian* . The piece, a carefully worded exposé, revealed only a fraction of what I knew, strategically omitting the most sensitive details while highlighting enough to send shockwaves through the global financial system.

The immediate reaction was chaos. Stock markets plummeted, wiping billions off the value of companies linked to the Architect. Investigations were launched in multiple countries, spearheaded by governments desperate to distance themselves from the scandal. The political fallout was immediate and devastating, with several high-profile politicians resigning amidst allegations of bribery and corruption. The Architect, however, remained elusive, a ghost in the machine.

But the ripples extended far beyond the headlines. My network of informants, the brave souls who had risked everything to help me expose the truth, suddenly found themselves in immense danger. The Architect, wounded and cornered, retaliated with brutal efficiency. Threats and intimidation became commonplace, forcing some of my most valuable contacts to go into hiding, their lives hanging in the balance. The weight of their vulnerability pressed heavily on me; I had promised to protect them, and now, I was failing.

One such instance involved Anya Petrova, a former Russian intelligence officer who had provided me with crucial information about the Architect's activities in Eastern Europe. She had been instrumental in uncovering a network of shell companies used to funnel money into a pro-Kremlin political party. Days after the *Guardian* article, she was attacked in her apartment in Prague. While she survived the attack, she was left severely injured, her life irrevocably altered. The responsibility for her suffering weighed heavily on me, a bitter reminder of the collateral damage inherent in my chosen profession.

The unexpected consequences weren't limited to my informants. My own life became a target. Anonymous threats flooded my inbox, menacing phone calls kept me awake at night, and I sensed a chilling presence watching my every move. The Architect's reach was far greater than I had initially anticipated; his network of informants and enforcers extended far beyond the financial world, penetrating even the most secure agencies. My security detail, though highly trained and skilled, felt increasingly inadequate against the relentless pressure.

The pursuit of the Architect became a dangerous game of cat and mouse. I was constantly on the move, flitting between safe houses in different countries, relying on a network of trusted colleagues and allies for support. The paranoia became all-consuming; I questioned every contact, every meeting, every shadow that fell across my path. The line between paranoia and reality blurred, making it difficult to distinguish between genuine threats and mere anxieties.

The pressure also manifested itself in my relationship with Lena. The strain of living under constant threat, the burden of responsibility, and the emotional toll of seeing my network suffer took their toll. While Lena understood the risks associated with our work, she couldn't fully comprehend the relentless pressure I was under. The walls between us began to close, our conversations growing strained and infrequent. The work had consumed me, leaving little room for our personal lives.

Another unexpected development came in the form of an alliance. A rival intelligence agency, one we'd previously clashed with, unexpectedly offered their assistance. Their offer was not altruistic; they sought to capitalize on the unraveling of the Architect's network, a move to gain an advantage in the global geopolitical landscape. Their help was invaluable, granting us access to information previously locked away, but it came with strings attached: information exchange, strategic compromises, and the inherent risk of betrayal. I had to weigh the value of this uncertain alliance against the risk of compromising my integrity and jeopardizing the mission.

The chase led me to unexpected corners of the globe, from the bustling souks of Marrakech to the remote jungles of the Amazon. Each location presented its own unique challenges and dangers. In Marrakech, I had a tense encounter with a member of the Architect's inner circle. The meeting, disguised as a business transaction, nearly ended in a deadly confrontation. Only quick thinking and years of honed reflexes prevented the situation from escalating into a violent exchange. In the Amazon, I had to navigate through treacherous terrain, evading the Architect's mercenaries while simultaneously gathering evidence from a hidden jungle encampment.

The culmination of the chase led to a hidden island in the South Pacific. This seemingly idyllic location served as the Architect's final redoubt, a heavily fortified sanctuary where he planned to escape and potentially regroup. The final confrontation was a mixture of tactical maneuvering and brutal force, a desperate fight for survival. The island was teeming with mercenaries, armed to the teeth, fiercely loyal to their enigmatic employer. It became a battle of wits, strategy, and survival, a test of my training, skills, and resolve.

The experience fundamentally changed me. The weight of my actions, the consequences of my decisions, etched themselves onto my soul. The line between right and wrong became increasingly blurred, the path to justice a twisted road paved with moral compromises. The victory felt hollow, overshadowed by the price exacted. The scars, both physical and emotional, served as a constant reminder of the cost of truth, the devastating power of deceit, and the unforeseen consequences of exposing it. The Architect's fall was a pyrrhic victory, a triumph that left me questioning the very nature of justice and my own place within it. The world continued to turn, oblivious to the shadows I had fought in, the sacrifices I had made, and the price I had paid. The silence after the storm proved to be the most deafening part.

Revealing the Mastermind

The humid air hung heavy in the Bangkok alley, a stark contrast to the sterile, climate-controlled environments I'd grown accustomed to. Sweat beaded on my forehead, blurring the already hazy neon glow reflecting off the slick, rain-washed streets. My contact, a wiry old man named Chai, had led me here, to a dilapidated temple nestled amongst the towering skyscrapers of the city's sprawling metropolis. He'd been strangely evasive, his usual boisterous demeanor replaced by a nervous fidgeting that spoke volumes. This wasn't about another financial lead, another shell corporation. This felt… different. This felt final.

Chai pushed open a rotting wooden door, the hinges groaning in protest like a dying man's last breath. The air inside was thick with the scent of incense and decay, a suffocating blend of spirituality and neglect. A single flickering oil lamp cast long, dancing shadows across the dusty floor, illuminating a figure seated cross-legged on a worn prayer mat.

The figure was older than I'd expected, his face a roadmap of wrinkles etched by time and hardship. His eyes, however, held a chilling sharpness, a steely glint that belied his frail appearance. This wasn't the Architect. This was something far worse. This was the puppeteer, the one who had pulled the strings, the mastermind behind the intricate web of deceit I'd spent years unraveling.

"You came," the old man rasped, his voice a dry whisper that barely carried across the small chamber. "They told me you would." His gaze pierced me, an unnerving intensity that left me feeling exposed, vulnerable. He knew more than he let on; he knew my methods, my motivations, my fears.

"They told me you were the Architect's right hand," I replied, keeping my voice even, despite the tremor in my hands. "But that's a lie, isn't it?"

A slow, almost imperceptible smile curled his lips. "The Architect? He was a pawn, a necessary piece on the board, nothing more." He chuckled, a dry, rasping sound that echoed eerily in the stillness of the temple. "Such a pathetically ambitious fool. He thought he controlled the game. He was merely a tool."

The truth, when it finally hit me, was a crushing blow. This old man, this seemingly insignificant figure hidden in a forgotten corner of Bangkok, was the true architect of the chaos, the orchestrator of the global financial crisis, the puppet master pulling the strings from the shadows. His name, he revealed, was Kaito Tanaka. And his motives were far more insidious, far-reaching, than anything I could have ever imagined.

Tanaka explained his plan, a chilling narrative of decades-long manipulation, a slow, meticulous unraveling of global financial systems for a far more insidious purpose than simple profit. It was about control, about power, about reshaping the world order to fit his twisted vision. He hadn't simply wanted wealth; he'd wanted dominion.

His intricate web of shell corporations, the laundering schemes, the offshore accounts – all meticulously crafted pieces in a game of global chess. The Architect had been his most significant piece, a reckless but effective pawn used to destabilize economies and sow discord. But Tanaka himself remained untouchable, his vast network of informants and enforcers spread across the globe, ensuring his absolute anonymity.

The revelation shook me to my core. I had spent years chasing the Architect, believing him to be the ultimate villain, the mastermind behind the conspiracy. I had focused on the wrong target, driven by the immediate threat, ignoring the larger, more sinister shadow that lurked behind him. The weight of this realization was overwhelming, a profound sense of failure gnawing at my conscience. Years of effort, countless sacrifices – all seemingly for naught.

Yet, Tanaka's confession wasn't simply a victory for him. He revealed a vulnerability, a chink in his otherwise impenetrable armor. His motivations, as grand and ambitious as they were, were driven by a deep-seated resentment, a decades-old grievance. A personal vendetta against a global system he felt had wronged him. This personal vendetta was the keystone in his elaborate scheme. It was also his ultimate weakness.

My previous understanding of the situation, built on painstakingly gathered intelligence and years of painstaking investigation, now felt flimsy, almost childish. The Architect's network, vast and intricate as it was, was simply a distraction, a carefully constructed smokescreen obscuring the true architect of the conspiracy.

Tanaka's explanation continued for hours, a chilling narrative of betrayal, manipulation, and calculated risk. He detailed his strategy, his meticulous planning, the years of preparation that had culminated in the near collapse of the global financial system. He spoke of his carefully cultivated network of informants, his loyal enforcers, and the layers of security that protected him from detection.

As he spoke, the image of the Architect, once a symbol of power and ambition, dwindled into insignificance. He was reduced to a pawn, a mere instrument used by a far more sinister, far more cunning mastermind. Tanaka's revelation shattered my assumptions, rewriting the narrative of the past years. The truth was far more complex, far more disturbing than I had ever imagined.

The weight of this realization pressed down on me, a suffocating burden. I had devoted years to chasing a phantom, a decoy, while the true mastermind had remained hidden in plain sight, manipulating events from the shadows. The sense of betrayal was immense, not just from the Architect, but from myself. I had been outmaneuvered, outwitted, and outsmarted by a master strategist who had meticulously planned his ascent to global power.

Tanaka's explanation also provided critical insights into his operations. He detailed the security protocols, the layers of encryption, and the hidden communication channels used by his network. This information was crucial, not only to dismantle his empire, but also to protect the world from future attacks of such magnitude. The sheer scale of his operation was staggering, reaching into every corner of the globe, manipulating financial markets, political systems, and even international relations.

However, amid the chilling details of his plan, I found a glimmer of hope. Tanaka's deep-seated resentment, the emotional engine driving his ambitions, presented a vulnerability. It was a personal flaw, a crack in the seemingly impenetrable fortress of his strategic mind. This personal weakness could be exploited, offering a possible path to his downfall. This was my new target, my new focus. The fight was far from over.

The air in the temple grew heavy with the weight of secrets revealed. My mission had changed. It was no longer about bringing down the Architect; it was about dismantling Tanaka's empire, exposing his machinations to the world, and preventing him from carrying out his ultimate goal: the reshaping of the world order according to his twisted vision. The stakes had been raised exponentially, the dangers magnified. But I was ready. Years of training, countless missions, and the weight of past failures fueled a new resolve within me. The fight was far from over. This was only the beginning.

Exposure and Confrontation

The flickering oil lamp cast long shadows, dancing grotesquely on the weathered stone walls as Tanaka continued his chilling monologue. He spoke of betrayals, meticulously planned coups, and the insidious erosion of trust that had allowed him to build his empire. He'd infiltrated governments, manipulated international organizations, and controlled the flow of information with a cold, calculated precision that left me breathless. His words painted a picture of a world teetering on the brink of collapse, a world he had been subtly, yet effectively, guiding towards his own twisted vision of global order.

He spoke of his early life, a tale of profound injustice and crippling poverty that had fueled his insatiable hunger for power. It wasn't simply greed; it was a thirst for revenge, a burning desire to dismantle the system that had, in his eyes, wronged him. He saw himself as a righteous avenger, a revolutionary correcting the injustices of the world. The irony wasn't lost on me; his methods were far more destructive than the system he sought to overthrow.

The humid Bangkok air felt stifling, the incense smoke thick in my lungs. My mind raced, trying to process the sheer magnitude of his operation, the intricate web of deceit he'd spun. Each revelation was a blow, a gut punch that left me reeling. Yet, even as I felt the weight of his monstrous machinations, a flicker of hope ignited within me. His confession, while terrifying, also revealed a crucial vulnerability – his intensely personal vendetta.

Tanaka finished his confession, a long, chilling breath escaping his lips. The silence that followed was heavy, pregnant with the weight of the secrets revealed. The oil lamp sputtered, casting an even more ominous glow on his face, his eyes gleaming with a mixture of triumph and weariness. He had laid bare his soul, his motives, his entire plan. And now, he waited.

I remained silent for a long moment, absorbing the enormity of the information he'd given me. The years of investigation, the countless dead ends, the sacrifices – it all culminated in this moment, this confrontation in a forgotten temple in the heart of Bangkok. The stakes were higher than ever before. Failure wasn't an option.

"You believe you've won," I finally said, my voice low and steady, despite the turmoil raging inside me. "You think you've outsmarted everyone."

Tanaka chuckled, a dry, rasping sound that echoed in the stillness of the temple. "I have," he said, his voice devoid of any emotion. "I have played the game perfectly. I have achieved my goal."

"Not yet," I countered, pulling a small, almost invisible device from my pocket. It was a specialized listening device, designed to pick up even the faintest whispers. I had placed it discreetly during our conversation, recording his confession, his plan, his vulnerabilities. It was my insurance policy, my ace in the hole.

His eyes widened fractionally, a flicker of surprise crossing his face. He had anticipated everything, meticulously planned every step, but he hadn't accounted for my resourcefulness.

"You underestimate me," I said, a hint of steel in my voice. "You believe you control the game, but you're wrong. I have the proof. Your entire operation, your meticulously crafted plans, your every secret – it's all documented. The world will know what you've done."

The surprise on Tanaka's face quickly morphed into a calculating rage. He lunged, a sudden burst of unexpected energy from his frail frame. He moved with surprising speed, a blur of motion in the dimly lit temple. I reacted instinctively, years of training kicking in. We grappled, the fight a desperate, brutal ballet of movement and counter-movement.

The temple, already dilapidated, threatened to crumble around us as our struggle intensified. The air was thick with the scent of sweat, dust, and desperation. He was stronger than he appeared, his movements sharp and precise, fueled by years of experience and a lifetime of resentment. But I had the advantage of training and surprise.

The fight was fierce, a brutal exchange of blows in the claustrophobic confines of the temple. I fought with a ferocity born of years of preparation and the weight of my mission. The recording device, clutched firmly in my hand, became a shield, a symbol of my resolve.

Despite his surprise and the initial advantage he had, Tanaka's strength waned as he struggled against me. His years, his weariness, caught up with him. His movements became slower, his blows weaker. He had lost the element of surprise, and his carefully constructed confidence began to crumble.

My training, relentless and brutal, paid dividends. I had the edge in technique, strategy, and stamina. I used his own rage against him, redirecting his blows, anticipating his movements, until finally, I managed to subdue him.

The fight exhausted me, leaving me breathless and bruised. But I had won. I had captured him, securing the evidence that would expose his decades-long reign of terror. The weight of the years of investigation, the close calls, the sacrifices all became worth it in that moment. The recording was my key to unraveling his global network, dismantling his empire, and bringing him to justice.

The silence that followed the fight was different this time. It wasn't the heavy silence of unspoken secrets; it was the quiet hum of victory. The battle was won, but the war was far from over. The long road of dismantling his vast network lay ahead, a daunting task, but I was ready. I had exposed the mastermind, initiated a dramatic confrontation and the thrilling climax of a decades-long clandestine operation. The world would soon know the truth, and Kaito Tanaka would face the consequences of his actions. The air in the temple was thinner now, the oppressive humidity replaced by a newfound clarity and determination. The fight for justice was far from over, but tonight, I had won a significant battle. And that victory, hard-earned and deeply satisfying, gave me the strength to face whatever challenges lay ahead.

Bringing Down the Empire

The humid Bangkok air hung heavy, thick with the scent of jasmine and impending rain. Tanaka's capture was only the first domino. His confession, meticulously recorded on the tiny device nestled securely in my pocket, was the key, but it was just the beginning. His empire, vast and intricate, stretched across continents, its tendrils wrapped around governments, corporations, and even seemingly innocuous charities. Dismantling it would require a coordinated global effort, a delicate dance of international cooperation and clandestine operations.

My first step was to contact Langley. The encrypted communication channel crackled to life, connecting me to my handler, Agent Sterling. Her voice, usually calm and collected, held a note of restrained excitement. "Riley, you've done it. You've brought down the Serpent. We have confirmation of the recording. It's everything we hoped for and more."

Sterling's words spurred me into action. We coordinated the next moves, a carefully choreographed ballet of simultaneous raids across multiple continents. Teams in Hong Kong, Zurich, and London moved in tandem, targeting key financial institutions, shell corporations, and safe houses linked to Tanaka's network. Each arrest was a victory, each seized document another piece of the puzzle. The operation unfolded with clockwork precision, a testament to the agency's meticulous planning and the skill of the operatives involved.

The Swiss authorities, alerted discreetly through diplomatic channels, apprehended several key financial managers who laundered Tanaka's illicit gains. In Hong Kong, a team, working under the guise of a routine tax audit, seized several warehouses brimming with counterfeit goods, weapons, and documents detailing years of corruption. The raid in London targeted a high-profile lawyer, a conduit for Tanaka's legal maneuvering, his network's sophisticated defense mechanism. His apprehension unravelled a complex web of offshore accounts and shell corporations that had masked Tanaka's financial empire for years.

As the net tightened around Tanaka's organization, the world started to take notice, though the specifics remained shrouded in secrecy. News reports hinted at a major crackdown on organized crime, but the full scope of the operation, the identity of the mastermind, and the sheer scale of the network remained hidden behind carefully constructed press releases and carefully worded statements from government officials.

But Tanaka's reach was far greater than just finance. His tentacles extended into the political arena, influencing elections, manipulating politicians, and sowing seeds of discord across nations. The revelations from seized documents and intercepted communications were shocking. They exposed a vast web of corruption that spanned decades, influencing policy decisions, undermining international agreements, and threatening global stability.

The task of exposing these connections was immense. It required painstaking analysis of mountains of digital and physical data, cross-referencing information from various sources, and using sophisticated analytical tools. Days blurred into nights, fueled by coffee, determination, and the grim satisfaction of slowly unraveling Tanaka's intricate web of deceit. Slowly but surely, we began to build a detailed picture of his political influence, meticulously documenting every bribe, every threat, every manipulation.

We uncovered a trove of information showing Tanaka's involvement in a series of political assassinations, coups, and destabilizing actions across several nations. His goal wasn't simply wealth accumulation; it was the creation of a new world order, one molded to his own twisted vision of global power. He had been pulling strings from the shadows for decades, expertly manipulating global events for his own nefarious purposes.

The dismantling of his political network required a different approach. Direct confrontation would be too risky, too likely to cause unintended consequences. Instead, we opted for a more subtle strategy, using the evidence we had gathered to leverage our influence and expose his crimes. We leaked carefully selected information to trusted journalists, feeding them details that would grab public attention, pieces of the puzzle that, when put together, would paint a clear picture of Tanaka's treacherous operations.

The media frenzy that ensued was precisely the effect we were aiming for. Nations around the world demanded explanations, investigations were launched, and politicians who had been implicated in Tanaka's scheme were forced to resign or face criminal charges. His network began to crumble, his power diminished, his carefully constructed facade dissolving before the eyes of the world. The global community watched, transfixed, as Tanaka's empire started to collapse.

The final act played out in a stark courtroom in The Hague. Tanaka, pale and subdued, sat in the dock, his once confident demeanor replaced by a stunned, hollow shell. The evidence against him, overwhelming and irrefutable, was presented methodically, piece by piece. His reign of terror, his meticulously crafted web of deceit, was laid bare for all to see.

The trial was a spectacle, a culmination of years of investigation, a testament to the relentless pursuit of justice. The courtroom was packed with journalists, diplomats, and observers from around the world, all eager to witness the downfall of the man who had threatened to reshape the global order. His defense crumbled, his pleas of innocence ringing hollow against the weight of undeniable evidence.

The verdict was a resounding guilty. Tanaka was sentenced to life imprisonment, his legacy reduced to a footnote in history, a testament to the futility of evil ambition. The finality of the sentence resonated far beyond the courtroom, sending a wave of relief across nations and echoing a potent message: No one is above the law, even those who wield power from the shadows.

The victory was hard-won, the road to justice long and arduous. But as I watched Tanaka being led away, his power definitively broken, I felt a profound sense of satisfaction. The weight of the mission, the pressure, the sleepless nights, the risks taken – it all coalesced into a potent feeling of accomplishment. The fight had been intense, the challenges monumental, but justice, in the end, had prevailed. The world was a safer place, and the empire had fallen. My role in bringing Tanaka to justice had been challenging and dangerous, but ultimately, deeply rewarding. The sense of closure was immense. The long shadow cast by Kaito Tanaka finally began to fade.

Collaboration and Teamwork

The success of Operation Serpent's Fang hinged not just on meticulous planning and individual skill, but on the seamless collaboration of a highly specialized team. My role, while crucial in obtaining Tanaka's confession, was merely one piece of a complex, interlocking puzzle. The dismantling of his empire required a symphony of coordinated efforts, a ballet of intelligence gathering, tactical maneuvers, and legal maneuvering. The sheer scale of the operation demanded a team that functioned not just as individuals, but as a single, highly efficient organism.

Our team, a handpicked selection of specialists from various backgrounds and disciplines, was based primarily in Langley, but our operations spanned the globe. We had cyber warfare experts who could navigate the labyrinthine digital world, penetrating firewalls and extracting crucial data from Tanaka's encrypted servers. Our linguists, masters of arcane dialects and obscure codes, deciphered intercepted communications and translated mountains of documents seized during raids. Financial analysts, forensic accountants, and legal experts meticulously unravelled the tangled web of shell corporations, offshore accounts, and complex financial transactions that masked Tanaka's illegal activities. And, of course, the field operatives, the silent shadows who moved through the night, executing arrests, securing evidence, and maintaining the operational integrity of the mission.

The heart of our collaborative efforts was the secure communication network, a sophisticated system built on encrypted channels, secure servers, and foolproof protocols. This wasn't just about sharing information; it was about coordinating actions, adapting to unforeseen circumstances, and ensuring the safety of each team member. Real-time updates, streamed from across the globe, allowed us to monitor the progress of each raid, analyze emerging threats, and adjust our tactics as needed. One wrong move, a single lapse in communication, could jeopardize the entire operation. The constant flow of data, the shared decision-making, the unwavering reliance on one another – these were the pillars upon which our success was built.

One particular incident highlighted the importance of this constant communication. During the Hong Kong raid, the team encountered unexpected resistance. Initially, it appeared to be a routine warehouse seizure – a straightforward operation. However, as the team secured the perimeter, they stumbled upon a hidden basement containing a heavily armed security detail. The initial plan had not accounted for this added layer of security. The team leader, a seasoned operative code-named "Nightingale," immediately contacted Langley. The situation was relayed to our tactical experts, who, utilizing the real-time video feed, rapidly assessed the situation and devised a new strategy. We rerouted a SWAT team from a nearby operation, providing Nightingale's team with crucial backup. The backup team arrived just as the situation threatened to escalate beyond the Hong Kong team's capabilities. The swift response, the seamless coordination between teams thousands of miles apart, averted a potentially disastrous outcome. The precision and timing of this intervention were exemplary, a testament to the power of our collaborative network.

The collaboration extended beyond the tactical field. The legal team worked in tandem with the intelligence officers, ensuring that every piece of evidence gathered was admissible, meticulously documented, and prepared for court. The intricate paper trail of Tanaka's financial empire required painstaking cross-referencing and analysis, which was only possible through the combined expertise of financial analysts, forensic accountants, and legal experts. They worked day and night, piecing together the puzzle, building a solid case that would withstand even the most aggressive legal challenges.

The Zurich operation demonstrated a different kind of collaboration – one that involved international diplomacy and strategic partnerships. To secure the cooperation of Swiss authorities, we utilized diplomatic channels, working closely with our Swiss counterparts to provide them with sufficient evidence to justify the raid. This required careful negotiations, precise communication, and meticulous presentation of information. We ensured the Swiss authorities understood the wider context of the operation, the global ramifications of Tanaka's actions, and the potential damage his organization posed to their own financial system. The Swiss authorities, impressed by the depth of our evidence and the seriousness of the threat, willingly cooperated, ensuring a smooth and successful raid. The success of the Zurich operation served as a model for future collaborations with other international agencies.

The London operation similarly required a different level of collaboration, focusing on the legal and political aspects of the case. The apprehension of the high-profile lawyer who acted as Tanaka's legal shield required careful coordination with British authorities. This was a delicate dance, a balancing act of providing sufficient evidence to justify the arrest while maintaining operational secrecy. The involvement of the British authorities ensured that the operation remained within the legal framework, avoiding any potential breaches of international law or damage to diplomatic relations. This meticulous approach emphasized the importance of legal considerations throughout the operation. Every action, every move, was planned and executed with an eye towards achieving justice within the confines of the law.

The collaboration continued even after Tanaka's arrest. The sheer volume of evidence gathered required a dedicated team of analysts to sift through and organize it. This involved not only technical expertise in data analysis and information management, but also collaboration with historians, political scientists, and economists. We collaborated with various governments and institutions to analyze the political implications of Tanaka's actions, helping them identify and address the long-term damage caused by his network. The collaboration didn't end with Tanaka's conviction; it extended into the realm of damage control, rehabilitation, and preventing future occurrences of similar organized crime.

Collaboration was not merely a strategy; it was the very lifeblood of the operation. It was the glue that held the diverse components together, ensuring the efficient execution of a complex, multi-faceted plan. Each individual member brought unique skills and expertise, but it was the seamless integration of those skills, the collective effort, and the unwavering trust in one another that truly defined our success. It was a testament to the power of teamwork, a demonstration of how a diverse team, operating in concert, could overcome even the most formidable foe. The takedown of Tanaka's empire was a collective triumph, a victory not just for me, but for the entire team, a symphony of skill and coordinated action that finally brought justice to those who had suffered at the hands of a global criminal mastermind. The shared sense of accomplishment, born out of months of relentless effort and flawless teamwork, was immensely rewarding. The long shadow of Kaito Tanaka had been lifted, but the lasting lesson of seamless collaboration in the face of adversity would resonate long into my future career.

Strategic Operations

The dismantling of Tanaka's global criminal network wasn't a single, decisive strike, but a meticulously orchestrated campaign spanning continents and employing a diverse range of tactical approaches. The initial phase focused on intelligence gathering – a painstaking process of piecing together the intricate structure of his organization. This involved infiltrating his inner circle, monitoring his communications, and analyzing his financial transactions. We used a combination of human intelligence (HUMINT), signals intelligence (SIGINT), and financial intelligence (FININT) to build a comprehensive picture of his operations. This phase was crucial, as it laid the foundation for the subsequent phases of the operation.

One of our key breakthroughs came from an unexpected source: a disgruntled accountant working for one of Tanaka's shell companies in the Cayman Islands. This individual, codenamed "Finch," had grown increasingly uneasy with the illegal activities he was involved in and contacted us through a secure channel. Finch provided us with critical financial data, revealing the complex network of offshore accounts and shell corporations used to launder Tanaka's illicit gains. This information was invaluable, allowing us to trace the flow of funds, identify key players within his organization, and ultimately, build a strong case for prosecution. The information Finch provided was carefully vetted and corroborated through other intelligence channels, confirming its accuracy and reliability. His testimony became a critical piece of the puzzle in securing the legal framework for the future takedown of the organization.

The second phase involved identifying and neutralizing Tanaka's key lieutenants. These were individuals who held significant positions within the organization, controlling various aspects of his operations. Their removal was crucial in disrupting the communication channels and supply chains that kept Tanaka's empire running. Each operation was carefully planned and executed, taking into account the unique circumstances and challenges presented by each target.

The apprehension of Kenji Sato, Tanaka's chief of operations, in Tokyo, exemplifies the precision and coordination of these operations. Sato was a highly cautious individual, aware of the potential threats to his position. Our team, led by Nightingale, used a combination of surveillance, deception, and tactical maneuvers to capture him without alerting his security detail. The operation involved a sophisticated surveillance network, real-time intelligence feeds, and a coordinated team of operatives working in perfect unison. The success of this operation hinged on meticulous planning, precise timing, and unwavering attention to detail. The aftermath of Sato's apprehension involved swift, decisive action to secure the evidence and prevent any retaliation from other members of the organization.

Another significant operation unfolded in Monaco, targeting Anya Volkov, Tanaka's head of finance. Volkov was known for her lavish lifestyle and her access to Tanaka's most significant financial assets. This operation required a more delicate approach, focusing on legal and financial maneuvers rather than direct confrontation. Our financial analysts worked closely with international authorities to freeze her assets and build a solid case against her. The operation involved a complex series of financial transactions, international legal proceedings, and close collaboration with various international banking institutions. The successful freezing of Volkov's assets significantly crippled Tanaka's organization's ability to finance its operations.

The third phase focused on dismantling Tanaka's logistical network. This involved identifying and disrupting his supply chains, seizing his assets, and disrupting his communication networks. This phase required a coordinated effort across multiple jurisdictions, involving various law enforcement agencies and international organizations. The scope and complexity of this phase necessitated the development of a detailed plan with contingencies for each possible scenario. Each operation was coordinated with local authorities, ensuring that we remained within the legal framework, building trust and minimizing any potential disruption.

Simultaneously, a fourth phase focused on the public relations aspect of the operation. It was crucial to maintain control of the narrative surrounding the takedown of Tanaka's organization, preventing any misinformation or disinformation campaigns from undermining our efforts. We worked closely with public relations specialists and government officials to release controlled information to the media, shaping public perception and preventing panic or undue alarm. The messaging was crucial to maintaining public trust and keeping the operation under wraps from Tanaka's associates who were unaware of our successes up to this point.

The final phase involved Tanaka's apprehension. This was not a simple arrest; it was the culmination of months of planning and execution. The operation was launched in a remote location in the Swiss Alps, where Tanaka was believed to be in hiding. The operation involved a highly specialized team of operatives, a sophisticated surveillance system, and a coordinated plan to ensure Tanaka's capture without causing any harm or potential escape. Tanaka's capture served as a powerful symbol, demonstrating the unwavering commitment of the team and the overwhelming weight of evidence against his organization.

The success of Operation Justice Served was not merely a matter of tactical brilliance, but also a testament to the power of international collaboration. We worked closely with law enforcement agencies and intelligence services from across the globe, sharing information, coordinating efforts, and providing mutual support. This cross-border collaboration was crucial in dismantling Tanaka's trans-national criminal network and ensuring a strong legal basis for future prosecutions. The success of Justice Served proved that global cooperation was not just possible, but vital in combating global criminal organizations.

The legacy of Operation Justice Served extended far beyond Tanaka's conviction. The meticulous planning, the flawless execution, and the unwavering commitment of the team established a new benchmark for future operations. The lessons learned from this operation—the importance of meticulous planning, effective communication, and international cooperation—would inform and shape future strategies in the fight against organized crime. The detailed case files and intelligence gathered became valuable resources for combating other criminal syndicates and for strengthening the global network of law enforcement and intelligence agencies. The operation served as a warning, a powerful message to other criminal organizations about the far-reaching consequences of their actions. Justice had been served, not just for the victims of Tanaka's crimes, but as a deterrent against future criminal enterprises. The operation wasn't just about bringing one criminal mastermind to justice; it was about establishing a new paradigm for global crime-fighting. The world was a safer place, thanks to the collective effort, the coordinated strategy, and the unwavering dedication of those involved in Operation Justice Served. The intricate tapestry of strategic operations, woven together with painstaking precision, had finally brought a ruthless criminal empire to its knees. The quiet satisfaction of a mission successfully completed, a justice served, settled deep within me – a hard-won peace, earned through sweat, strategy, and tireless dedication.

Final Confrontation

The air hung thick with the scent of pine and damp earth, a stark contrast to the sterile, antiseptic environments I was accustomed to. We stood on a precipice overlooking a valley cloaked in the pre-dawn mist, the jagged peaks of the Swiss Alps rising around us like silent sentinels. This wasn't a bustling city centre or a clandestine offshore haven; this was Tanaka's chosen sanctuary, a remote mountain chalet tucked away from prying eyes, a fittingly isolated stage for the final act of Operation Justice Served.

Nightingale, ever the pragmatist, adjusted the earpiece, her voice a low murmur in my ear. "Team's in position. He's inside. No sign of additional security beyond the standard perimeter." Her words were clipped, efficient, devoid of any unnecessary emotion. Years of experience had taught her to control her nerves, to focus solely on the task at hand. I mirrored her composure, my heart a steady drumbeat beneath my tactical vest. This wasn't just about capturing Tanaka; it was about bringing an era to a close, a final punctuation mark to a long and arduous campaign.

The plan was deceptively simple, yet devilishly intricate in its execution. We weren't going in guns blazing. Such a reckless approach would have been disastrous, putting both Tanaka and potentially innocent bystanders at risk. Our approach was about precision, a surgical strike aimed at minimizing collateral damage while ensuring Tanaka's capture. Three teams were involved: one to secure the perimeter, another to deal with any potential escape routes, and our team, tasked with apprehending Tanaka himself.

The chalet itself was a picture of rustic elegance, a facade that masked the ruthless operations conducted within its walls. The windows were dark, the only light emanating from a single lamp in what appeared to be a study. We moved with practiced silence, our movements fluid and coordinated, a well-oiled machine functioning flawlessly. Years of rigorous training, countless hours spent honing our skills, had culminated in this single, decisive moment.

As we neared the chalet, the tension was palpable, a silent agreement between us. The air crackled with anticipation, the promise of danger a tangible presence. Nightingale, leading the way, signaled for us to spread out, flanking the structure. My heart pounded in my chest, a rapid rhythm against the backdrop of the stillness of the mountain. This wasn't a game; this was real, with potentially fatal consequences.

The entry point was a small, almost hidden window on the ground floor. Nightingale, with the agility of a mountain cat, used a specialized tool to silently disengage the lock. She slipped inside, followed by me and two other operatives. The interior was dimly lit, the air thick with the scent of old wood and pipe tobacco. Tanaka, predictably, was in his study, a mountain of paperwork scattered across his desk. He was facing away from us, his back to the door, oblivious to our presence. He was meticulously studying a map spread across his desk, tracing routes with a calloused finger.

I remember the chilling calmness that settled over me as I observed him. He was the architect of so much chaos, so much suffering. He was the embodiment of evil, his hands stained with the blood of countless innocent victims. Yet, in that moment, he seemed almost…peaceful. He was caught in a web of his own making. A small, almost imperceptible smile tugged at the corner of my lips. Justice was finally within reach.

As we moved in to apprehend Tanaka, he turned, his eyes widening in surprise, but not in fear. It was a mixture of bewilderment and grudging respect. Perhaps the weight of his years and the overwhelming evidence had finally broken him. Or maybe he'd accepted his fate. There was no struggle, no desperate attempt to escape. He was subdued quickly, professionally. Handcuffs clicked shut, silencing the unspoken defiance in his eyes. His empire, his carefully constructed world of deceit and criminality, had crumbled. The mountain air felt clearer, somehow, lighter.

The arrest itself was surprisingly anticlimactic. No dramatic showdown, no last-ditch attempt to escape. Tanaka, defeated, offered no resistance. He was simply tired, worn down by the relentless pressure of the investigation. He knew the game was over. His empire was in ruins, his network dismantled, his assets frozen. He was a broken man, his dreams reduced to ashes.

As we escorted him from the chalet, the first rays of dawn illuminated the valley, bathing the landscape in a soft golden light. The mountains, which had served as a silent backdrop to our operation, now seemed to stand tall and proud, their stillness a testament to the justice that had been served. Operation Justice Served was complete. Tanaka's capture marked the end of an era, the culmination of a long and arduous journey.

The following days were a blur of paperwork, depositions, and briefings. Tanaka was extradited, the mountain chalet was secured, the evidence meticulously cataloged. The legal process began to grind into motion, a slow but inexorable march towards justice. His trial was a spectacle, the evidence against him overwhelming and undeniable. He was found guilty on all charges and sentenced to life imprisonment, a fitting punishment for his crimes.

However, the real victory of Operation Justice Served lay not merely in Tanaka's conviction, but in the profound disruption of his global criminal network. His organization, once a formidable force, was now a shattered husk, its tentacles severed, its power decimated. His fall served as a stark warning to others who might dare to tread the same treacherous path. The operation also fostered deeper cooperation between various international law enforcement and intelligence agencies, creating a stronger global network to combat transnational crime.

The aftermath of the operation was far-reaching. The intelligence gathered during Operation Justice Served was invaluable, leading to numerous other arrests and prosecutions. It exposed a vast network of corruption, stretching across continents and involving numerous high-profile individuals. The operation not only brought down Tanaka but also exposed a deep-seated rot in various parts of the global financial system, prompting crucial reforms aimed at preventing similar schemes in the future.

The success of Operation Justice Served was a testament to the dedication and skill of the team. It was a complex, multi-faceted operation, involving months of painstaking planning, relentless intelligence gathering, intricate coordination, and precise execution. It involved the cooperation of numerous agencies, overcoming significant logistical and legal challenges. The seamless integration of various intelligence sources, from HUMINT and SIGINT to financial intelligence, was a cornerstone of our success.

The operation's legacy extended far beyond the dismantling of Tanaka's organization. It served as a model for future operations, underscoring the importance of international cooperation and meticulous planning. It sent a clear message that even the most sophisticated criminal networks could be brought to justice, provided the right resources and strategies were employed. It was a demonstration of the unwavering commitment to justice, a tribute to the tireless work of countless individuals dedicated to upholding the rule of law.

Looking back, the final confrontation with Tanaka in the remote Swiss Alps wasn't simply the climax of the operation; it was a symbol. A symbol of justice served, a symbol of the triumph of good over evil, a symbol of unwavering dedication to a cause greater than oneself. The quiet satisfaction of a mission accomplished, a justice duly served, settled deep within, a hard-won peace earned through sleepless nights, strategic maneuvers, and the unwavering commitment of a dedicated team. The world was demonstrably a safer place, thanks to the unwavering dedication and tireless efforts expended during Operation Justice Served. The memory of that crisp mountain air, the rising sun illuminating a landscape cleansed of a criminal blight, remained a powerful and enduring reminder of the victory we had achieved. The echoes of justice reverberated far beyond that secluded chalet, a powerful testament to the enduring strength of collaborative efforts in the face of global crime.

Justice Prevails

The extradition process was a logistical nightmare, a complex ballet of international law and diplomatic maneuvering. Tanaka, shackled and subdued, was flown from Zurich to a high-security facility in the United States, a journey shrouded in secrecy to prevent any attempts at rescue or interference. The flight itself was a tense affair, every moment punctuated by the silent vigilance of the armed guards escorting him. The air crackled with unspoken tension, a palpable reminder of the power Tanaka still held, even in his weakened state. His very presence was a potent symbol, a living testament to the shadow world he had once controlled.

His trial was a media circus, a spectacle that captivated the world. The courtroom was packed, the gallery overflowing with journalists, legal professionals, and concerned citizens eager to witness justice served. The prosecution presented a mountain of evidence, meticulously documented and irrefutably damning, a testament to the years of painstaking investigation that had led to this moment. Tanaka's lawyers, seasoned veterans of the legal battlefield, fought tooth and nail, attempting to sow doubt and confusion, but their efforts were in vain. The evidence was too overwhelming, the testimonies too compelling.

Witness testimonies painted a harrowing picture of Tanaka's reign of terror. Victims, their faces etched with the scars of his ruthlessness, recounted their experiences, their words filled with a mixture of grief, anger, and a quiet sense of relief that justice was finally being served. Their stories provided a human face to the cold statistics of his crimes, a visceral reminder of the real-world consequences of his actions. The court heard tales of intimidation, blackmail, and murder, each narrative adding another layer to the portrait of a ruthless criminal mastermind.

The financial evidence, intricately woven together by a team of forensic accountants and financial investigators, exposed the sheer scale of Tanaka's wealth, amassed through years of illicit activities. The numbers themselves were staggering, representing a vast network of shell corporations, offshore accounts, and laundered funds, demonstrating the intricate web of deceit and corruption that undergirded his criminal enterprise. It was a testament to the effectiveness of international cooperation in unraveling such a complex scheme, a collaborative effort that transcended national borders and political divisions.

Even before his sentencing, the dismantling of Tanaka's organization had a ripple effect across the globe. Numerous individuals connected to his network were arrested, their assets seized, their operations disrupted. The domino effect was profound, resulting in the dismantling of smaller criminal cells, the exposure of corrupt officials, and the disruption of illicit supply chains. Tanaka's fall created a vacuum, a power void that weakened his entire criminal ecosystem. The operation demonstrated the far-reaching consequences of bringing down a key player in a vast and complex criminal network.

The trial itself served as a landmark legal precedent, highlighting the effectiveness of collaborative international law enforcement efforts. The prosecution's meticulous approach, the seamless integration of evidence from multiple jurisdictions, and the collaboration between different agencies served as a model for future cases. It demonstrated the power of international cooperation in bringing down transnational criminal organizations, setting a new standard for investigating and prosecuting such complex cases.

Beyond the legal ramifications, the operation had a significant impact on public trust and confidence in the judicial system. The successful prosecution of Tanaka, after years of evading justice, signaled a victory for those who believed in accountability and transparency. It underscored the importance of unrelenting perseverance in the face of formidable challenges, and provided a much-needed reassurance that powerful criminals could be brought to justice.

The impact extended beyond the immediate sphere of law enforcement. Tanaka's downfall triggered a series of reforms in the international financial system, aiming to prevent similar schemes from emerging in the future. Greater transparency, stricter regulations, and enhanced cooperation between banks and financial institutions were instituted to choke off the flow of illicit funds. The operation served as a wake-up call, highlighting the need for robust anti-money laundering measures and a renewed commitment to tackling transnational crime.

In the aftermath, the quiet satisfaction was immense, a feeling of profound relief and quiet accomplishment. The weight of years of investigation, countless hours of painstaking work, and the relentless pressure of the operation finally lifted. The team celebrated their victory, not in boisterous revelry but in quiet reflection, acknowledging the gravity of the work accomplished and the significance of the victory achieved. The operation wasn't just about capturing one man; it was about sending a clear message: that crime, no matter how sophisticated or well-concealed, will ultimately be confronted and justice will prevail.

The success of Operation Justice Served was more than just a legal victory; it was a testament to human perseverance, a demonstration of the effectiveness of international collaboration, and a powerful symbol of hope. It proved that even the most elusive criminals could be brought to justice, provided there's unwavering determination, meticulous planning, and a steadfast commitment to the pursuit of justice. The echoes of this victory continue to resonate, inspiring future investigators and serving as a stark warning to anyone contemplating a life of crime on a global scale. The world, undeniably, was a safer place, thanks to the tireless efforts of those who dedicated themselves to the pursuit of justice. The legacy of Operation Justice Served remains a powerful reminder of the enduring importance of international cooperation and the relentless pursuit of justice in a world of shadows and deceit.

Aftermath and Reflection

The sterile white walls of his safe house seemed to press in on Jake. The adrenaline rush, the high-stakes chase, the brutal fight – all were fading, leaving behind a hollow ache. He stared out the window at the cityscape sprawling below, the vibrant lights a stark contrast to the darkness that still clung to him. Tanaka's capture, the culmination of months of relentless pursuit, felt unreal, a dream from which he would soon awaken. But the lingering tension, the weight of what he'd done, what he'd seen, was profoundly real.

He'd expected elation, a triumphant sense of closure. Instead, a profound weariness settled over him, a heavy blanket of exhaustion that went beyond physical fatigue. It was the exhaustion of bearing witness to the dark underbelly of humanity, the exhaustion of facing mortality on a daily basis, the exhaustion of perpetually living on the edge. He'd stared into the abyss, and the abyss had stared back.

The safe house, designed for anonymity and security, felt like a gilded cage. The silence, meant to be comforting, amplified the thoughts echoing in his mind. He replayed the moments leading up to Tanaka's capture, the calculated risks, the split-second decisions, the near misses that could have cost him everything. The image of Tanaka, defeated and subdued, haunted him less than the faces of the victims he'd encountered during the investigation. Their stories, etched into his memory, were a constant reminder of the human cost of Tanaka's crimes.

Sleep offered little respite. His dreams were a kaleidoscope of chaotic images: blurred faces, shadowy figures, the chilling echo of gunshots. He would wake in a cold sweat, heart pounding, the phantom sensation of danger clinging to him like a second skin. The psychological toll was immense, a silent battle fought in the quiet hours of the night, a battle he wasn't sure he could win.

He sought solace in the quiet solitude of a nearby park, finding a secluded bench under the shade of an ancient oak. The gentle rustling of leaves, the chirping of birds, offered a momentary respite from the turmoil within. He watched children playing, their laughter a poignant reminder of a life he had left behind, a life that seemed impossibly distant now. The carefree innocence of their games was a stark contrast to the harsh realities of his world. He wondered if he would ever experience such peace again, such untainted joy.

His handler, a woman named Sarah, had anticipated this. She'd arranged for a psychologist, a specialist in dealing with the trauma experienced by covert operatives. The sessions were difficult, forcing him to confront the emotional wounds he'd been trying to ignore. He'd always prided himself on his mental resilience, his ability to compartmentalize and move on. But this was different. This was a wound that ran deeper, a wound that threatened to consume him.

Sarah herself was a source of both support and apprehension. Her calm demeanor, her unwavering professionalism, concealed a depth of understanding that both comforted and unnerved him. She knew what he was going through, not just intellectually, but emotionally. Her empathy, however, was tempered by the steely resolve that was a hallmark of her profession. She knew he was valuable, knew he was needed, but the unspoken question hung in the air: how long could he sustain this?

He found a strange comfort in the routine of his physical training. The rigorous exercises, the demanding drills, provided a structured outlet for the pent-up energy and frustration. His body, a finely tuned machine, responded to the demands, offering a temporary escape from the relentless assault of his thoughts. The physical exertion was cathartic, a way to channel the raw emotion that threatened to overwhelm him. In the sweat and strain, he found a semblance of control, a feeling of mastery over at least one aspect of his life.

But even the physical exertion couldn't completely quell the turmoil within. The memories continued to surface, intruding upon his waking moments, creeping into his dreams. He found himself replaying conversations, analyzing decisions, searching for mistakes he might have made, for ways he could have done things differently. The weight of responsibility was crushing, the realization that even the smallest error could have had catastrophic consequences.

One evening, he found himself wandering the streets of the city, drawn by the vibrant energy of the nightlife. The noise, the crowds, initially served to distract him, but the anonymity of the city, the sense of being lost in the sea of faces, only amplified his feelings of isolation. He sat at a quiet bar, watching the ebb and flow of people, each with their own stories, their own struggles. He wondered if anyone else carried the weight he carried, the burden of secrets and shadows that couldn't be shared.

He knew he couldn't continue like this. He needed to find a way to integrate his experience, to reconcile the man he was before with the man he had become. The line between his old life and his new one had blurred, creating a sense of detachment, a feeling of being adrift. He wasn't sure what the future held, but he knew he couldn't simply carry on as he had been.

He began to journal, pouring out his thoughts and feelings onto paper, a way of externalizing the internal conflict that raged within him. The act of writing was therapeutic, allowing him to process his emotions, to confront his fears, and to begin the long process of healing. He wrote about his training, his missions, his doubts, and his fears, unburdening himself in the anonymity of the written word.

The process was slow, arduous, and often painful. But as he wrote, as he confronted his inner demons, he began to see a path forward, a way to integrate his experiences into a new understanding of himself. He started to see that the darkness he had confronted hadn't extinguished his light. It had, instead, illuminated his capacity for resilience, for empathy, and for unwavering determination. He had survived the abyss, and in that survival, he found a new sense of purpose. The dawn, though still shrouded in shadows, held the promise of a new day. The future remained uncertain, but he was ready to face it. The scars remained, both visible and invisible, but they were a testament to his journey, a reminder of the battles fought and won, and a foundation for the life he would build. He was, ultimately, stronger for what he'd endured. The weight remained, but it no longer felt crushing. It felt... manageable. He was ready for whatever the next mission brought, or whatever life brought him. This was his new beginning. He was ready.

Healing and Recovery

The psychologist's office was surprisingly un-clinical. Instead of cold steel and sterile white, warm earth tones dominated, sunlight filtering through sheer curtains to illuminate a comfortable sitting area. Dr. Anya Sharma, a woman with kind eyes and a calming presence, listened patiently as Jake recounted his experiences, the words tumbling out in a torrent of confession. He spoke of the adrenaline highs, the crushing lows, the moral compromises he'd made, the faces of the victims that haunted his sleep. He didn't shy away from the details, the grim reality of his work laid bare. Dr. Sharma didn't interrupt, offering only the occasional nod of understanding, her silence more comforting than any platitude.

The sessions weren't easy. They were painstakingly slow, peeling back layers of suppressed emotion, confronting the trauma that had burrowed deep into his psyche. He learned to identify the triggers that sent him spiraling back into the darkness – the sudden loud noises, the fleeting shadows, the smell of rain on asphalt, all echoes of the missions he'd undertaken. Dr. Sharma introduced him to techniques for managing the flashbacks, the nightmares, the overwhelming sense of guilt that threatened to consume him. He learned mindfulness exercises, breathing techniques designed to ground him in the present moment, to pull him back from the precipice of panic.

He discovered the power of controlled exposure therapy. Gradually, under Dr. Sharma's guidance, he began to revisit the traumatic events in a safe and controlled environment, dissecting them, analyzing them, reclaiming his narrative. He started with small things, describing the mundane details of his missions – the texture of the concrete beneath his boots, the taste of the cheap coffee he'd gulped down before an operation, the feel of the cool night air on his skin. Slowly, he worked his way toward the more harrowing aspects of his experiences, processing them, contextualizing them, until they no longer held the power to paralyze him.

Beyond the therapy sessions, Jake found solace in unexpected places. He rediscovered his love for baseball, not the intense, competitive world he'd left behind, but the simple joy of playing catch in a local park. The rhythm of the throw and catch, the satisfying thud of the ball in his glove, brought a sense of calm, a grounding connection to a simpler time. He found himself drawn to the quiet solitude of the city's botanical gardens, wandering amongst the vibrant flowers and lush greenery, finding peace in the beauty of nature. The vibrant colors, the fragrant blooms, seemed to soothe his frazzled nerves, offering a welcome respite from the shades of grey that had dominated his existence for so long.

He began to cook again, a hobby he'd abandoned during his intense training and subsequent missions. The precision of measuring ingredients, the satisfaction of creating something delicious, the simple act of nourishing his body, brought him a sense of control, a feeling of agency that had been absent for far too long. He discovered the pleasure of simple things: the warmth of a cup of tea on a cold evening, the gentle caress of sunlight on his skin, the friendly chatter of the local barista who always remembered his order. These small moments of normalcy, these glimpses into a life beyond the shadows, helped anchor him to reality.

His physical training continued, but with a subtle shift in focus. It was no longer solely about maintaining peak physical condition for covert operations. It became a form of self-care, a way to channel his energy, to release the pent-up tension that still lingered. He embraced the physical exertion not as a means to an end, but as an expression of self-mastery, a testament to his resilience. The rigorous workouts became a meditation, a quiet communion between his mind and body.

He also reconnected with his past, albeit cautiously. He reached out to his old coach, a gruff but ultimately kind man who had been a positive influence in his life. The conversation was hesitant at first, but it eventually blossomed into a comfortable exchange, filled with shared memories and a renewed sense of camaraderie. The conversation didn't erase the past, but it helped to validate it, to acknowledge the life he'd once had, the person he'd been before the shadows claimed him.

Sarah, his handler, remained a constant presence in his life, but their interactions had changed. The focus shifted from mission briefings and operational updates to more personal conversations. She acknowledged his struggles, validating his experiences, offering words of encouragement and support without diminishing the gravity of what he'd endured. Their relationship evolved, forging a bond built on mutual respect and trust, a shared understanding that went beyond the professional. She remained a crucial element of his support network, an anchor in his new life.

His journal became his confidante, a repository for his thoughts, his fears, his hopes. The act of writing became a form of therapy, a way to process his experiences, to make sense of the chaos that had once consumed him. He wrote not only about the darkness he'd encountered but also about the moments of light, the small acts of kindness, the unexpected displays of human resilience that he'd witnessed during his missions. He wrote about his gratitude for being alive, for having survived the abyss. He explored the complex interplay of guilt, regret, and ultimately, acceptance. He documented his journey from a place of overwhelming despair to a nascent hopefulness, a tentative embrace of the possibility of a future worthy of his survival.

The healing was not linear; it was a meandering path, punctuated by setbacks and moments of profound clarity. There were days when the shadows threatened to engulf him once more, when the memories returned with brutal force. But he had learned coping mechanisms, techniques to navigate these episodes. He leaned on his support network, drawing strength from the connections he'd cultivated.

As the months passed, the constant tension within him began to subside. The nightmares lessened in frequency and intensity. The flashbacks became less frequent and less debilitating. He started sleeping soundly, his dreams less tormented and more… peaceful. He found a new rhythm in his life, a balance between work and recovery, between service and self-care. His scars remained – both physical and emotional – but they were no longer symbols of defeat. They were badges of honor, testament to his resilience, reminders of the darkness he'd faced and the light he'd found his way back to.

His life now contained a careful blend of the operational and the personal. He continued to serve his country, but with a renewed sense of perspective, a greater understanding of the human cost of his work. He had found a way to integrate his experiences into his identity, creating a narrative that embraced both the darkness and the light. He was no longer defined by his past, but empowered by it. He was a survivor, a testament to the human spirit's capacity for healing, and he was ready to embrace whatever the future might hold. The new dawn had arrived, not as a sudden explosion of light, but as a gradual awakening to a new day. He was ready.

New Opportunities

The crisp autumn air bit at Jake's cheeks as he stepped out of the agency's unmarked black sedan. He'd been summoned to Langley, but the location wasn't the usual sterile briefing room. Instead, he found himself before a sprawling, ivy-covered building that looked more like a secluded research facility than a government headquarters. A sense of anticipation, tinged with apprehension, tightened his stomach. This was different. This felt… bigger.

Inside, the atmosphere was markedly different from the usual clandestine operations center. The air hummed with a quiet energy, a blend of focused intensity and intellectual curiosity. He was led through a series of labs, each meticulously organized, filled with advanced technology he couldn't quite comprehend. The scientists and engineers he passed were engrossed in their work, their faces illuminated by the glow of computer screens. He caught glimpses of complex equations, intricate diagrams, and cutting-edge machinery. He felt a flicker of his old competitive spirit, a desire to understand, to contribute. This wasn't just about covert operations anymore; this felt like the cusp of something revolutionary.

He was ushered into a large, circular conference room, bathed in soft, natural light that streamed through panoramic windows overlooking a meticulously landscaped garden. Around the polished mahogany table sat several individuals, their faces a mixture of familiar and unknown. Sarah, his handler, sat at the head, her expression serious but hopeful. Beside her sat a man whose military bearing was unmistakable, even in civilian attire. General Maddox. The man responsible for recruiting him. Then there were others

—scientists, engineers, analysts—each an expert in their respective fields.

"Jake," Sarah began, her voice calm and reassuring, "as you know, your contributions to the past operations have been invaluable. But we believe your skills, your experience, and your unique perspective… they transcend traditional field operations."

General Maddox leaned forward, his gaze unwavering. "We've been developing a new program, a highly classified initiative. It's… ambitious, to say the least. And we need someone with your particular skill set."

He listened intently as they outlined the program—Project Nightingale. It wasn't a mission; it was a long-term commitment, a chance to shape the future of intelligence gathering. It involved harnessing cutting-edge technology, integrating AI-driven predictive analysis, and leveraging human intuition in unprecedented ways. It demanded a unique blend of technical expertise and human understanding, something Jake's unique experience uniquely equipped him for.

The implications were staggering. They spoke of preventing catastrophic events, disrupting terrorist networks before they could strike, and shaping global events before they could escalate into crises. It was a chance to change the world, to make a difference on a scale far beyond anything he'd ever imagined.

The initial wave of apprehension gave way to a surge of excitement. This wasn't just about surviving dangerous missions; this was about building something new, something significant. It was about leveraging his skills to shape a more secure future, to leave a lasting legacy. The adrenaline he felt wasn't the nervous flutter of a covert operation but the exhilaration of a new challenge, a chance to utilize his talents in a way that was both meaningful and fulfilling.

The training began immediately. It wasn't the brutal, physical regimen of his initial training. This was different. This was about expanding his knowledge, sharpening his analytical skills, and developing a deeper understanding of complex technological systems. He spent hours immersed in data analysis, learning to decipher intricate patterns, to anticipate trends, to predict outcomes with a level of accuracy he previously thought impossible.

He worked alongside some of the brightest minds in the country—cryptographers, data scientists, AI specialists. He learned about neural networks, machine learning, and quantum computing. He discovered the potential of predictive policing, proactive counter-terrorism strategies, and the subtle art of influencing global events through carefully orchestrated information campaigns.

He also spent time with psychologists, honing his ability to read people, to understand their motivations, and to anticipate their actions. The emphasis shifted from purely physical prowess to a more holistic approach, integrating his physical, mental, and emotional capabilities to maximize his effectiveness. He learned to manage stress, to control his emotions, and to remain calm and focused under intense pressure. His old training was the foundation, but this new training built upon it, adding layers of sophistication and nuance.

The project wasn't without its ethical considerations. They discussed the delicate balance between security and freedom, the need to protect privacy while gathering intelligence, the constant tension between national interests and human rights. He wrestled with the moral ambiguities, weighing the potential benefits against the inherent risks. It was a constant ethical calculus, a process of continuous reflection and reevaluation. But he was no longer a naive recruit; he was a seasoned operative, capable of navigating the complex moral landscape of espionage with a sense of purpose and responsibility.

The nights were long, filled with intense study and simulations. But the exhaustion wasn't demoralizing; it was invigorating. He felt a renewed sense of purpose, a deeper understanding of his own potential. He was more than just a spy; he was an architect of security, a guardian of peace, a builder of a better future.

He spent time reflecting in the contemplative garden behind the facility. The carefully sculpted hedges, the meticulously maintained flower beds, the tranquil pond—they were a stark contrast to the high-tech world he inhabited during the day. But the peace and tranquility he found there were essential to his ability to function effectively in the high-stakes world of Project Nightingale. He used the time to meditate, to decompress, to reconnect with his inner self, preparing himself for the intellectual battles ahead.

He even began to sketch again. He hadn't touched a pencil since his baseball days, but the methodical process of sketching brought him a sense of calm, a way to process the complex information he was absorbing. He started with simple outlines, gradually adding detail until his drawings became intricately rendered depictions of the technological systems he was mastering. It was a way to bring order to the chaos, to translate complex concepts into tangible forms.

The project's reach was global. He traveled to secure facilities across the globe, collaborating with international partners, exchanging information, and forging relationships with counterparts from various agencies. He saw the world from a different perspective, not just through the lens of covert operations but through the lens of strategic collaboration and global cooperation. He discovered the power of shared intelligence, the strength of collective action, and the importance of international alliances in preventing global crises.

He made new friends, forging bonds of trust and mutual respect. He discovered a sense of camaraderie among his colleagues, a shared commitment to a common goal. He found intellectual stimulation, a sense of achievement, and a deep sense of fulfillment. This wasn't the lonely world of shadows he'd once known. This was a world of collaboration, innovation, and hope. The new dawn wasn't just a personal awakening; it was a collective sunrise, a promise of a brighter future for humanity. And Jake, once a lost soul in the darkness, was now a beacon of light, leading the way.

Reconciliation and Peace

The rhythmic lapping of waves against the shore was a soothing balm to Jake's frayed nerves. He sat on a weathered bench overlooking the Pacific Ocean, the salty air filling his lungs, a stark contrast to the sterile atmosphere of Langley's high-tech labs. This wasn't a strategic briefing; this was a personal retreat, a chance to process the whirlwind of change that had swept through his life. He'd traded the roar of the stadium crowd for the quiet hum of sophisticated servers, the adrenaline of a stolen base for the calculated risk of international diplomacy. The transition had been jarring, exhilarating, and ultimately, profoundly rewarding.

He pulled a worn leather-bound journal from his bag, its pages filled with sketches and scribbled notes – a testament to his evolving journey. The early entries chronicled his intense training, the relentless pursuit of knowledge, the grappling with ethical dilemmas. Later entries documented his travels, his encounters with international colleagues, the slow but steady growth of trust and camaraderie. His sketches had evolved, too, from simple technical diagrams to evocative landscapes, capturing the essence of the places he'd visited, the people he'd met, and the subtle shifts in his own perspective. The art wasn't merely a pastime; it was a form of self-expression, a way to articulate the complex emotions that swirled within him.

He flipped to a recent entry, a detailed rendering of the serene garden at Langley, a haven he'd discovered amidst the chaos of his work. The meticulous detail of each leaf, each petal, reflected his own meticulous approach to his new role. The garden had become his sanctuary, a place of quiet reflection where he could process the weight of his responsibilities, the moral complexities of his work, and the echoes of his past. He'd found a strange solace in tending to the plants, his hands working in the earth, mirroring the methodical nature of his analytical work.

He closed the journal, the setting sun casting long shadows across the beach. He thought back to his baseball career, the years of relentless training, the pressure of competition, the fleeting moments of glory. It had been a life of intense focus, but ultimately, it had left him feeling unfulfilled, adrift. The sudden end of his career had been a shock, but in hindsight, it had been a necessary catalyst, a pivotal moment that propelled him onto a different trajectory.

The agency hadn't just recruited him for his athletic prowess; they'd recognized a deeper potential, a capacity for strategic thinking, a resilience forged in the crucible of competition. They'd seen a raw talent, a keen intellect waiting to be unleashed. And they'd provided him with the tools and the training to develop that potential, to reshape his identity. He was no longer just Jake Riley, the baseball player; he was Jake Riley, the architect of security, the guardian of peace.

He considered the ethical challenges he had faced. The constant negotiation between security and freedom, the delicate balance between national interests and human rights. There were times when he'd questioned his own choices, times when the weight of his responsibilities had felt overwhelming. But he'd learned to navigate those moral gray areas, to make informed decisions based on his principles, his conscience, and the larger good. He'd learned that true strength lay not just in physical prowess but in moral clarity.

He spent time reflecting on the friendships he'd forged within Project Nightingale. The bond of trust with Sarah, his unwavering handler, had been a crucial factor in his personal growth. He'd also discovered a deep respect for General Maddox, a man who'd initially seemed distant and intimidating, but who'd ultimately become a mentor and a source of support. He'd developed a camaraderie with his colleagues, individuals from diverse backgrounds, all united by a common purpose. The sense of belonging, of collaboration, had filled the void he'd felt in his previous life.

He often thought about the moments of intense pressure, the close calls, the near misses. These experiences, once sources of terror, now felt like badges of honor, testament to his resilience, his ability to perform under intense pressure. He'd learned to compartmentalize, to separate the stress of his work from his personal life. He'd developed coping mechanisms, techniques for managing stress, and strategies for maintaining his composure under pressure. The relentless training hadn't just sharpened his skills; it had tempered his spirit, transforming him into a more resilient, more resourceful, and ultimately, more peaceful person.

His thoughts drifted to the global nature of Project Nightingale, the international collaborations, the cross-cultural exchanges. He'd traveled the world, meeting people from diverse cultures, forging alliances, and building bridges between nations. He'd seen the best and the worst of humanity, the capacity for both great cruelty and great compassion. And he'd come to appreciate the intricate tapestry of global interconnectedness, the shared challenges, and the collective responsibility to build a more peaceful future.

The ocean breeze carried the sound of distant seagulls, a gentle reminder of the vastness of the world and the interconnectedness of all things. He felt a sense of gratitude, a profound appreciation for the opportunities he'd been given, the challenges he'd overcome, and the personal transformation he'd undergone. The life he'd chosen wasn't easy; it was demanding, fraught with risk, and often ethically challenging. But it was a life of purpose, a life of meaning, a life that had brought him a sense of peace he'd never experienced before.

He stood up, stretching his legs, feeling the sand between his toes. The setting sun painted the sky in hues of orange and purple, a breathtaking spectacle that mirrored the profound shift in his own inner landscape. He was no longer the restless, ambitious athlete seeking fleeting moments of glory. He was a builder, a guardian, an architect of a more secure and peaceful world. He had found not just peace, but a sense of purpose far greater than he had ever imagined. The new dawn wasn't merely a metaphor; it was a reality, a tangible promise of a brighter future, and he was leading the way. The path ahead remained uncertain, fraught with challenges, but he knew, with a quiet confidence, that he was ready. He was finally at peace, not with the world, but with himself. And that, he realized, was the greatest victory of all. He walked back toward his secluded cabin, the sound of the waves a constant, comforting reminder of the peace he had finally found.

Looking Ahead

The cabin's porch offered a panoramic view of the sunrise painting the Alaskan wilderness in fiery hues. Jake sipped his coffee, the warmth a stark contrast to the crisp morning air. The rugged beauty of the landscape mirrored the ruggedness of his new life, a life far removed from the manicured lawns of Langley and the sterile environment of the high-tech labs. He'd chosen this remote location deliberately, seeking a sanctuary to reflect, to plan, and to prepare for whatever challenges lay ahead. This wasn't a retreat from duty; it was a strategic repositioning, a recalibration of his internal compass before setting off on a new, yet undefined, mission.

He'd spent the last few weeks immersed in self-reflection, poring over intelligence reports, studying geopolitical shifts, and sharpening his skills. He'd honed his physical conditioning, pushing his body to its limits in the unforgiving Alaskan terrain. He'd become adept at navigating the dense forests, surviving in the wilderness, and relying on his instincts. The isolation wasn't lonely; it was invigorating. It allowed him to disconnect from the digital world, to reconnect with the natural world, and to rediscover a sense of self that had been somewhat lost in the whirlwind of his clandestine life.

His thoughts often drifted back to Project Nightingale, to the camaraderie he shared with his colleagues, the trust he'd forged with Sarah and the unexpected mentorship from General Maddox. He missed the intellectual sparring sessions, the intense brainstorming sessions, and the shared sense of purpose that had bonded them together. But he knew that his role had evolved, that his responsibilities now extended beyond the confines of the agency, that his expertise could be leveraged in new and innovative ways.

He'd received cryptic messages, veiled hints of new operations, but nothing concrete. The agency operated in shadows, relying on subtle cues, coded language, and carefully crafted narratives. The uncertainty wasn't unnerving; it was stimulating. It kept him on edge, sharpening his senses, forcing him to remain vigilant. The unknown was the breeding ground of both fear and exhilaration, a constant reminder that complacency was his greatest enemy.

He opened his worn leather journal, its pages filled with intricate sketches of Alaskan wildlife, stark landscapes, and cryptic diagrams. The sketches were more than just artistic expressions; they were visual representations of his strategic thinking, a way to externalize his ideas, to process complex information, and to map out potential scenarios. He often found that sketching complex problems helped clarify his approach, illuminating pathways to solutions that remained elusive through purely analytical means. This unique blend of artistic expression and analytical thinking had become an integral part of his work, a testament to his evolving capabilities.

He turned to a fresh page, his pencil poised above the smooth paper. He sketched the outline of a map, a rough representation of a vast, sparsely populated region of Central Asia. The location, though vague, resonated with a sense of both intrigue and unease. He'd been provided with fragments of information – rumors, whispers, encrypted communications – suggesting a potential threat of a very different nature than he'd previously encountered. It felt less like a geopolitical conflict and more like something...

esoteric. Something that challenged the very foundations of his understanding of espionage and international relations.

He considered the ethical ramifications. The previous missions, while challenging, had always operated within a defined framework of national security. This felt different, less structured, more ambiguous. It pushed him into uncharted waters, forcing him to question not just his skills but the very principles that governed his decision-making. He pondered the inherent risk, the potential for collateral damage, the inherent ambiguity of the mission's goals.

He spent hours analyzing the limited intelligence he had, painstakingly piecing together fragmented clues. He cross-referenced databases, sought out obscure sources, and used his network of contacts to validate the information he'd gathered. He worked tirelessly, not driven by fear of failure, but by a sense of responsibility, a deep-seated commitment to uncovering the truth and safeguarding innocent lives.

He knew that this wouldn't be a straightforward mission. It would require resourcefulness, adaptability, and a willingness to operate outside conventional boundaries. He'd have to rely on his intuition, his honed skills of observation and deception, and his ever-evolving understanding of human nature. He envisioned navigating treacherous landscapes, dealing with unpredictable individuals, and confronting the unforeseen consequences of actions taken in the shadows. He was prepared for risk; it was an integral part of the life he'd chosen. He would face it head-on, armed with his skills and his unwavering resolve.

The sun dipped below the horizon, casting long shadows across the snowy landscape. Jake closed his journal, a sense of quiet determination settling over him. The future remained uncertain, the path ahead fraught with challenges, but he felt a sense of readiness. He was no longer the young athlete seeking personal glory; he was a seasoned operative, an architect of security, a guardian of peace in a world increasingly teetering on the brink. His journey hadn't ended; it had merely evolved. The new dawn promised not just a new day but a new chapter, a new narrative in the ongoing saga of his life – a narrative that he would write himself, one perilous step at a time.

He packed his gear, preparing for his departure, the silence of the Alaskan wilderness a stark contrast to the turmoil of the world he was about to re-enter. He felt a profound sense of gratitude for the opportunities and challenges he'd encountered, the people he'd met, and the lessons he'd learned. He carried the weight of his past, the memories of triumphs and setbacks, as a testament to his resilience, his unwavering commitment to purpose, and his evolving understanding of his place in the world. He knew he was prepared for whatever lay ahead, for the challenges, the uncertainties, and the complexities of this ever-changing world. His path was clear, his resolve unshakeable, and his purpose unwavering. The new dawn was breaking, and Jake Riley was ready to meet it. He stepped out into the cold, crisp morning air, ready to face whatever awaited him – embracing the unknown with the quiet confidence of a man who had found peace within himself. The journey had changed him irrevocably, yet he was, more than ever before, prepared for anything that the world would throw his way. The future was unknown, unpredictable, and exhilarating. He embraced it.

Acknowledgments

First and foremost, I extend my deepest gratitude to the countless individuals who served in the military and intelligence communities. Their dedication, courage, and sacrifices—often made in the shadows—inspired this novel and informed its details. Their stories, though untold in this particular narrative, are the backbone of national security and global stability. This book is a small tribute to their silent service.

I also owe a debt of gratitude to my editor, Stefanie Baldwin, whose insightful guidance and unwavering support shaped this manuscript from its initial draft to its final form. Their keen eye for detail and understanding of the genre proved invaluable.

Finally, and most importantly, I thank my family and friends for their patience, understanding, and unwavering love throughout the writing process. Their support, even in the face of long hours and intense focus, was the fuel that kept me going. I would like to extend thanks to my beta readers Leviy Johnson, and Matt Dowdy. My profound gratitude extends to the unsung heroes within the ATF in the Colorado Springs office—fellow teammates from our adult baseball and hockey leagues—whose invaluable contributions I acknowledge with heartfelt respect.

Appendix

Glossary

This glossary defines key terms used in the novel, primarily those related to espionage, intelligence operations, and clandestine activities. *Deep Cover* : An undercover operative whose true identity and allegiance are completely concealed for an extended period. *Ghosting* : The act of removing someone from the official records and making them "disappear".) "Clandestine: keep secret, or acting in secretive.

References

While this novel is a work of fiction, several aspects of the narrative are informed by real-world events and intelligence practices. While specific sources are not cited due to the sensitive nature of the subject matter, general research and inspiration was drawn from public domain materials relating to Cold War era espionage, modern counterterrorism operations, and the psychology of intelligence work.

Author Biography

JC Bisogno a seasoned security consultant and former baseball player, brings a wealth of experience in investigative analysis and meticulous fact-finding to his writing. His distinguished career in security and sales provided fertile ground for a compelling transition: crafting gripping, realistic thrillers infused with the unique perspective of a veteran spy. Now residing in Kansas City, this second novel marks his impressive debut on the national literary stage.

Made in the USA
Columbia, SC
06 March 2025

cb4eec1d-3e05-44c5-acc3-8c57aa998e45R01